DAY AND KNIGHT

DIRK GREYSON

Hugs & Love
Dirk Greyson

Published by
DREAMSPINNER PRESS

5032 Capital Circle SW, Suite 2, PMB# 279, Tallahassee, FL 32305-7886 USA
http://www.dreamspinnerpress.com/

ISBN: 978-1-63216-706-4
Digital ISBN: 978-1-63216-707-1
Library of Congress Control Number: 2014922887
First Edition May 2015

Printed in the United States of America
∞
This paper meets the requirements of
ANSI/NISO Z39.48-1992 (Permanence of Paper).

To Lynn, a superior editor and a special friend. The hours we talked made this story possible.

Chapter 1

DAYTON INGRAM had never thought of this area of Milwaukee as particularly dangerous. The restaurants and businesses on Mitchell Street were bustling with customers, but two blocks made a real difference. He should have waited to find a parking space closer to the Wild Chili, but it had been light out when he arrived at the restaurant, and now that darkness had fallen, the welcoming feeling faded as he walked into a neighborhood he wasn't familiar with. Dayton picked up the pace and began walking faster toward his Ford Fusion. He'd was just approaching it when a cry reached his ears. He stopped, listening intently the way he'd been taught, to pick up the direction, hoping he would hear it again.

It came again, louder this time and much more frantic. "I have done nothing to you," a young voice pleaded in Spanish. "Leave me alone."

The reply came, also in Spanish, menacing, growly. "Why should we?"

Instantly Day headed in that direction. He reached for his phone and pulled it from his pocket. He pressed the button to wake it up, and it remained dark.

"Shit!" he swore, kicking himself for not checking it earlier. He'd felt it vibrate a few times during dinner but had figured it was Facebook or something like that. Instead the damn thing had been telling him it was almost out of power. He needed to see about getting a new battery for the piece of shit—he'd charged the fucking thing just before he'd left the house.

"Leave me alone." The cry repeated, this time in distress and accompanied by the sounds of a scuffle and an overturned trash can rumbling on concrete as it went. Day took off in the direction of the sound, rounding the corner of a small alley that stank of garbage and

God knew what else, where two heavyset men in ratty sweatshirts and stained pants hanging halfway down to their knees loomed over a teenager, or someone not much older than that.

"Just give us your money, and we'll let you be, *maricón*," the man spat, puffing up his chest in a display of machismo. "Otherwise we'll cut your balls off." The man held up his hand, a knife flashed, and Day stopped a few feet away, just out of arm's reach.

"*Huye*!" he cried at the top of his lungs to the kid. "Get out of here," he added as the men advanced on him. Dayton kept his cool and widened his stance, carefully watching the glazed eyes of both men. The one with the knife came first, jabbing it at him a little clumsily. Dayton danced back out of his reach and waited for another pass. It looked like the fat man's friend was going to see what happened before he entered the fray. Stupid mistake. They might have been able to get to him if they worked together—might. But alone, no way in hell!

"It's two against one, gringo," the man warned, and Dayton caught a hint of alcohol on his breath. "Give us your money too, and we'll let you live." He swung the knife, and Dayton caught his arm before it reached the apex of the arc. Holding the man's hand firmly in his, he twisted around and flipped him over his shoulder. The knife flew out of the assailant's hand, clattering to the concrete, and he landed on his back with a hard thud and didn't move. Day swung around to the other man, ready for his attack, but none came.

He expected the man to flee, but whatever he was on must have made him brave and too stupid to know better. He'd grabbed the kid and was holding him as a shield. "Stay still," Dayton said and locked gazes with the man. His eyes were wide, and Dayton guessed he'd been drinking, at least, and maybe had taken a hit of something else. As he took a step closer, not looking away, the man's eyes widened enough that they caught the light. His pupils were huge. Yeah, he was definitely high.

Dayton breathed evenly, remembering his training, pushing aside the nerves that threatened to cloud his concentration. What he'd been taught and practiced had worked once already. He did his best to keep his racing heart from pounding too loudly in his ears.

"Back up, gringo."

"Let the kid go, and you can leave," Dayton said levelly, even as he was starting to wonder if this whole situation was getting out of control. He'd meant to help the kid, not make things worse.

"Instead I maybe break his neck," the man said, smiling to show a mouth full of rotten teeth.

Dayton crouched slightly, and when the man's gaze shifted to the kid, Dayton took a step forward. He swept his leg out in a kick that caught the mugger's leg. The man lost his balance, falling to the ground. Dayton was ready in case the kid fell too, but he managed to jump away. "Call the police," Dayton ordered, and the kid nodded, pulling a phone out of his pocket while Dayton grabbed the man, rolled him over, and held his hands. "Give me your belt."

"What for?" the kid asked but then opened his belt and handed it over. Dayton used it to fasten the man's hands behind him. The other one groaned, and Dayton warned him not to move unless he wanted more. He thought he heard the man mutter, "*No más*."

Sirens sounded, and Day looked around. "Are you okay, kid?" He nodded. "I have to go. Tell them what happened, and the police will see to it that these two are taken care of."

"You're leaving? You saved my life," the kid said in English as he continued shaking a little.

"I'm glad I could help," Dayton said with a smile. Then he turned and walked calmly down the street, got in his car, and drove slowly off as police vehicles began to arrive behind him. As he drove, Day plugged in his phone, got the beginning of a charge, and called in to the office.

"I need to speak to Gladstone," Day said when the call was answered and then waited to be transferred. He steered his car onto the freeway as his boss answered. Day switched the phone to hands-free as he sped up. "Remember you said to tell you if anything unusual happened…," Dayton began and then relayed the incident.

"Did the police see you?"

"No. I left before they got there," Dayton answered.

"Okay. We'll take care of it, but come into my office first thing in the morning." The call ended abruptly, and Dayton hung up and drove the rest of the way to his South-Side home.

He pulled up to the house, sliding past it before turning down the alley. He parked his car in the garage that he paid a little extra to use and then walked to the house. He unlocked his ground-floor door and then took the stairs up to the second floor of the duplex. It was a nice place—compact and affordable. Once inside he closed the main door and walked back to the bedroom. He set his keys in their place on the dresser, along with his wallet. Then he plugged in his phone and arranged it in its place next to his wallet. Finally, he took off his shoes, filling in the space they'd left on the floor of his closet, then left the room and returned to his living room.

He sat on the serviceable but old sofa he'd found at a thrift store and covered with a slipcover to make it look less hideous. He'd done the same thing with the two chairs. They were comfortable enough, and that was all that mattered to him. He made do, and there was something familiar and almost homey about it. The same could be said of the mismatched chairs pushed into place around the table in his small dining room. And no one would know how old and scarred the tabletop was unless they lifted the sapphire tablecloth to peer under it.

Day turned on the television and did his best to relax, but the incident in the alley kept running through his mind. He'd been trying to help, and in the end he had, but he'd also put the kid in more danger, if momentarily. His boss hadn't said anything about whether he thought Dayton had done the right thing. Well, it was too late now, and if he'd screwed up with his rashness, so be it. He'd helped the kid and had gotten him away from the men.

Laughter came from the television, pulling him out of his thoughts for a little while. He turned his attention to the rerun of *Will and Grace,* laughing a few times before changing the channel once the show was over. He settled on an episode of *The Mentalist*. It was an unrealistic portrayal, but it was entertaining. Secretly, however, he wanted to be just like Patrick Jane—keenly observant, a student of human nature—and have the ability to get in other people's heads. After watching the episode, he turned off the television.

The tiny second bedroom in the apartment acted as Dayton's office. Before going to bed, he sat at his desk, started up his laptop, and checked his personal e-mail. It was mostly junk, but there was a note from his brother about his latest lame scheme to make himself a pile of money so he could continue his wandering lifestyle forever. Like all the other "opportunities," Stephen made it sound as though it were the deal of the century, but Dayton could see the holes in it a mile away and shook his head. He should call him, but he wasn't in the mood to have that conversation tonight. So after checking the last of his e-mail, he closed the computer lid and headed to the bathroom, where he cleaned up and got ready for bed.

THE FOLLOWING morning, pressed and dressed, he left his apartment and drove to a brick office building that had once housed a bank. It still looked like a bank, which was probably why it worked so well for its new purpose. The sign out front read "S L S Inc." It stood for Scorpion Logistics Services. But everyone inside knew those words meant something very different than the public might take them to mean. People asked him if they were a trucking and shipment management company, and Dayton always answered yes but was vague about what he did.

He parked in his space alongside the building and pulled his badge out of his wallet. He scanned it at the door reader, and it clicked. He pulled the door open and entered the building. He scanned his card at the next door and placed his thumb on the pad. When the door clicked open, he walked farther into the building.

"Good morning," the receptionist said professionally, barely looking up from her keyboard as she typed.

Dayton knew she wasn't being rude, just efficient, and he returned her greeting before continuing on to his cubicle. He sat down and started up his computer, entered himself into the system, and checked the programs he'd set to run overnight. They had finished, and he smiled before picking up the phone.

"Gladstone."

Jason Gladstone. Everyone just called him Gladstone, and a few people dared to call him Glad, but Dayton never had and doubted he ever would.

"You wanted to see me this morning?" Dayton said.

"Uh… yeah. Come to my office in an hour. Uh… good morning." He hung up, and Dayton placed his phone back in its place. His boss was a weird duck. Smart as they came, but social niceties tended to get lost in his intensity. Not that Dayton minded. He went back to work analyzing the data he'd collected, and then, once he'd finished the report, he sent it off to the requestor. He saved the information in case it needed to be reworked but set it for auto-purge in a month. Then he went to Gladstone's office.

"Dayton," Gladstone said after he knocked on the doorframe. "Come with me."

He stood slowly and nodded, following his boss through the building and into one of the small conference rooms. Gladstone closed the door and motioned Dayton to take a seat while he sat just opposite him. Fuck, he was in trouble. That was the only explanation.

"We got some additional information on the incident last night from the police. Apparently you left out some details when we talked last night." Gladstone stared at him intently.

"I believe I told you everything."

Gladstone smacked a file onto the table and slid it over to him. Dayton glanced down at it and saw it had his name on it. "You never told any of us that you speak Spanish."

Huh? Dayton covered his confusion. Even in the office, he'd learned to maintain a façade of strength and unflappability. "It's a new skill. I decided to learn about a year ago, and I've been practicing with a number of people conversationally online. I was surprised at how quickly I could pick it up." He didn't smile, even though he was fucking proud of himself. He spoke a number of other languages as well, so he did have a gift for them.

Gladstone pulled the file back and opened it. "You were hired away from the NSA six months ago, and the reason you gave for wanting to join us was that you wanted to do fieldwork, and that wasn't going to happen there. Well, up until last night, no one thought you had what it took for fieldwork, but you've changed some minds." Gladstone didn't look happy. "And your newly acquired skill seems to have sealed the deal."

"All right. Do you have a new project for me?" Dayton kept his excitement out of his voice. He loved gathering and analyzing data, especially when there was an external challenge involved.

"Don't know yet. A team is being assembled, and you're on the short list for consideration. Doesn't mean you'll be chosen, but the powers that be are moving quickly on this, so be ready to go, and make sure your affairs are in order to be away from home for a period of time."

"How long would I be away?" Dayton asked.

"That wasn't shared with me," Gladstone answered flatly. "But they were also interested in your more clandestine computer skills as well as… your looks." Gladstone's possum-like eyes bored into him. Dayton didn't flinch. Gladstone was never going to win any beauty contests. He'd been in the clandestine-operations business for quite a while and knew his way around, but the man had most definitely been hired for his skills.

"My looks?" Dayton asked. That seemed the most unlikely of all his traits to have garnered him consideration for a field operation. "I work hard, and I'm fucking good at what I do." His hackles raised in a split second.

"Cool down, Ingram. I wasn't casting aspersions on your qualifications, just stating facts." Gladstone's expression softened slightly.

"So what do I do now?" He really wanted to get into fieldwork.

"Nothing. If you're chosen you'll be contacted, and they'll arrange to meet and brief you. That division of the organization is as secretive and closemouthed as they get. They tell no one anything they don't need to know, and that even goes for me." Gladstone paused. "You're here in part because of your skills, and in part because you know how to keep your mouth shut. There may be training involved, but I don't know for sure." He stood up, a signal that the meeting was over. "Just be prepared to pick up and go at a moment's notice." Gladstone picked up the file and left the room, closing the door behind him.

Dayton wanted to crow to the rooftops. He was actually being considered for fieldwork. How fucking awesome was that? Of course, he kept his cool and left the room a minute after Gladstone, his expression schooled and his walk as normal as he could make it. He went back to his desk and got to work.

"What did the Weeble want?" Kyper Morris asked, popping his head over the cubicle. How Kyper had gotten his job, Dayton didn't know. He was gossipy and tended to talk. A lot. Granted, Dayton never heard him say anything he shouldn't, but how he could talk so damned much and not accidentally spill something he shouldn't was beyond Dayton. "Did you do something? I heard there was an incident last night."

Just like any office, there was a rumor mill here as well, but it tended to be quite subdued. "He wanted to talk," Dayton answered.

"You're no fun," Kyper said, and Dayton heard the chair squeak, which meant Kyper had plopped himself onto his chair in a show of disappointment. "You know, we all took this job because of the potential excitement, and what do we see? The same four walls and reams of data. We might as well be working at Walmart." The clicking of keys was nearly deafening. When Kyper got pissed about something, he typed as hard as hell.

"Give it a rest," Dayton called as lightly as he could. The pounding eased off, but the typing continued. Dayton went back to work, searching for the data locations he could use to put together the analysis request he'd just been sent.

"So, was it good news?" Kyper asked a few minutes later. The man was like a dog with a bone—he never let anything go. Dayton ignored him and continued working. It hadn't worked before, and it wasn't likely to work now. Kyper's special skill was that he never gave up. If there was a way to get something he needed, he would stop at nothing until he had it in hand. The only time he'd ever given up on anything was when Gladstone had threatened his ability to have children. Even then, he'd only backed off, and a few days later he was crowing about solving the problem.

Dayton took a break and got a cup of coffee from the snack area. He brought it back to his desk and settled in to work for the rest of the morning. He left for lunch and returned with takeout that he ate at his desk. When he was done, he wadded up the paper and tossed it into the trash.

"Two points."

Dayton turned around and shivered as a man with a pair of black, almost hollow eyes stared right back and through him. It was the coldest gaze he'd ever seen in his life. "Dimato," the man said with no emotion whatsoever. Dayton knew instantly that it wasn't his real name.

"Ingram," he said, standing up and offering his hand.

The man stood there and did nothing. "Come with me."

Dayton lowered his hand and followed Dimato out of the cubicle area and up the stairs. They passed through various secure areas, with Dimato getting them access.

They entered an office, and Dimato closed the door. "All right," he began, pointing to a chair. Dayton sat, and Dimato pulled another from around the polished conference table and lowered himself into it, getting comfortable. "As you've been told, we have been looking at you for an assignment." Dayton had expected him to have a file or some information, but he simply sat and watched him. Dayton forced himself not to squirm. Dimato's attitude was designed to make him uncomfortable, but he'd be damned if these kinds of games would have an effect on him, so he waited, refusing to break eye contact.

"Yes. I was told nothing other than it would require me to be away for a period of time."

Dimato nodded. "We have a situation, and we need someone with your particular blend of skills."

"And what would that be?" Dayton pressed, leaning forward.

"Your computer skills are top-notch, you speak multiple languages, including Spanish, which tipped the decision in your favor, and frankly, your appearance was a plus as well." He crossed one leg over the other. "We do have concerns, one being your lack of fieldwork. But we were all new once, and you have good instincts. The other is… harder to explain. In the field you must put the mission and the safety of the team above everything else. Last night, according to the information gathered, you were cool under pressure and saved the kid. But by getting involved, you put yourself in unnecessary danger. In the field, choosing your battles can mean the difference between success and failure. This isn't a game. It's dangerous." Those emotionless black eyes were making Dayton's skin crawl.

"I understand that." He'd always known what was required. "When will I meet the others I'll work with? I'm assuming I won't be sent in alone."

"I'm expecting him at any time," Dimato said. He didn't move, but his gaze did shift slightly. Dayton had noticed a set of world clocks on the wall when he'd come in, so Dimato was checking the time.

"He's late," Dayton said flatly. Dimato didn't react, other than a slight twitch of his lips. The office door opened. Dayton turned in his chair as an older man stepped in and closed the door.

"This is Knighton from Records and Research," Dimato said. "He'll be your partner on this particular assignment."

"Him?" Dayton asked, eyes widening. That was hard to believe. He seemed a little old, with gray hair at the temples and a slight slouch to his posture. He seemed a little like he'd been rode hard and put away wet. Granted, he was handsome enough, with a strong, chiseled jaw covered with stubble that looked like he hadn't bothered to shave as opposed to a fashion choice, and piercing eyes that Dayton doubted missed much.

"Yes, me," Knighton said firmly in a rich baritone. He sat down at the chair across from Dayton and made himself comfortable. "What's the deal, so I can decide if I want to take it?" He leaned back in his chair, hands behind his head.

Dimato stood up and walked to where Knighton sat. He braced his arms on the edge of the table and leaned over it. "This is your final chance for fieldwork." So there was emotion Dimato somewhere. "You've buried yourself in the research department for almost two years, and it's time you either shit or got off the pot."

Dayton wasn't sure he should be here for this. He swallowed hard and turned away. But like a train wreck, it was hard not to watch.

"This requires your skills, and we need you. So get over yourself and get back on the horse. Once this is over, you can go back to research for the rest of your life for all I care."

Dayton turned slightly. Knighton's expression hadn't changed, except his lips curled up into a slight smile, making Dayton wonder if this was all some act for his benefit. He didn't see what the motivation could possibly be, but it seemed to him this sort of conversation should have been held behind closed doors.

"Since you asked so nicely…," Knighton began.

Dimato moved back to his seat as though nothing had happened.

Dayton acted the same way and turned toward the man he assumed was his boss now.

"One of our departments picked up some chatter coming out of Mexico. We get it all the time and turn most of what we suspect over to the DEA, but this is different and doesn't seem to be drug-related. It's centering on an attack of some type on the electronic intelligence infrastructure here in the US." Dimato stood and retrieved two folders from his desk. He handed one to each of them. "These are to be destroyed if you are in danger or compromised in any way."

"Understood," Dayton said as he took the file with a slight tremor of excitement in his hand. "May I ask why the CIA isn't involved?"

"We brought it to their attention, and they, in their infinite wisdom, punted it back to us, claiming budget cuts. The truth is they don't see this as the threat we know it is." Dimato shook his head. "So we're sending you in to neutralize it. We believe—and the details of what we have are in the folder—that they plan to make this attack in the next two weeks."

"When you say electronic infrastructure, you mean the Internet, correct?" Knighton asked.

"Yes."

"But isn't there security already? Websites have security and so do their back-end systems. It isn't flawless, but how can someone attack that when it's so dispersed?"

Dayton gasped and looked at Dimato, but he just sat quietly.

"That's easy. Any security system can be gotten around. It's a multibillion-dollar business," Dayton said to Knighton. "Hackers and threats get more and more sophisticated each year, and so do the security precautions that guard against them. It's a never-ending cycle." Dayton then turned to Dimato. "There are a number of systemic holes that could be exploited. Some I suspect have been anticipated but others probably haven't. The terrorists may have hit on some as yet undiscovered hole and are working on a way to exploit it."

"Could you do that? Exploit a security hole?" Dimato asked.

Dayton smiled. "I do it every day. That's how I get some of the critical data we need. We don't use it for nefarious purposes, and I schedule it all for deletion once we are through with it, but if I can do it, so can others. Do we know the exact threat?"

"No," Dimato said. "That's part of the problem. Gentlemen, we need you to determine the source of the threat. It's originating in the Yucatan Peninsula of Mexico, and we believe it's near the border with Belize. That area is sparsely populated, with plenty of remote areas where a plot like this could be hatched and carried out. The team here will supply support, but we need boots on the ground, and that's you two."

"How are we getting there? By plane?" Knighton asked.

"No. We need to make sure you slip into the area under the radar. If this group, and that's our assumption, is savvy enough to do this, then a plane or anything out of the ordinary would be spotted."

"We could fly over at night, and you could drop us out of the plane. We'd hit the ground, ditch the chutes, and no one would be the wiser. That area is dark as shit at night." For the first time, Knighton seemed really engaged.

"We can't take the chance. We'll only get one shot at this. If we blow it, they'll move, and we will have to start all over again. The team is still trying to figure out how to get you in with no one noticing."

"How about a cruise ship?" Dayton suggested. "You said this is near the border with Belize. There are cruise ships that stop in Costa Maya, which is in that area. A friend took one last year. They run Sunday to Sunday. I think she left out of Fort Lauderdale. We could arrive on the ship in Costa Maya. No one would be looking for us in a group of tourists. We simply book an excursion inland and then disappear. When we don't return, the ship will sail on without us."

"Aren't ships like that booked?" Knighton asked.

Dayton shrugged, but Dimato was already out of his chair and picking up his phone. "Research cruises leaving this weekend from any port, docking in Costa Maya, Mexico, and arrange for a cabin. If they're full you'll need to arrange for existing passengers to be waylaid or shifted off the cruise. Everything must be done not to raise suspicion." He hung up and sat back down. "We'll arrange for both of you to have access to the transmissions we've intercepted."

"Excellent, sir," Dayton said. He was anxious to see what they were getting into and to look for clues about this mysterious threat.

No one said anything more, and Dayton wondered if the meeting was over. He waited for Dimato to stand and then did the same. Dayton stepped toward the door, with Knighton remaining behind.

"By the way," Dimato said. "Your desk and things have been relocated to this floor. See Eileen just outside. She'll show you where it is and give you a new badge and explain the security requirements to get on this floor. It's good to have you on the team."

Dayton pulled the door open, stunned, and stepped outside, where Eileen was waiting for him. The middle-aged woman screamed efficiency, from the tailored way she was dressed, down to her highly polished, sensible shoes. She led him briskly toward what appeared to be an office. There were two desks inside. "This space will be for you and Knight. We find that operational teams need to be kept together so information can be shared in a secure environment." She stepped inside and directed him toward the desk closest to the window. "We set up your things there. Here's your new badge." She took the old one and bent it in half. "I'll have this shredded. You won't need it any longer."

"Will I be restricted from any parts of the building?"

"Only the computer operations center. Everything else will be open to you. If you need something and you aren't getting cooperation, let me or Dimato know, and we'll take care of it." She paused. "Is there anything else I can do for you?" She obviously didn't anticipate anything because she was already turning to leave the room. She closed the door, and it took all Dayton's self-control not to jump up and pound his fist in the air. Instead, he booted up his computer to clear the work he'd left undone and then opened the file folder he'd been given and began to read.

AN HOUR or so later, the door bounced open. He jumped and then looked up, and Knighton walked in, surveying the space as though he owned it.

"I see you already took the desk near the window."

Dayton was about to argue and say that his things had been put there for him, but he kept quiet and returned his attention to the file.

"You aren't going to find much in there other than the standard information and a little more detail about what we've already been told," Knight said. A folded piece of paper landed on Dayton's desk.

Dayton ignored it for the time being. "Do you always enter a room like a herd of elephants? I understand we all have skills. Is that listed among yours?" He raised his eyebrows and then went back to the file. He was nearly done and wanted to make sure he had all of the information in his brain before he went to work on the messages that had been intercepted. A series of encrypted files from Eileen had been waiting on his computer in his new office. He'd only glanced at them and realized he needed the background information before he could dig into the transmissions themselves.

"Look, kid, I have years of experience at this sort of thing. So let me do what I do best, and you can do the computer stuff, and maybe we'll get out of this alive and back home so we can go on with our lives." Knight dropped the file on his desk and schlumped into his chair.

"If you don't want to do this, then tell them instead of acting like a grumpy old man," Dayton countered. Then he sighed. This was not the way to start what should be a partnership. "Let's start over rather than snapping at each other. I'm Dayton Ingram. My friends call me Day." He walked over to the other desk and extended his hand.

The other man stared at it for a second, and then he stood as well. "Knighton. People call me Knight."

"Is that your first or last name?" Day said as he shook the offered hand.

"Just Knighton," he said, and then he dropped the hand. "So did you find any pearl of wisdom in there?"

"Not really, just background information. But some of it might be helpful." He returned to his computer, opened one of the encrypted files Eileen had sent, and turned the monitor so Knight could see it. "The signals they intercepted have been traced to this area, here. But according to what's in the file, it isn't coming from the same place each time."

"So they're moving around. That's going to make it more difficult to find," Knight commented as he walked over to Day's desk.

"That's a possibility, but it could also be that there's something distorting the signal."

"Like what?"

"I don't know. But we'll get some answers when we get there. There are a number of reasons why the signal could be distorted or intermittent." Day made a note on a pad on the desk. "I'll research and see what I can find."

"Good," Knight said. Thankfully this time no attitude accompanied it. "Are you going to see what you can make of the transmissions?"

"Yes," Day answered, already pulling up the files after turning his monitor around. Knight walked toward the door. "What are you going to do?"

"Travel arrangements." Knight pulled open the door and closed it after he left. Day watched him go, wondering what in hell he had gotten himself into. Knight was handsome enough—Whoa, he needed to stop right there. He'd be working with Knight for weeks, and anyway, he had no intention of putting one single toe outside the proverbial closet, not while what he wanted was within his grasp. He'd kept his sexual orientation to himself for a long time. The last time he'd ventured out, things had not gone well at all. He would keep his interest, whatever the hell that was, to himself.

Dayton glanced at the paper Knight had plopped on his desk. It was some basic information about travel expenses. He knew what to do; he wasn't dumb. Shaking his head, he returned to his computer and went to work on the messages to see if there was anything he could learn. He spent much of the rest of the day on them, doing his level best to ignore Knight's comings and goings in the office.

"Are you going to knock off for the night or sleep at your desk, newbie?" Knight asked, breaking Day's concentration. "I have our travel arrangements all set, and the company even sprang for a decent stateroom."

"We're only going to be on the ship a few days. It seems like a waste to—"

Knight cut him off with a wave of his hand. "You've been busy and haven't heard the latest. The sailing we're on is a gay cruise, so you and I are playing the part of lovers on a vacation together."

Day's stomach did a flip, and he tried his best to keep his discomfort off his face. "Sounds… interesting." God, what in the hell did he say to that?

"Don't worry, we don't have to take it too far, but it was the easiest way to get us on the ship we need, and it will help us blend in with the other passengers." Knight handed him a set of papers. "Put this someplace safe. That should be all your travel arrangements."

Day nodded, reading through the details.

"I'll see you tomorrow," Knight said. "And you're welcome."

Day looked up from the travel documents and opened his mouth to say thank you, but Knight was already leaving the office with the grace of a panther on the prowl. Day was transfixed, his mind instantly stripping away the dress shirt and pants, imagining what might be hidden beneath. Probably acres of rich olive-toned skin with just enough short dark hair on his chest to make things really interesting. Day's mind conjured up a scent that made his head swim.

"Practicing for the cruise?" Knight asked from the doorway, and Day blinked once as he fell back to reality.

"Just wondering if being an ass came naturally to you or if you actually worked at it?" Day flashed a smile, thankful he'd been able to come up with something to cover his little daydream. Shit like that had to end. He needed to keep things together. He could do this.

"It's a talent gifted by the gods," Knight countered and left the room before Day had a chance to respond.

Day ground his teeth for a few seconds. That guy was going to drive him insane. He wished he had someone else as his partner for his first assignment. Day closed the transmission files he'd been working on and saved them onto a USB stick so he could take them home. A grin formed on his face as he opened a window into the Scorpion internal systems and went to work, searching for information on Knighton. If he was going to be working with the man, he was going to find out everything there was to know about him. Fuck if he'd stumble around like some newbie and let Knight get the better of him all the time.

Chapter 2

KNIGHT LEFT the Scorpion building as itchy as a three-legged dog with fleas. He was being sent back into the field under pressure, and they'd saddled him with an agent in diapers. Fuck, now he was supposed to ensure that the mission was a success, help the newbie along, and somehow make sure they didn't get killed in the process. Hell, he didn't know what skills the newbie had other than a smart mouth and the ability to click computer keys. From the rumor going around the building, he'd helped some kid being attacked on the South Side the night before, so Day must have guts, and he obviously had a brain in that movie-star head of his. Knight pulled open the door to his ancient truck, climbed in, and slammed the door closed. His frustration had to come out somehow.

Movie star.... He chuckled slightly at the thought and jumped at a slight knock on his window. He cranked it down and stared out at Mark. "What's up, Mark?" he asked, even though he already knew.

Mark Cale leaned on the lowered window, resting his forehead on the doorframe. "Heard you're going back out in the field."

"Yeah." Knight tilted his head toward the other door. "Get in. I could use a drink. How about you?"

"I bet you could." Mark pushed away and walked around the back of the truck. He was decades older than Knight, with years of experience etched into every line on his face and gray hair on his head. The passenger door ground open, and Mark climbed in, pulling the protesting door closed. "Damn you, kid, you need to get rid of this death trap and get a new fucking truck. This thing is going to blow to pieces around you one of these days."

It was a familiar comment and loosened some of the knot in Knight's stomach. "They don't make them like this anymore."

"That's because new cars have things like power windows and a fucking fan that works." Mark cranked his window down, but that one only went halfway. "Jesus Christ, I'm going to suffocate in this death trap." He turned to Knight. "Start the damn engine, and get this piece of crap moving."

Knight didn't argue. With anyone else he would have, or at the very least retorted with a smart remark, but not with Mark. The idea of talking back to him never crossed his mind. Knight started the engine, which purred like a kitten, and backed out of his space before shifting into first and moving forward. They didn't talk as they rode to the same bar as always. "What about your car?"

"Carolyn drove me in this morning because the dang thing needed its checkup. Kept dinging at me all the time. So when we're done, if you could drop me home…."

Knight nodded and continued the mile to the freeway and then turned toward downtown. They got off at the exit for Whitefish Bay and drove to a small restaurant that also served liquor. This part of town had always been upscale, but in the past few years it had become even more so with an upgraded shopping district, new fancy restaurants, and even a Trader Joe's. Knight loved the place but wouldn't tell anyone. It felt too much like selling out. He wasn't quite sure why. Maybe it was like selling out his memories of the way things had been, which were all he had left now.

He pulled in the parking lot and turned off the engine. They got out and walked inside.

"Mr. Knight," the hostess said. "Are you here to eat?"

"We'll just sit at the bar and decide on food later." He managed a smile, and she waved them toward the bar with the same smile she had for him every time he came in.

"She's growing up," Mark commented.

"Yeah. I remember when she was just old enough to peek over the hostess stand, and now she's graduating from college and is engaged to be married." Knight took a seat at one of the small tables off to the side, and Mark sat across from him.

"So what's crawled up your butt?" Mark asked and then had the decency to look away when the pretty waitress stopped at their table.

He ordered a whiskey, neat, and damn if Knight wasn't a split second from ordering one too. He wanted one—hell, he *needed* one, but he pushed that aside. He might think he needed it, but he'd be damned if he was going to drink because he needed it. He ordered an iced tea and left it at that. Mark noticed but didn't say anything, which was good, because Knight would probably have punched him if he'd said anything condescending or sappy. Mark tilted his head in that way he had that said "talk."

"Shit, Mark…." He didn't know where to fucking begin. It wasn't like he was used to talking about his feelings. Everything—years' worth of crap that had rolled downhill—was all bottled up inside, and if the container cracked, they would all be up to their armpits in a smelly mess.

"Start with what has you wigged about this mission," Mark said as the waitress set the amber liquid in front of him. "Thank you, darlin'." A hint of Mark's old Texas accent crept into his speech as it sometimes did when his guard was down or he was truly grateful for something. That was how Knight had always known when he'd done something really well—Mark's Texas accent would come out. It didn't matter what Mark said, Knight had always listened for the accent that was the true tell.

"It's the first one," Knight answered.

"Yeah, I know that, but it's been two years. Don't you think it's time you took off the black dress and veil and went to purple at least?" Mark always had these sayings that rarely made sense. "It's time you rejoined the living and stopped mourning." Mark lifted his glass to his lips and sighed after taking a sip. "Damn, that's good." He sighed and then let his gaze wander back to Knight. "Kid, you need to get back to life, or you'll end up a grumpy old man before you're forty."

"Shit." Knight sighed and drank from his tea. "That's what Dayton called me today."

"Who's Dayton? Your partner in this mission?" Mark barely stopped long enough for Knight to nod. "Then that kid pegged you fast." Mark seemed pleased about that… too pleased.

"What?"

"At least this Dayton isn't going to take any of your crap. You need that." Mark grinned, the small scar at the corner of his mouth showing. It was a souvenir he had gotten from a bar fight in Mexico when he'd rescued Knight after he'd done something stupid as a newbie. "Any partner that will let you walk all over them isn't the partner you need."

"You walked all over me," Knight said plaintively.

Mark paused with his glass halfway to his lips. "Did I?" He raised his eyebrow slightly to the left, catching Knight in a whine without saying a word. "You were fresh out of the Marines and as gung ho as they came. Damn, you were scary as shit, always raring to shoot or blow shit up." Mark smiled. "Came in handy in Ecuador, though." He sipped his whiskey again, still grinning. "You needed a firm hand. Still do. Now, sometimes we end up with the partner we need, and sometimes we end up with the partner we get. It's up to you to decide which this is."

"He's the partner I got…." Knight gulped from his glass, the liquid coating his suddenly dry throat. "Just like I was the partner you got, and you were the partner I needed."

"Are you sure about that, kid?" Mark's expression was unreadable. "You sure we didn't both get what we needed?" He downed the rest of his whiskey and signaled the waitress for another. After she brought it, he said, "Don't be too hard on this Dayton, but don't go easy on him either. Fieldwork is fucking hard. Everyone thinks it's excitement and glamor, but it's really days of waiting surrounded by moments when shit happens."

"Tell me about it. He's so excited he's probably spending the evening reading files and reviewing intercept transmissions."

Mark stared at him. "That sounds smart to me. The question I have for you is, why aren't you doing the same thing? It sounds like the kid is getting himself ready and doing the preparation you'd want a partner to do." He lifted his glass to his lips but then sat it back on the table without taking a drink. "He may be new, but maybe the one who isn't ready for this mission is you." Mark folded his hands. "You never shirked on any mission we had. You pulled your weight and then some. That's what he's trying to do."

That hit Knight like a punch in the gut. "Shit."

"I ain't saying you need to be a newbie about this. It's your job to act as the seasoned pro. Help him along, but don't be an ass about it… well, not all the time. Asking you not to be an ass is like asking you not to breathe. But at least keep your assness to a minimum."

"Fuck…." Knight sighed and ran his hands through his hair.

"And while you're at it, get yourself a haircut, and make yourself presentable. You look like hell and have for months. It's time to take care of yourself again. Everyone left you alone, including me, because that's what you said you wanted. Maybe we were all wrong, and what you needed was a kick in the behind." Mark smiled. "And believe me, there are plenty of people who would line up do that. Hell, we could hold a raffle and solve world hunger at the same time."

Knight chuckled at Mark's penchant for exaggeration. He'd missed that.

"Yeah, I was being funny and trying to get under your skin like the old days, but I can't do that any longer. Your hide is way too thick for that, at least against the darts I can throw at you." Mark's gaze drilled into him without wavering, and he seemed to be looking for something.

Knight was determined not to shiver or even breathe under the intensity of the stare. "What was that for?" he finally asked, staring back at Mark.

"Just checking to see if the Knight I knew was still in there."

"What the fuck are you talking about?' Knight shot back. "I lost my wife and kid. I…." His cheeks heated, and he leaned over the table, nearly spilling the glass as he did, but not giving a damn. "There's no shame in trying to heal so you don't put anyone else in danger."

"No. But you've gone beyond that. You're hiding, and it's time you stopped. Cheryl and Zachary are gone, and they aren't coming back." Mark slapped his hand on the table. "All that is history, and so is everything that happened between then and now. You have an assignment that's going to be dangerous and will require the Knight I remember, the one I trusted with my life and would still trust today."

Fuck. Knight ran his hand down his face in a vain attempt to wipe away the doubt that seemed to dog him at every turn. Mark was right; he had to get it together. “What do I do?”

“You’re asking me, Marine?” Mark said, and Knight sat straighter in his chair as old instincts kicked in. “See? Now you’re getting it. When all else fails…”

“…go back to the basics. They’re what everything we do is built on,” Knight finished, and Mark nodded.

“Now let’s get some food before this whiskey goes to my head, because if you bring me home drunk, Carolyn will have both our hides, and we both know we don’t want that to happen.”

“God, no.” Carolyn, Mark’s wife, was a force of nature, like a category-five hurricane, and not to be messed with in any way. “Be right back.” He stood and told the hostess they were ready for a table. She walked back through the bar, got Mark, and then led them to a table near the front windows. “Thank you,” he said to her as he sat down.

“Anytime,” she said with a smile that seemed a little flirtier than usual and then left.

“Is there anyone in your life?” Mark asked. “You know, it wouldn’t hurt you to start dating. It might make your life feel less—”

“You sound like my mother, and I don’t need another one of those in my life right now,” Knight broke in and then leaned to the side of the table. “Nope, I don’t see where you turned into a chick. So stop matchmaking. I’ll date when I’m ready.” Knight had been telling his mother and most of his family that for months now. Everyone needed to back off.

“Okay… okay. It’s just something to think about. I’m not turning into a yenta. Carolyn does that well enough for the both of us.”

Knight took the menu from the server and opened it. He hadn’t told anyone that he had no intention of marrying again. He’d been happy enough with Cheryl, and he’d loved their son to the ends of the earth. But that kind of relationship had been a one-time thing for him, and that part of his life was over.

HE AND Mark had a pleasant meal after that. He took Mark home and managed to say hello to Carolyn without being dragged into the house and having to talk all night. He needed time to think… desperately. Mark had been right about some things. He needed to move on, and the place to start was the kitchen. Once he got home, Knight opened the cupboard under the sink and pulled out the trash, staring at the full bin, mostly bottles. He'd been taking too many of his meals in liquid form lately, and that needed to end. A sociable drink was one thing, but there were dozens of bottles here, and he had emptied each and every one of them on his own, sitting alone in his chair.

The bottles clanged into the recycling bin when he took the can out back and upended it. Then he went back inside and threw away the other mostly empty bottles still in the cabinet. The sipping whiskey and scotch he kept, but all the rest went down the sink and then the bottles joined the rest. It was more than past time he got his shit together. Once he was done, Knight grabbed the case file he'd brought home, sat on the sofa with a glass of iced tea, and began to read.

He woke a few hours later, the house quiet, file spread across his chest, a crick in his neck from lying fully on the sofa. He moved slightly, and the papers spilled onto the floor. Knight sat up and wiped his face, wondering what had woken him.

Since enlisting in the Marines, he'd found he could sleep anywhere and almost at any time. It didn't take much, and in the Corps, you slept when you could, because it could be days before you did again. He'd been dreaming, he knew that, but for the life of him he couldn't remember what it was. All he was left with was the warm feeling of someone else taking care of him. Whatever it was, the dream had been nice. As he thought about it, he remembered a pair of deep brown eyes, happy eyes, shining at him. At first he thought they must have been Cheryl's, but both hers and Zachary's had been blue—deep, sapphire blue that shone in the sun. These had been warm as melted milk chocolate.

Knight picked up the papers and put the file back in order before stretching his back. He placed the file in the safe in his office and then went into the bathroom to clean up and get ready for bed.

TWO DAYS later Knight strode down the airport corridor toward the gate with his carry-on bag in his hand. His flight was set to take off in ten minutes, and getting through security had been a huge pain. But he'd made it and was hurrying as quickly as he could. At the gate he showed his boarding pass and walked onto the plane. He found his seat and stowed his bag. He groaned when he realized his was the one in the middle.

Day stood and smiled up at him.

"I thought I…." Knight threaded his way to the middle seat and sat down.

Day sat down next to him, fastened his seat belt, and rested his head on the back of the seat, that grin never leaving his face. "You know I'm very good with computers," he whispered, turning his head toward him.

Knight sighed. He had to give the kid credit. "If you're so damned good, why didn't you get us an upgrade?" He shifted in the seat, trying to get comfortable as the flight crew began their safety announcement. Then they left the gate, taxied, and took off. Almost as soon as they were in the air, Knight put his seat back, closed his eyes, and went to sleep, waking just before landing.

"Fucker," Day said when he put his seat forward.

"It's one of the benefits of the Corps. After being awake for days on end, you learn to sleep when you can and, by extension, pretty much whenever you want to." Knight stretched as they taxied to a stop at the gate. "Fastest flight ever."

The fasten seat belt sign was turned off, and Day stood and began getting things out of the overhead. Knight waited until the rows ahead of them had cleared before getting his bag and following Day down the ramp. He knew he shouldn't look, but he couldn't help watching the perfect backside in tight jeans bob in front of him. Well, he allowed it for about two seconds and then centered his mind on the task ahead of him. Those kinds of thoughts about his partner on this mission—or any man for that matter—had been pushed from his mind a long time ago and they needed to stay away. But damn, Day had dropped his jacket and bent over to pick it up. Knight took a peek and then averted his eyes until Day had straightened up. Then they continued down the Jetway and into the Fort Lauderdale airport.

They walked briskly toward baggage claim and got their luggage. Then once they had everything, they took a cab to the hotel.

"Is there a package for me?" Knighton asked at the desk as they checked in. The clerk left and returned a few minutes later with a box. Knight handed it to Day with a smile and then took the passkeys the clerk handed them and led Day to their room.

"What's in the box?" Day asked as soon as they were in the room behind closed doors.

"Weapons," Knight answered. "We couldn't take them on the plane without raising a ton of scrutiny and suspicion, so I had them shipped." Knight checked that both pistols were in working order and had arrived in suitable condition before stowing both of them in the safe at the bottom of the closet.

"I assume one of those is for me?" Day asked.

"Possibly," Knight answered. He'd probably end up giving Day one of them, but not until he had to. "Now, we board the ship tomorrow morning, so we have the day to ourselves. Is there anything you want to do?"

"Yes," Day answered and opened his bag. "I've been working on these intercepted transmissions, and I believe I may have been able to retrieve some additional information."

"Do you ever stop working?" Knight asked. Not that it was a bad thing; he was simply curious. He had known Dayton for only a couple of days, but the guy never seemed to take a break. His diligence was impressive, and Knighton nodded. Maybe he could use a little of that himself.

"I…." Day seemed surprised by the question. "This is what we're here for. Not to go to the beach or take walks in the sun, no matter how pleasant it may be." Day paused to peer out the window. "It does look nice, though, after leaving bare trees behind back home." Fall had definitely arrived, and they had already had their first snow. For the past few days they had been enjoying what would be a temporary reprieve from the cold weather before winter set in hard.

"Yes, it is," Knight agreed and pulled out one of the chairs from around the small table in the corner of the room. Day brought over his computer and booted it up.

"As I said the other day, I was looking over the transmissions, and I may have come across a clue. Dimato said they might be planning an attack on electronic infrastructure, but I believe I can narrow it down a little further. In this particular message. See?" He showed him the transcript.

"I've read it," Knight said. "But I found nothing specific."

"That's because you weren't looking at it as closely and with a data expert's eye." Day smirked slightly, and for a split second Knight noticed a glint in his deep brown eyes, then turned away quickly. "They aren't planning an attack on, say, transmission lines or the Internet, but on data."

"You mean by hacking websites?" Knight asked. "That seems rather inefficient and something that rarely happens today. How could hacking individual websites be a terrorist attack on the entire country?" He didn't really expect an answer. "Did you decipher which websites?"

"They don't say. But I've requested copies of any additional transmissions." Day continued looking at the monitor.

Knight watched him, wondering how he could see with his floppy brown curls in his eyes. Fuck, the man was handsome. If he let himself admit it, Day was the sexiest man he'd ever seen, with warm skin and hair just a few shades darker, a chin chiseled out of marble, and full luscious lips. He should not be having thoughts like these. He'd left them behind when he'd made his decision to do the right thing a decade ago.

"The thing is, I'm not sure they are attacking a particular set of websites."

Day's words snapped Knight back to the present.

"Then what are you saying? If they're going after data and they aren't attacking websites or particular companies… are they attacking the government?"

Day shook his head. "I don't know. I'm going to need some time to try to figure this out."

"We don't have time," Knight snapped. "The days are ticking down, and we're no closer than we were."

Day jumped to his feet. "Don't yell at me. I don't see you doing anything to help." He leaned over the table, his eyes blazing. "There is no more information in the transmissions, and I can't conjure it up out of thin air. These are transmissions we intercepted almost by accident.

Once we're closer to the source, I hope we can pick up more and get a better sense of what's going on."

So Day had a temper. He'd seen it before, but this time he hummed with energy because of it. Knight could feel it fill the room. Day stared at him, half daring him to argue.

"How are you going to do that?" Knight asked harshly in return. "Pull the communications out of your ass?" Fuck, the man tried his patience faster than anyone he'd ever met in his life.

Day walked to one of his bags, unzipped it, and displayed what appeared to be a communications center of some type. "You're not the only one who arranged for special equipment."

"How did you get that through security, and how will you get it onto the ship?"

Day grinned. "When they X-ray the bag, they'll see a normal suitcase filled with clothes. That particular item was a gift from an old friend. I'll set things up on the ship and try to monitor the terrorists' communications. We'll also have communications of our own without having to rely on those aboard ship, so it should be more secure."

"What kind of old friend?" Knight asked, a pang of ridiculous jealousy touching his belly and then retreating. That was so wrong on so many levels.

"If I told you, I'd have to kill you," Day responded. "Anyway, at least we have a way of gathering additional data. If you like, I can put the weapons in there too. They'll glide right through security. Now, how do you plan to get us where we need to go once we're separated from the tour group?"

"We'll leave when we're near a village or even from the tour itself. From what you've said, the tour we're booked on is going to take us within a few miles of the area we think we need to get to. So I thought if there were enough people, we could get lost in the crowd and then simply fade away when the time comes." Knight was still working through the details in his mind, but he knew he would have to take advantage of the particular situation at that time. It wasn't possible to predict the assets that would be available. "At the very worst we'll need to walk." Knight expected a reaction of surprise, but he only got a nod, and then Day returned to his seat in front of his computer. His jaw remained set, and Knight turned away. He walked to the window and drew back the curtains, opening the sliding door before stepping out onto the small balcony. Knight slid the door closed and leaned against the railing. The balcony, if you could actually call it that, was barely big enough for him to stand on. The thing was mostly decorative and rather stupid when Knight thought about it, but he soaked up the sun and remembered the last time he'd been in Florida.

Laughter rang in Knight's ears. It wasn't really there, but he could hear it just the same. "Let's go higher, Dad." Zachary pushed the bar forward, and Dumbo rose into the air. "I wanna fly someday, Dad. Like Dumbo. I wanna fly." Knight gripped the balcony railing as he moved closer to his son. He didn't remember what he'd said. He shifted his gaze toward the passing clouds, wondering if Zach was hitching a ride on one of them.

The door opened behind him, and the daydream popped like a soap bubble. "What do you want?" Knight asked between clenched teeth. Day stayed back, and Knight used the moment to blink away the emotions that had worked their way to the surface.

"Sorry, Your Highness, I didn't realize you were greeting your public."

The door closed, hard. Knight didn't turn around or react. Instead, he stood there looking out over the palm trees and tropical foliage. When he was ready to go inside, he turned and opened the door, stepping out of the heat and into the air-conditioned comfort of the room.

Day sat at the table. He didn't look up as Knight came back in.

"Have you figured out anything new?" Knight asked.

"No. I decided to send a few e-mails to friends. It will help explain why I went away on such short notice." He continued typing.

"What are you telling them?" Knight asked, and for a second, stubbornness filled Day's eyes, and Knight figured he wasn't going to tell him just to be obstinate.

"The cover story we agreed on. The company sent me to Florida on a last-minute business trip. I kept it simple and explained that I would be gone for a couple of weeks. They all wished me a good trip and said for me to send them pictures when I got some free time." He closed the top on his laptop and opened his suitcase, pulled out some clothes, and then walked to the bathroom. The door closed with a thud, and Knight wondered just what all this was about. He knew part of it was the result of his "assness," to use Mark's word. But he also thought Day was acting like some pretty boy prima donna and needed to get the hell over it.

Knight opened his bag and pulled out a pair of shorts. He toed off his shoes and dropped his pants, then bent over to pull on the shorts so he'd be more comfortable. The bathroom door opened, and he stumbled and nearly fell forward onto the bed but caught himself and pulled up the shorts, then fastened the waist. He turned around and stopped for a second.

Day stood barefooted in shorts and a tank top that left little to the imagination, showing off a developed chest, nipples raising the crisp white fabric to slight relief. Wide shoulders and a narrow waist completed the package. "I'm going to take the shuttle bus to the beach area. I figure I can take some pictures that I can send to friends in a few days. Help solidify the cover story." He slipped his tanned feet into flip-flops, then grabbed a small carryall from the top of the suitcase and began shoving things inside. Then he stopped and looked up from his task. "Do you want to come?" Knight was almost shocked. He'd figured Dayton would want some time away from him. "If you're going to come, get your butt in gear, and I'll meet you in the lobby in ten minutes." There was no smile, and Knight figured Day was simply being nice. He didn't need a pity trip to the beach or anyone's sympathy.

Day shut down his computer and stowed his gear before he grabbed his bag, his wallet, and one of the key cards, then he left the room, the door closing with a bang that reverberated like a gunshot in the small room.

Knight stood alone, much as he had for the last two years. He pulled open the sliding door and once again stepped out onto the balcony and into the heat. Zackary and Cheryl would have loved it here. He could just imagine Zachary sneaking out to drop water balloons over the atrium railing, with Cheryl doing her best to try to head off whatever mischief he was going to get into next. Theirs had been a game that had gone on for most of the time they'd been in his life. But that had ended, and it wasn't coming back. He would never hear Zachary's unguarded laughter or see Cheryl's smile when he came home.

Knight turned and checked his watch. It had only been five minutes. He still had a few more if he wanted to get out of here and join Day at the beach. Knight turned back to the view. "What the hell are you doing moping around like a huge putz?" he heard Cheryl say. He could see her with her hands on her hips, tapping her right foot. She did that whenever she thought he was doing something dumb. Her eyes shone with her own version of gentle love. Theirs hadn't been a grand passion but a warm, friendly kind of love. One he missed every day like a soft blanket wrapped around his shoulders on a winter day. "What are you waiting for?" Cheryl asked, still tapping her foot. She could do that all day.

"All right," he said out loud and stepped back in the room, closed the balcony door, and grabbed a light T-shirt from his bag. He slipped off the shirt he was wearing, pulled on the fresh one, and after hurrying to change into old deck shoes, grabbed his wallet and key card before leaving the room.

The elevator was slow, but the doors finally parted. He jumped in and pressed the button for the lobby, watching through the glass as the car descended, hoping to catch a glimpse of Day. Knight wasn't sure why he was so excited about going to the beach, but he strode out of the elevator and around to the empty lobby.

"Did you see a man in shorts and a white tank top?" Knight asked one of the desk clerks.

"The one sexy enough to curl your toes?" she asked and then her cheeks colored.

"Yes, that would be him," Knight answered with a slight eye roll.

"He asked where to catch the shuttle bus and then left a minute ago. I told him the stop is on the corner." She flashed him a smile a few watts brighter than he would have expected. Knight moved away, strode through the front door, and headed toward the corner. Day stood near the sign, hair going every way possible in the breeze, sun shining on him. "Radiant" was what came to mind. He slowed his walk and shoved those thoughts out of his head. He was not going to have them. He actually thought about turning around and going right back inside. Day hadn't seen him. He could go to the beach on his own and have a more pleasant day than spending it with a man who wanted nothing more than to drink himself into oblivion to forget… everything.

"You decided to come," Day said as he stood rooted to the spot. "Just in time. Here's the bus." Either Day hadn't seen his indecision or had chosen to ignore it. Either way, he stepped forward and climbed on the shuttle to the beach. It was hard to tell if Day was pleased that he'd come, but the decision had been made. Knight took a seat across the aisle from Dayton, the door closed, and the shuttle moved forward.

The ride from the hotel to the beach area took ten minutes or so, and Knight got out when Day did, following him across the street from the shops that sold beachwear and T-shirts and the restaurants where people sat on covered verandas drinking and talking.

The sand was warm, and Knight wished he'd worn flip-flops the way Dayton had as he walked toward the ocean's pounding waves, which drowned out the sounds of people. Dayton slipped off his flip-flops and stood at the edge of the surf, the water swirling around his feet. Knight pulled out his phone and snapped a picture of Dayton looking out over the water.

"Do you want any pictures?" Dayton asked.

There was no one to send them to. Mark was his closest friend, and he knew where he was, so Knight shook his head.

"I'll take some of you, though," he offered. Dayton walked over and handed him his phone. Knighton brought up the camera app and took a step back, snapping a picture of a smiling Dayton standing at the edge of the water. "I need a few different ones," he called over the ocean's sounds. He stepped back and snapped a few pictures up and down the beach. Then he panned the screen of the phone back onto Dayton and nearly dropped it. Day had pulled off his shirt and now held it in his hand. He was…. Words failed him. Not that it mattered. Day could be as sexy as fuck, which he was, but Knighton shouldn't be looking, and, God, the guy was most likely straight. Besides, he was his partner in this mission. The reasons why he shouldn't be taking his time lining up this shot before pushing the button were piling up against him, but he still took his time, framing Dayton in the picture perfectly before snapping it.

Dayton reached around and shoved his shirt in his back pocket. Then he held out his hand, and Knight placed the phone in it. "Let's see what's up that way."

Knight nodded, and they walked north up the beach. Skateboarders and inline skaters rolled by on the sidewalk. Men and women paused what they were doing, watching Day as he strutted by, and Knight took a few seconds to admire musculature and a physique that could have served as the model for many a work of art. Little beads of sweat broke out on Day's skin, making it glisten in the bright sunshine.

"Are you hungry?" Dayton asked after looking over his shoulder.

"I could eat." He tried to remember the last time he'd had food. He'd grabbed a granola bar before leaving the house that morning. He figured they would find a table at one of the many restaurants nearby, but Day had other ideas and led them to a snack bar, where he ordered them each a hot dog and a soda. "Is this your idea of lunch?"

"What?" Day asked after taking a bite. "Nothing tastes like a beach dog." He moved closer. "Besides, I thought field people ate at places like this."

Knight chuckled. "When we're on expenses, we eat as well as we possibly can. That's the reality. Besides, if you eat this stuff all the time, you'll get fat, and what would that do to our hale and hearty, rough and ready to go image?"

"I don't think you have to worry," Day said, and Knight felt Day's gaze shift to his belly. Day certainly didn't have to worry. His stomach could appear on a poster for the perfect set of abs. Knight kept his mouth shut and didn't comment. Instead, he ate the hot dog, listening to the waves on the shore, the screech of the gulls, and the laughter and chatter of people. It was almost normal. He felt almost normal, something that he had started to think would never happen again.

He sucked the diet soda through his straw and worked on the hot dog, keenly aware of how close Day was standing to him. If he wanted, he could reach out and touch him, but he didn't. He never would. It would be too close to a betrayal, and he had never knowingly betrayed anyone in his life. He was a Marine, and only the role of father had ever meant more to him. Marines were about duty, honor, and integrity. He lived those virtues—at least he strived to—in every part of his life. Knight ate the last of his hot dog, finished the soda, and then threw all the paper away.

"Did you even taste it?"

Knight humphed as a stab of pain went through his chest. Cheryl had asked that with almost every meal they had together. All those years and meals eaten in minutes because there was no time. For most of his life he'd wolfed down food because it was what was required. Growing up there had never been enough, so he'd learned to eat fast so he could have first dibs on seconds if there were any. In the Marines, he ate fast because… well… he had to eat fast or not eat at all. "Yes, it was good."

"Okay, then," Day said, taking another bite of his. "I don't eat like this very often. Mostly I try to eat vegetarian and limit red meat. It's healthier and closer to nature. I also avoid processed foods as much as possible, but sometimes I just need a hot dog." He popped the last of it into his mouth, and Knight found the waves and surf incredibly interesting to look at. "Do you want to move on?"

"Sure." His throat was dry again, and Knight thought about ordering another soda, but fuck, it wouldn't do a bit of good. Every single time he looked over at Day, with his warm skin, powerful chest with nipples that screamed to be touched, licked…. Knight stood up and turned away, waiting for Dayton. When he didn't start out, Knight led the way up the beach. This was better—at least he didn't have to watch him all the damned time.

"Are we heading for something special, or is this a forced march?"

He hadn't realized how fast he'd been walking and slowed down. They were approaching the volleyball area of the beach, where games were in progress. Men and women crowded the areas, running, diving, and yelling as they played. Knight sat down at one of the tables to watch. He expected Day to do the same, but when some of the players waved, Day jogged off and had soon joined one of the games.

"We could use another guy if you wanna to play," a college-age kid said. Knight knew he was being looked over and most likely seen as too old to keep up with them.

"Sure," Knight answered and followed the kid over. "Knight," he said to the other guys.

"That's Pete, Grift, Luke," the kid said as he pointed to the tanned guys in the front row. "Hunt is serving, and I'm Skip. Take the spot on the end over there." Knight moved into position, the score was called, and the ball was served over the net only to be returned right at him. Knight set the ball up front, and Grift spiked it over the net. It should have been a point, but Day got to it and popped it up. The ball came to him again, and Knight set it high. Hunt got it and pounded it over the net for the point.

"Man…," Luke said, whipping around to slap Knight's hands. "And you didn't want him because you said he was too old." Luke lightly shoved Grift before cuffing him on the side of the head. "Let the rest of us do the thinking. You just play." That got Luke a return cuff.

"If you two are done with your lovers' spat, let's go," Hunt called, and everyone got into position as the ball was served again. The serve went to the other team after Knight was unable to reach a shot at his feet. The other team rotated, and the game resumed. The score went back and forth, tension ramping up as the ribbing continued. Knight pulled off his shirt when he got too warm and tossed it off to the side before taking his position in the center of the front row, nose to nose with Day.

"I'm going to take your head off, old man," Day said with a huge bright smile. "I'm gonna feed you the ball for dessert."

"No. I think it's you who's going to be having dessert, diaper boy," Knight teased back.

Day tilted his head slightly to the side. The score was called and the ball served. The ball was set up by the other side, and Day leaped into the air, arm over his head to spike it at him. Knight was already reacting before Day touched the ball, and as soon as he hit it, Knight connected with the ball, sending it slamming into the ground just in front of Day. The guys on his team all slapped his hand, grins all around.

The sun went behind a cloud, and the wind rose off the water. Knight glanced upward, seeing dark clouds filling the horizon.

"Great game," his teammates called to one another as they went to grab their things.

"You better go for cover. These afternoon storms don't last long, but they pour like nobody's business," Grift told him.

Knight grabbed his shirt and pulled it back on before following the others toward the sidewalk. The beach emptied in minutes, a steady flow of people taking to the sidewalk and crossing the street, flowing into the shops and bars.

"Let's go back to the hotel," Day suggested. Knight saw one of the buses coming, and they hurried across the street as the sky darkened further. The first drops of rain fell as the bus pulled to a stop, and by the time Knight and Day were in their seats seat, rain pelted the roof before running down the windows in sheets.

Day tugged on his shirt as Knight stared out the window, keeping his thoughts centered, refusing to allow them to wander where he didn't want them to go. All this wishing, lusting, and fantasizing was for nothing. It was stupid. Knight closed his eyes, drawing on his Marine training to center his mind. It worked, and as they pulled away from the bus stop, he focused on the mission ahead. "We should check to see if there are any new communications when we get back," Knight said softly. Day turned toward him as though he'd stated the most obvious thing in the world. There was a barb waiting at the tip of Day's tongue; he could feel it there. The only thing stopping Day was the very public venue they were in. He turned away and once again stared out the window.

As the bus rolled down the street, he continued watching the water, white waves against the black sky. Zachary loved playing in the sand, and Knight had to carry him off the beach in order to get him to stop building sandcastles and trying to keep the moat filled. His blond hair would be full of sand by the time he and Cheryl got him back to the hotel, and his smile would last for days. That smile had made everything worth it.

By the time the bus stopped near the hotel, the rain had stopped, and the sun shone again. The air-conditioning fought the sun until they exited the bus. The heat slapped into him instantly, and Knight gasped for a second before inhaling deeply and remembering the heat was part of why he'd wanted to come here. His heart had been cold and empty for a long time, and he'd hoped maybe the warmth would revive it. It hadn't happened.

Knight pushed that thought aside, as he'd been doing a lot lately, entered the hotel right behind Day, and they headed directly for the elevators. Inside their room Knight set up his computer, and Day hooked it to his portable secure network. Knight checked his messages, but there were none. "Do you have anything?"

Day typed furiously. "Yes. Additional transmissions have been intercepted." He continued typing. "It's going to take me a little while to work to decode and then figure out if they tell us anything new." He didn't stop typing for a second. "Like, most of the time, we aren't getting the entire conversation, and it isn't as though they're sending out a blueprint of their plan. All we can hope is that we'll get some detail that will fill in the picture further."

Knight knew all that. "NSA?" he asked. Had to be. They were the true experts on interception of terrorist transmissions and data. It was what they did. "That detail was left out of your file."

Day looked up from behind his laptop screen. "There were a lot of details left out of your file too." He lowered his gaze and continued working. "Like your first name. I looked for it in all the files I could find, but all I ever found was Knighton."

"You're not the only one who can work magic with systems." Knight mimicked what Day was doing and checked to see if he had any work waiting for him. Then he logged into the archives and began digging into anything they had on groups in this area of Mexico. "The groups in this area have been more interested in running drugs and increasing their influence in Mexico City than in terrorism, mostly for their own protection and to bring money into the area, which they use to line their pockets."

"So why are they doing this now? Why not continue doing what they do best instead of hatching a scheme that's guaranteed to bring the wrath of the US and the world down on them?" Day continued working. "Something has to have changed."

"Fuck," Knight groaned.

Day was right. Until recently, the groups in this area had shown no interest in anything other than feathering their own pockets and pushing their product across the border. The prime motivator had been money, but if that had changed, then they needed to find out what the new motivator was. "I somehow doubt we're going to get that from their transmissions."

"Maybe, maybe not," Day mumbled without looking up. "The transmissions are broken pieces of voice. Unfortunately, something is definitely interfering with the transmission. Which means they're talking locally, probably over a satellite phone. It's not a cellular communication. There are no towers in that area. If there were, it would be easy enough to hack into the data for the tower and get what we need. They have to be using sat phones, which is what they suspected back at the office." Dayton paused. "I'm going to try to string these transmissions together and see what I get."

Day played the intercepted transmission, but it didn't sound like much to him. "I can pick out a few words, but not much more than that. It's almost gibberish, we have so little of the conversation." Day didn't stop typing. "I'm going to try to run this through some programs to see if there's enough to make sense out of this."

"What sort of programs?" Knight asked, keenly interested.

Day lifted his gaze. "You don't want to know." He then lowered his head and went back to work.

"Excuse me," Knight began. "Are you saying that only someone as computer literate as you could understand what you're doing?" Sometimes the man could be a real pain in the ass.

"Jesus, no. It's just something you… don't… want to know…." He paused, and Knight humphed and went back to the data he was able to get from Research and Records. In this business, sometimes new information wasn't needed. Instead, the information you already had, looked at differently, could yield results, but he was coming up with nothing, and he hated that. The kid was making progress, and he needed to do the same.

The click of keys was constant and unending. Day worked, head down, and he did the same.

"I'm coming up empty," Knight said a little while later. "All the data I have is pointing to the same thing—drugs and money. We've been able to trace some weapons purchases, but they're mostly small stuff."

"I'm making progress. The programs are coming up with likely scenarios, but most of them are meaningless chatter." Day put on earphones and held up his hand as he listened once again. Then he took them off and handed the phones to Knight. "Listen to this." Knight put on the phones, and Day played the track.

"I don't understand that much Spanish," Knight admitted.

"They're saying they have to move up their plans. They aren't saying what they are, but to get everyone busy and ready to go." Day paused. "I think it means that our mission just got more urgent, and we need to get into Mexico and locate these bastards as soon as we can."

"Is there any indication of how soon?"

"No. Which means whatever they're planning could happen at any time. But it doesn't sound like they're ready yet."

Well, that was something at least. Knight stood up and paced around the room. He felt like a caged animal. He wanted to get out there, boots on the ground, find out what the fuck was going on, and then put an end to it so he could get back home to his normal life and away from temptation. Day stood as well, and Knight watched him stretch his arms over his head. Then he pulled his shirt over his head and tossed it aside before stretching some more and then limbering up. "Do you need the bathroom? I'm going to take a shower."

"No," Knight answered, his throat dry once again. Was Day doing this to him on purpose? He couldn't be. No one was aware of his feelings. They had been buried for so long, hell, even he wasn't sure what they were. But fuck if his body wasn't screaming inside his head that it sure wanted Day. "Go ahead." Once again, he turned and walked away, pulled open the sliding balcony door, and stepped out into the heat. He closed the door and gripped the railing. This was not supposed to be happening. He stayed outside for a long time, until his heart rate returned to normal and he could swallow without his throat scratching like sandpaper.

Knight heard a light tap on the slider and turned around. Day had dressed and now stood on the other side of the door. Knight opened the door and stepped inside. He opened his suitcase and pulled out fresh clothes before heading to the bathroom. As soon as he closed the door, Knight blew out his breath. He stood in front of the mirror. He hated how old he looked. His hair hadn't had the tinges of gray a few years earlier. That had all grown in since… he'd lost his family.

Knight stripped off his shirt and shorts before starting the shower. He made sure the bathmat was in place and got a towel within grabbing distance, then stepped under the water.

The heat felt great, but it didn't do a single thing about the tension that had settled in each cell of his body, and that shit wasn't going away. A few days earlier, his life had been quiet—boring as hell, but predictable and ordered. Now he was back in the field with a partner who had awakened longings he thought he'd willed out of his life a long time ago. Knight grabbed the bar of soap and ran his hands over his body. He was too self-aware and grounded in reality to imagine it was someone else's hands on his body. But his dick reacted as though it was. He did his best to ignore the erection that sprouted within seconds.

Knight washed his hair and willed his dick to go back to sleep, but the damned thing was not going to do that. Instead, his dick throbbed when he washed his chest and legs, swinging back and forth as he stepped from foot to foot. *Fuck.* He groaned softly and soaped his hands good. He turned around, the water pelting his back, and wrapped a hand around his dick, gripping hard and then stroking fast.

"Damn," Knight groaned softly, hoping like hell the water covered any of the sounds he was making. He focused on the usual images as he jerked himself, but nothing was happening. He'd done this plenty and knew what he liked, but, fuck, that wasn't getting it done. He kept pulling on his dick, but nothing seemed to work. However, as soon as an image of Day filled his mind, he was up and raring to go. Energy flooded thorough his veins, and his right leg shook.

His breath came in small pants. Knight moved back in the tub until he could lean against the wall. Fucking hell, his vision was beginning to narrow, and his fingers felt like fucking magic. He'd been jerking off for decades, but nothing had ever felt like this. The floaty feeling was already starting. He heaved for breath, heart pounding in his ears. He wasn't quite there yet, but the climax of his little shower show was approaching fast. He pressed back against the tile, needing the wall to steady himself as he thought about Day standing in the shower with him, acres of honey- brown skin, ringlets plastered to his head, lips parted, coming closer. "Fuck me," he whispered.

As soon as the imaginary Day reached for him, Knight closed his eyes, letting the energy from the entire day coalesce in a single place at the base of his spine. Within seconds heat spread throughout his entire body, his legs shook, and he gripped his dick like a vise and came like he'd never come in his life. Knight opened his mouth, inhaling deeply as lights flashed behind his eyes. His feet slipped forward, and he slowly slid down the wet tile wall, managing to hold the shower door to keep from crashing on his ass. He ended up sitting on the floor of the tub, water washing over him. He gasped, head bent forward so he could breathe without sucking water. He had no energy to stand, so he sat for a few minutes and then reached forward to turn off the water. What had collected in the tub washed down the drain, and still he couldn't move. Fuck, he didn't want to. His skin still sang, and his head whirled in little circles whenever he opened his eyes.

Eventually his head righted itself. Knight stood slowly, getting his feet under him before stepping out of the tub and onto the mat. He dried his ultrasensitive skin, turning on the fan to pull the moisture out of the room. He should have turned on the fan before he started the shower, so he waited a little for the moisture to dissipate, leaning on the counter. Then he got dressed and stepped out of the bathroom. He found Day sitting at the table behind his computer, headphones on his ears.

"Find anything new?" He was grateful Day wasn't paying attention to him for so many reasons. This fascination he seemed to have wasn't being returned, and that was good. It would make it easier for him to dismiss it from his system because, just as he thought, the interest wasn't reciprocal. Not that he expected it to be. It was a foolish notion. Day's immersion in his work also gave Knight cover for his still wobbly knees and a chance to catch his breath.

Day nodded. "I called Dimato and let him know what I found. All he said was to get the hell on the ship and stick to the plan."

"That's what he would say." Dimato was a man who changed plans as rarely as possible. Knight was more a "fly by the seat of his pants" kind of guy. He made plans and preparations—they had their value—but he wasn't married to them, and his ability to think on his feet was one of his greatest assets. At least he liked to think so.

"I just want to get this moving," Day said. "We can't do any good sitting here."

"Yes, we can. We can go to dinner, get something good to eat, and then come back here and get a solid night's sleep." He bet Day had been so excited since being given his first field assignment that he hadn't slept much. Knight stuffed his wallet and the key card in his pocket. "Close that up for a while, and let's get going."

Day nodded and typed briefly, then closed the lid on the computer before sliding it back into his bag. He then shut down the communications equipment and secured it back in its case.

"Go on down to the lobby. I'll be right behind you," Knight said. Day nodded and left the room. Knight grabbed their computer bags and the communications bag and slid them into the cupboard beneath the sink in the bathroom to keep them out of sight. He pulled the cabinet door closed, lacing a scrap of paper between the door and the frame as he did so. He wasn't expecting trouble, and no one could use the equipment without security protocols, but better safe than sorry. He placed the "Do Not Disturb" sign on the room door as he closed it before heading to the elevator. He met Day in the lobby, and they walked to a nearby sports bar, where they sat at the bar, ate, and spent an hour or so watching sports on the televisions located all around. Not that Knight was a huge sports fan—it was simply easier than trying to come up with topics for chitchat. Cheryl had been the social butterfly in their marriage. Knight avoided most social situations when he could or he'd simply let her do the talking, because she knew what to say for both of them.

After dinner they walked a little in the growing darkness. The heat of the day had dissipated, but it was still a lot warmer than back home. Knight was in no hurry to go back to the room and go to bed. He knew he should take the same advice he'd given Day, but his mind didn't want to settle. The two of them were only walking together, but he was acutely aware of where Day was all the time and even how close to him he got. Knight didn't have to see it—he closed his eyes and he could feel Day like he had some invisible force around him that pinged off Knight's skin whenever he got close.

This shit had to end. He couldn't think when Day was around him, and that had to change. He had to get his head screwed on straight and stop mooning over someone and something he couldn't have. He'd made his choice years ago, and he wasn't going to betray the memory of his family by going back on that now.

They arrived back at the hotel and went up to the room. The sign was still on the door, and inside, the tiny scrap of paper fluttered to the floor when he opened the cabinet door. He pulled out the equipment and handed it to Day. Then he checked the rest of the room. Nothing seemed to have been disturbed, and yet he had the feeling, something unsettling in his gut, that someone had been in the room. Maybe it was housekeeping. Maybe they'd knocked and come in anyway. Knight checked the bed, but it hadn't been pulled down. He also peered into the bathroom, but the towels were where they'd left them. "Check your stuff just to be sure," he told Day. Something was off, and he wasn't sure why. It must have been his imagination.

"Everything is where I left it," Day said.

Knight nodded and flopped down on the bed, turning on the television. The team was taking their cover story a little far. They had booked a room with a king-size bed. Not that Knight hadn't slept in a bed with other guys before. He'd slept on concrete floors with other Marines, huddled together for warmth. It was what they did, and he wasn't going to let the thought of sleeping in the same bed with Day get to him.

Eventually he got up and changed into a pair of shorts and a T-shirt before pulling down the covers and sliding between the sheets.

Day still sat at the table in the corner, his computer screen casting a glow on his upper body and face as Knight turned out the light, rolled onto his side, and closed his eyes.

He was asleep in seconds, dreaming of chocolate eyes just like he had before, only this time, he knew who they belonged to. He'd spent hours trying not to look into them, and it had been those eyes he'd seen in the shower. He was so fucking screwed.

Chapter 3

DAY WAITED for a while after Knight turned out the lights before quietly going to the bathroom to change. He brushed his teeth and rinsed his mouth before returning to the room. He climbed into the far side of the bed with as little movement as possible. Then he rolled onto his side away from Knight and closed his eyes.

But fuck if sleep would come. He lay there without moving for a long time, eyes closed, but it did no good. Fatigue must have caught up with him eventually, because he closed his eyes, and the next time he opened them, light was peeking at the top of the curtains. It took him a few seconds to figure out that something was wrong. A strong arm wound around his waist, hand resting on his belly. He shifted slightly, and Knight mumbled behind him and tugged him closer, pressing his chest to Day's back.

Day gently lifted Knight's hand and moved away from his embrace. It was really nice, but Day was not ready for Knight to wake with him in his arms. Hell, he wasn't sure if he was ready to wake up being held by another man. At least not this man. Yeah, Knight was handsome all right, but he'd been married, he'd read that in the file—wife and son deceased, that's what it had said in the politically correct language of human resources. Still it was nice being held. It made him feel like someone actually gave a damn about him, regardless of whether the guy knew what he was doing, which Day doubted.

He managed to disentangle himself from Knight and got off the bed without disturbing him. He went into the bathroom, used the toilet, shaved, and brushed his teeth, then got dressed before booting up his laptop and checking for messages. There was nothing important, but he occupied himself at the computer, looking up briefly when he heard Knight shift on the bed and then get up. He pretended to be working, head lowered a little, but he was really hoping to catch a glimpse. The day before, when they were playing volleyball, he'd nearly lost it when Knight pulled off his shirt. The man was sexy as fuck. Day shifted slightly to get comfortable, glad the table hid everything. It had been obvious that Knight had lived a life of hard work. Muscles bulged in all the right places. Day had worked hard at the gym to get the body he had; Knight had worked hard in life to get what he had.

"Are you done in the bathroom?" Knight asked, yawning as he scratched his belly, giving Day a glimpse of the dark treasure trail over light olive skin.

"Yes. It's all yours," Day answered, doing his best not to look up. "I'm just checking on a few things. There isn't anything really new."

"Okay. I'll clean up, and we can get some breakfast and then head to the ship." Knight turned and went into the bathroom. Day breathed a sigh of relief and began packing everything up. It didn't take long before his bags were ready. All he needed was to get his kit and things from the bathroom. Once Knight came out, Day got his things and finished up.

THEY WENT down for breakfast and then finished packing before making their way down to the front desk to check out of the hotel. A shuttle bus took them over to the port, where they got in line and checked in for the cruise. They were early, but someone must have pulled some strings because they were apparently in the system as frequent cruisers and ended up being seated in a comfortable area to wait for boarding. The process was incredibly efficient, and soon they were logged onto the ship and headed up the gangway.

"Pay attention to the people around you," Knight whispered to him.

"Do you really think there's a threat?" Day asked.

"There's always a threat," Knight countered. They got on board and found out they couldn't get into their cabins for a few hours yet. They ended up riding a glass-enclosed elevator up to the buffet and having lunch.

"I'm going to go to the gym," Day said as they exited the buffet. He wanted some exercise, and there was still time before they could get into the cabin. Knight nodded absently, and Day took a few steps. "Do you want to come?" The guy appeared a little lost as he stared out at the port buildings.

"I'll stay here and take charge of the bags with the equipment. We don't have to do everything together the entire time we're on board," Knight said a little snippily.

"I was just being nice. If you don't want to come, don't come," Day retorted in a low voice before turning to walk away. "You know, you get further being pleasant than being a spawn of Satan." God, the man could be the biggest pain in the ass. Day strode across the deck, checking one of the ship maps before taking the stairs down to the fitness center area.

There wasn't a locker room for him to use to change, so he used the restroom and stored his things in a temporary locker. As soon as he came out, it was readily apparent that this was a gay cruise. The gym was filled with guys in various stages of dress, or undress, as the case may be. Most wore as little as possible to show off as much as they could. The view was magnificent, and even though he wasn't sure how comfortable he was with everyone thinking he was gay, it was liberating too. He could just be who he was, and no one was going to judge him. Hell, from the leers Day was getting, he could have just about whatever he wanted.

The thing was, he was so uncomfortable he didn't know what to do. Part of him wanted to chuck the veneer he'd spent so long perfecting and dive headfirst into the buffet of men on display and seemingly ripe for the taking. But he was here to get a job done, not to fuck his way across the Caribbean. Secondly, the guys on the ship might think he was gay, and that was the cover he was supposed to convey, but having Knight find out he really was gay was so not going to happen. Scorpion was populated by men who were *men,* and they expected everyone else to be the same. Most were ex-military, and regardless of the death of Don't Ask, Don't Tell, in Scorpion they didn't ask, they just assumed.

Day found a bench and did some light warm-up lifts before moving to something heavier.

"Do you need a spot?" a man asked after his second set. His gaze didn't meet Day's. Instead he was looking everywhere but, taking him in like he was lunch. Day felt so damned exposed that he was seconds from blushing his fool head off.

"That would be nice," he answered and lay back on the bench to do another set. The man stood over him, and as Day lifted the bar, the man moved a little closer, giving Day a view of everything the good Lord gave him. Day nearly choked, and only supreme effort kept the bar from crashing down on his chest. Instead, he took a deep breath, cleared his mind, and did the set. He had not expected that. "Thanks," Day said and stood up. "Do you need one?"

Apparently the offer and view was an invitation. "No, I'm good," he crooned with a lascivious grin. He seemed to be waiting for Day to take him up on his offer.

"Well, thanks," Day said and moved to another machine. He watched the man move on, and as Day worked at an incline chest machine, the man seemed to have gotten someone else to accept his offer.

"Dayton?"

He finished the last two reps in his set and looked to where he'd heard the voice. "It is you." An old "friend" from college, Blain, stepped into his view. Fuck, why in hell did he have to be here? Of all the people to be on board ship, one of them had to be Blain fucking McIntyre. "I never thought I'd live to see you on a cruise like this." He grinned, flashing everyone within twenty feet his perfect dentist-manufactured smile.

"I'm on vacation with a friend." He needed to keep his cover and not make a big deal about this. There were five thousand or more passengers on this ship. It wasn't like he would be seeing Blain a great deal. *Keep cool, and stick to the story.* "He invited me along with him."

"You do know the kind of cruise you're on, don't you?" Blain moved closer. "I never expected you to step far enough out of the world's biggest walk-in closet you had yourself stuck in to go on something like this." Yeah, he was still bitter and as bitchy as ever. He narrowed his gaze. "So you're here with a friend. Is he a boyfriend or just a friend?"

Day did his best to smile. He'd been hoping to spend the time on board in near anonymity, but that had just flown out the window.

Furthermore, his big secret, the one thing in his life he hadn't wanted to deal with, was most likely going to become an issue of epic proportions, and knowing Blain, major drama. "Knighton is a friend. We both got vacation at the same time and booked the cruise."

Blain looked at him and then threw his head back and laughed. "You had no idea what kind of cruise it was, did you?" The bastard laughed harder. "That explains why you're here."

"And why are you here? Finished sleeping with the men in the northern half of the country so you came down here to find someone new?" He could be mean and bitchy too. "Don't forget, there are two sides to every issue, just like there are two sides to your revolving bed." Blain went slightly pale and looked across the gym to where another man was working out. "So you're with someone? Does he know about your past and the trips to the clinic?" From the way Blain's eyes darkened, the guy he was with had no idea.

"It's very new."

Day breathed a sigh of relief. "Good. I wish you all the happiness in the world." He really did. But he also met Blain's gaze with the hardest stare he could muster. Blain turned and walked over toward the man working out with the dumbbells. It wasn't likely Blain would be seeking him out after that little exchange, which bought him some time, at least for now. Day continued his workout, conscious of the men around him. A few chatted him up between sets, and he talked with them but remained distant. He wasn't like them. They all seemed to know each other, even if they were complete strangers. They spoke a language Dayton didn't understand and wasn't sure he was interested in learning. He was gay, he knew that, but being gay and acting on it were two very different things. He'd done the acting-on-it part, with Blain. What a mistake that had been, and meeting him again had solidified his resolution to focus on his career and keep who he was to himself.

"Are you done with that machine?" one of the men asked in a rich deep voice.

"Sure, sorry." Day stood and took a step away.

"Don't be," the man said, after sitting down. "Name's Ryland," he added with a deep, most likely Texas accent. "Are you here with someone or on your own?" He shifted his arms behind the pads of the pec deck fly machine and smiled a little. "Because if you're alone, I'd be mighty pleased to keep you company for a while. Maybe get a drink when we're done in here?" He got the machine working, and Day couldn't help watching as the man's chest got bigger and harder with each movement.

"I'm with someone. Thanks, though," he said, forcing a smile. "You have a good workout." He needed to get the hell out of there. Back home, the gym was a place of refuge, but here it was nothing more than a meat market. He found it unsettling. For him, the gym was where he worked his body to try to cleanse his mind, but that wouldn't be possible on board ship, at least not on this cruise, short as it was going to be for him.

Day grabbed his bag out of the locker and left the gym, then climbed the stairs to the ninth deck. The doors were open, and he walked down the passageway checking the cabin numbers until he found his. He inserted his card, the door clicked open, and he entered the cabin.

Knight stood in the center of the cabin. "I wish our luggage would get here."

"They won't deliver them until this evening. That's what it said in the cruise documents." He set his bag on the edge of the bed and looked around the cabin. "It seems they booked us a suite of some sort."

"They did, and if you notice on our passes, we're members of their frequent cruiser club."

"How did that happen, I wonder?" Knight asked, raising his eyebrows.

Day knew he'd been caught. "I figured we might as well have the best cruise experience possible for the few days we're on board ship." He lifted his carry-on bag off the bed and pulled open the bathroom door. It was roomy, and he stripped off his sweaty workout clothes and changed into fresh shorts, shirt, and underwear. He wanted to take a shower and wished there had been one in the gym area, but he also figured he would swim and use the whirlpools later, so he decided to wait.

"Did all your toys make it through?" Day asked as he stepped out.

"You're not the only one with a few tricks. I locked them in the safe. Don't touch them until I have a chance to go over how to use them with you, and we can review the safety mechanisms. I don't want you taking your own foot off." The derision in Knight's voice rankled him, but Day ignored it. "How did yours fare?"

"Don't know. I had to lock it in my luggage. We'll see in a few hours." He walked over to the sliding door, opened it, and stepped out onto the small balcony and into the Florida sunshine.

"How was the gym?"

"Pickup central," Day retorted. He didn't want to go into any more detail, and he certainly wasn't going to mention anything about Blain. If he could get through the next few days without a major drama fest, he'd consider himself lucky. His sexuality was his own business. If he wanted to keep how he felt quiet, that was his business. "They have a nice gym, though. What did you do?"

"Learned where things were." Knight began pacing through the cabin. "This waiting is driving me crazy. We should have arranged for a better way to get there that didn't take so much time."

"We can't just sneak into the country or fly into that area. It might be remote, but this was the best way not to raise anyone's suspicion. No one will think twice about a group of tourists, and the excursion we're booked on is going to have hundreds of people spread over multiple buses. We can easily slip away." Day huffed. "Why can't you simply enjoy yourself for a few days? You seemed ready to do that in Florida."

"That was when we thought we had more time. They could be launching whatever they're planning while we're trying to get there. And we don't even know what the fuck they're going to try to do." Knight continued pacing like a caged animal. "We have got to find a way to figure out what they're up to. At least then we can head off part of this."

"As soon as my bag is delivered, I'll get the equipment set up and have it monitor the frequencies they've been using. We may get lucky." He turned away.

"What if that isn't enough?" Knight asked. "What if we do everything we can and this… thing… attack still goes off and all hell breaks loose?"

Day didn't have the answer, so he remained quiet. He had thought along those lines multiple times. "We can only do our best. We wouldn't have been assigned to this if we couldn't handle it."

Knight laughed almost evilly. "You really think that? They assigned this to us because they thought it would be easy. The threat is in a localized area. All we need to do is locate and neutralize it. I'm a man who's been out of fieldwork for a few years, and you're a baby agent. They gave us something simple."

"But it wasn't," Day protested. "They didn't know what the threat was."

"The threat itself doesn't matter. We're supposed to figure out where they are, and take them out. It's that simple. See, that's how the muckety-mucks' minds work. They boil everything down to the lowest common denominator because they think no one else is capable of thinking." Knight whirled toward him. "Are you up to that?" He squinted. "Can you shoot a gun?" Day opened his mouth to protest. "I know you're as smart as they come, that's obvious, but can you shoot… and can you kill?"

Day came through the balcony door, pulling it closed behind him with a bang. "I want to shoot you right now. Does that count?" he countered with half a smile, since he was half kidding.

"Fine, but can you hit the side of a barn?" Knight pressed.

Day stepped closer. "I can shoot just fine."

"We'll see," Knight said.

"Oh, we will? And where is this going to happen, and why is my word not good enough?" He let his annoyance show freely. "I'm getting a little tired of your condescension. I can shoot just fine, and if you want to know if I can kill, I suggest you unlock the safe and stand on the balcony. I wouldn't want to make a mess of the ship."

Knight glared at him. "In Grand Cayman there's a shooting club. We stop there before Costa Maya. I had booked us a little practice time while we're there, but since you're so adamant about it…."

Day leaned against the sliding door. "You are the north end of a horse going south. In fact, I think it's your goal in life."

"Probably," Knight deadpanned. "But that doesn't change the fact that I want to make sure you can shoot and handle a gun before I put one in your hands. So get the hell over it, Diaper Boy," he added in the tone a parent uses with a small child.

"You want a competition?" Day snapped. "Fine. What do I get if I win?"

Knight grinned. "My respect and one of the weapons to use. And if I win, you take me to the premium steakhouse on board for dinner and let me teach you how to shoot before we get in the thick of things and you shoot me in the head." Knight paused. "I reserved extra time at the gun club."

The smug bastard. "Fine." Day didn't really see much of a downside. "But until then, no more jokes or stupid nicknames. If I win you have to pay for dinner with drinks. And I get to come up with a nickname for you that I can use back at the office." Day crossed his arms over his chest. That should shut him up.

"As long as you're willing to do the same," Knight said with a glint in his eye. "But you should know two things: I had sharpshooter training in the Corps, and I learned how to drink in the Corps as well. That little shipboard card of yours is going to get quite a workout."

Day rolled his eyes. "What time is dinner tonight?" he asked to change the subject. He went to the schedule for the day, which sat on the coffee table, and looked it up. "Eight thirty, and there's a muster drill in half an hour." As he set down the sheet, an announcement was made, and they left the room to head to their station.

After the drill, which consisted of watching a video and listening to announcements, as well as a lot of standing around, they were dismissed, and shortly after that, they left port. Day went back to the cabin and found their bags had been delivered. He began unpacking and setting up the communications equipment, which had arrived in perfect working order. He had no idea where Knight was, and the longer he stayed away, the better Day liked it.

Once he had everything set up, Day logged on to the secure satellite network he'd brought with him and sent a few messages to tell the team back in the office that he was online, and everything was working. They had intercepted some additional communications, and he set about piecing them together.

Knight came in the cabin as he was making progress, the door banging closed behind him. "Do we have anything?" He pulled his laptop out of his pack and booted it up once Day got him connected.

"There have been more interceptions, but they don't say anything new, other than they're having trouble getting the 'sharing logic' to work. I have no idea what that means." He pulled out a dictionary and then looked up a website of Spanish slang to make sure he was translating the words correctly. "Yes, that's what they said, but I'll be damned if I can make anything out of it. Does it mean anything to you?"

"Sharing logic," Knight repeated. "Is there something special like that in computer coding?"

"There's shared logic where core modules are written and then used in multiple programs, or simply called from multiple programs or job controls. But they're definitely using a different tense of the verb. It could be the same thing and I'm translating wrong, but I ran it through a translation program and got the same thing."

"Let's log it with the other things we know, and hopefully it will make sense with more information. It really does seem like things are heating up. The communications are becoming more numerous. That should happen before any plan is carried out. I would suspect radio silence if the final attack is imminent. So the fact that they're talking is good news, in my experience."

"Okay," Day said with relief. Whoever they were, they were chattier than he would have expected. "We are still only getting parts of the transmissions. Let's hope we get more as we get closer."

"Since we're moving now, that should happen each hour. Maybe we'll get lucky soon. Have you been able to get a better fix on location?"

"A little. I'm sure at least part of the transmission is coming from this area." Day pulled up a map of the Yucatan and turned his screen around. "The one thing we got a break with is that it's relatively close to Costa Maya."

"Well, they'll need a town nearby where they can get supplies. It doesn't help having a base in the middle of nowhere if you have to go hundreds of miles for food all the time, and much of the area is swamp and lowland. The only hills are over ruins. That's how archeologists know where to look—just follow the hills. Everything else is flat."

"I've been thinking that maybe they're using some ruins somewhere as a base. That would help explain some of the interference," Day said. "They would need shelter, and they could be partially underground. If they were communicating over short distance, they could probably get a signal, but it would weaken as it got farther, and if there was stone or earth in the way, that might help explain the difficulty triangulating the source." He turned his screen back around and logged what he'd found out in a fact sheet. He also added their suspicions about the interference, did some additional research, and called up satellite images of the area. Mostly what he got were images of vegetation, but he was able to identify a few areas that had potential and overlapped the area where he thought the transmissions originated. That was progress.

"We should get ready for dinner, and we need to get this equipment out of sight." Knight was already packing up, and Day did the same, disconnecting the communications equipment and slipping it into his suitcase under the bed. It wasn't the greatest hiding place, but then no one should be looking for it. All they wanted to do was keep it out of sight. Then they got ready to leave to go to the dining room.

They arrived and found their table, where they were seated with six other people. Introductions were made, and after the requisite comments on the symmetry of the names Day and Knight, the other couples spent most of dinner chatting between themselves or with the others at the table. Day felt amazingly awkward. The couples talked about how they'd met, how long they'd been together, all that stuff. When Willy, seated next to his partner, Bobby, asked how long they had been together, Day hadn't known what to say.

"Dayton and I have been together just a few months." Knight had placed his arm around Day's shoulder just as easy as could be. The touch was so gentle and caring, Day had leaned into it without really thinking. "He was able to get some time off work, and I wanted to do something special, so we were lucky enough to be able to book the cruise." Knight turned to him and smiled. Day found he was smiling back, and what surprised him was that he wasn't forcing it. He liked this kind of attention from Knight, even if it was all just an act. "Our schedules are both so busy that by the time we were able to arrange time off, we seem to have been some of the last to get on the cruise."

"This cruise has been booked for months," Kevin, a bottle-blond, said from across the table.

"A cabin opened up, and we were lucky enough to get it," Knight answered smoothly and turned to Day, smiling sweetly. The others around the table sighed.

"I remember when you used to look at me like that," Bobby whispered, and Willy pulled him into a gentle kiss.

"I still do and always will," Willy said, and the others "aww'd" softly.

The waiter went around the table and took their orders. The conversation moved away from them, and Day sat and listened. He expected Knight to slip his hand away, but it stayed where it was. Day didn't move and forced himself not to tense. They were playing a part that was integral to their cover for being on board ship. That was all. There was nothing more to it than that.

"So what do you have planned tomorrow?" Kevin asked, as perky as a cheerleader.

Day almost answered that he had work to do but managed to stop the words from crossing his lips. That wasn't the type of answer people gave on board ship. "Just hanging out," he answered. "On Grand Cayman Knight has arranged for something special." Day didn't say it was at a shooting range. Let them think it was something romantic rather than work related. The others talked about their plans, and the conversation didn't drop off a bit once the food arrived. It simply shifted to talk of food and who cooked, their specialties, and all that.

Knight seemed to rise to the occasion for the sake of the mission. He talked and talked about mundane things. Apparently Day made a killer veal piccata that Knight just adored. He even glanced at him softly as he spoke about it. The man deserved an Academy Award for his performance, and after a few minutes Day explained about the chicken that Knight made using his mother's recipe. When Day glanced at Knight during that exchange, he was shocked at the dark look that flickered in his eyes. It didn't last long, but it was surprising and cold as hell in its intensity. Day wondered what he'd said and turned to him more fully, looking for some additional explanation in Knight's expression, but the look was already gone, and Knight smiled as though nothing had happened.

Day remembered reading Knight's file, and what had surprised him was how little there was in it. His parents were listed, but no details had been provided, and no other family members had been included. It was like that part of the file had been scrubbed clean. He'd thought it strange when he'd checked, given the other information that had been included regarding Knight's professional history. Someone, probably Knight himself, had gotten the records altered to include only the information he wanted known. There were other sources of info, though, and Day's curiosity had been raised.

"Day, honey," Knight said, pulling him out of his thoughts, "they were asking if we'd like to surf the FlowRider tomorrow."

"Sure, I'm game if you are," Day said with a smile. Knight didn't look too happy, but he kept the smile plastered on his face. "What time would you like to meet?"

"It opens at eleven," Kevin said, looking around the table. "The line gets longer in the afternoon, so why don't we meet then?"

They all agreed, and once dessert had been served, the couples began leaving the table. He and Knight did the same, saying good-bye to everyone and walking together back toward the cabin. It was nice, and Knight led the way to the elevator. They got off at their deck and went right to the cabin, Day still a little flushed from all of Knight's small touches during dinner.

"That went well," Knight said as soon as the door closed, his tone all business.

"It did," he agreed and began pulling the equipment out to get it set up once again. He paused at a knock on the door. Knight opened it to the steward, who was just making sure they had everything they needed. Knight closed the door, and Day noticed the king bed for the first time. He should have expected that.

"I can ask him to separate the bed into two twins," Knight offered and stepped to the door.

"It's fine," Day told him. Maintaining their cover was important. No one must suspect that they were anything but a happy couple out on a cruise together. People talked, and the last thing they wanted was people talking about them. He got out the communications equipment and set it up once again. Then he sat at the desk and got to work. No additional transmissions had been intercepted, but he spent some time doing additional research on the area they were going to be traversing while Knight settled on the sofa with his laptop resting on his legs.

"Are you finding anything?" Knight asked.

Day shook his head. With the research he could accomplish done for now, he'd changed his topic. "I'm not having any luck at all." He squinted and began typing again. "They've done a lot to cover their tracks." He was able to find a little information about Knighton—a few articles written in the Allegan, MI, newspaper about his military service, but very little else. He pulled up the article, hoping to at least discover his first name, but fuck if they didn't use "Knight" or his last name as well. In fact, they used PFC "Knight" Knighton as his name. Fuck all. How in the hell did he do that?

"I guess the people we're dealing with are rather sophisticated."

"Either that or they're lucky," Day said, glancing up at Knight, who was immersed in his work. Day brought up a network sniffer program, just to see if Knight was messing with him somehow. He didn't seem to be. He was able to see that Knight was simply surfing the net for anything about groups in that area of Mexico. "I keep thinking they have help from someone." He knew Knight must have had help removing all his personal family data from the files. But that puzzle could wait for another day.

Knight looked up from his screen. "That's always possible. Any number of terrorist groups could be providing aid or expertise. Sometimes I think if those groups worked together instead of fighting one another…." Knight paused and shivered. "What are you thinking?"

"I don't know. My mind is running in circles and not getting anywhere." Day rubbed his eyes and stood up. He closed his laptop and went into the bathroom. He always looked for deeper meaning in things. That was what had made him very good at making the connections the NSA needed from him. And there was some connection here he needed to make, but it wasn't coming to him. He turned on the water and splashed some on his face.

"Day," Knight said through the door after a quick knock.

"I'll be right out." He turned off the water and wiped his face before opening the door and stepping out.

"You should go to bed, and get some rest."

He had been hoping for some words of wisdom. "Is that all you have?" Day asked him.

Knight shrugged. "Sometimes there are no answers, and the more you try to find them when there aren't any, the more attention and energy you draw away from the real problem." Knight grabbed his shoulder. "Go to sleep. There's nothing we can do for the next few days except gather information. So we'll continue to do that, but you can't exhaust yourself now."

"That's your advice?" Day sniped.

"It worked for me in the Corps. You have to pick your battles, and keep yourself strong. The best way to do that is to sleep and rest before battle. Once we land and are on our own, it will be a battle, against the heat, nature, and eventually our quarry." Knight stepped in front of him. "Fieldwork is grunt work. Days of waiting leading up to minutes of action. But we have to remain strong during the waiting."

"But there's something I'm missing—we're missing," Day said. "I know it."

"There probably is. Maybe more than one thing. But we aren't going to figure it out just because we want to. Sleep on it, and things will be clearer in the morning." Knight stepped away and closed up his laptop. Then he went into the bathroom, and Day got ready for bed. He set the temperature in the room so they would be comfortable and climbed under the covers before turning out most of the lights.

Day listened to water running and closed his eyes, rolling onto his side to face the wall. The bathroom door opened, light flooding the room for a few seconds before it went dark again. He heard Knight walk through the cabin and felt the bed shift when he sat on the edge and then lay down. Day didn't move as Knight got comfortable. Eventually he closed his eyes, and fatigue got the better of him.

THE FOLLOWING day was busy, but fun. He and Knight worked, but they also played around on the ship. They checked for additional intercepted communication and worked on what they received, but it was of little help. Day set up his equipment to try to pick up additional signals but hadn't gotten anything yet. He managed to relax and get some rest, and he did feel better, but something continued to gnaw at the edges of his mind. Just when he thought it was within reach, whatever he'd been grasping for would skitter away again. It was frustrating as hell, and he went to bed the second night just as frustrated as he'd been the night before.

The rocking of the ship that had accompanied them the past two days was absent. That was the first thing Day noticed when he woke. The next was that Knight had plastered himself to him, holding him tightly around the waist with one arm. Day had never brought up the last time this had happened, and he was certain that Knight didn't remember; at least he hadn't brought it up either. Day didn't move for a while, soaking in the attention and care, even if it was unintentional. Just like before, Day carefully disentangled himself from Knight's arm and moved away before getting up. As soon as he was away from the bed, he hurried to the bathroom and closed the door. What the fuck was he going to do? He doubted Knight intended to spend half the night holding him, and yet it felt good, and he liked it—really liked it, from the way his dick was hard enough to pound nails. Not that it mattered. Knight wasn't gay, and Day had no intention of opening his mouth and adding additional tension and weirdness to the situation.

Things were weird enough already. He was a gay man who was supposed to be straight on a gay cruise, playing half of a gay couple, and the other half was straight. All this to present a proper image for a mission that would occur after they disappeared from the cruise ship. This was totally nuts and too *Victor Victoria* for words. Day brushed his teeth and shaved before getting in the shower, thinking maybe he'd feel better.

It didn't really work, and by the time Day reentered the room, Knight was back on his side of the bed, covers pooled around his waist, lying on his back and snoring to beat the band. Day took a few seconds to look and dream before quietly grabbing his laptop and moving to the far side of the room to check for any new messages. There weren't any, so he tried to see what he could find out about the man asleep in the bed a few feet away, though he had a hard time focusing on his computer instead of on Knight.

Knight was gorgeous, toned, a line of black hair marking the center of his powerful chest. Day had picked on him, calling him old because of the tinges of gray in his hair, but Knight was anything but old. There was power in him, and when he rolled onto his side, Day was treated to a view of his wide back, skin sultry against the white sheets, a beautiful contrast if he'd ever seen one. Day gave up trying to work and watched Knight sleep. He wanted more in his life than the loneliness he had now. Hell, he'd woken up only three mornings in his life to someone holding him: twice had been Knight and he probably didn't even remember it, and once was Blain. That had been after they'd both had too much to drink. Blain was not the kind of man who did mornings-after very often. Day found that out the hard way when Blain explained the facts of life, at least those according to him.

"What time is it?" Knight murmured groggily.

"It's a little after eight. There's no hurry." Day returned his attention to the computer. "The chatter isn't telling us anything new right now."

Knight pushed the covers down and got out of bed. God, he was even better looking standing up. Hell, the man was hot. Sex-on-a-stick hot. Pictures-in-a-magazine hot. Day made sure to keep his head down as Knight walked to the closet in boxer briefs that were almost indecently tight. He got out some clothes and went into the bathroom. As soon as the door closed, Day blew out the breath he'd been holding and adjusted the computer on his lap to keep it from rocking back and forth on his dick. This whole situation was messing with his mind and driving him crazy.

Day finished up what he was doing, then closed his computer and began packing things away. Once he was done, he pushed the curtains aside and opened the balcony door, stepping out into the tropical heat. The cove around the harbor was filled with gleaming resorts and grand tropical homes with palm trees towering over them, all surrounded by a sea of lushness that set off the deep blue of the water. A tropical paradise if he'd ever seen one.

"Are you ready for me to kick your ass?" Knight asked with way too much glee. Day sighed and left the balcony. It was time to pay the piper. "Let's eat, and then we can go. Our appointment at the shooting club is at ten."

"Fine," Day said stiffly and followed Knight out of the cabin. They had breakfast at the buffet and then returned to get the things they'd need before exiting the ship and finding a taxi in port. "Cayman Shooting Club," Knight told the driver, and he sped off through town and up into the hills.

The club sat on a plateau, elegant, with interior as well as outside ranges.

"May I help you?" a doorman asked.

"The name is Knighton. I arranged for some target practice."

"Yes, sir, we've been expecting you," a man in spectacular white said as he approached. "I am Manuel. I have been instructed to assist you any way I can." He motioned them inside. "You instructed that you wanted to start at the pistol range, and you specified the use of .44 caliber pistols. We have those here and set up for you."

The surprise must have shown on Day's face, because Manuel turned to him. "We have a full stock of weapons at the club. Many of our customers arrive here unable to bring their weapons with them. So we provide them for use at the club."

"Excellent," Day said and followed Manuel through the lavishly appointed interior to a shooting range accessed by a surprisingly exquisitely carved staircase, the muffled sound of pistol shots reaching his ears.

They entered the range through heavy doors once the shooting had quieted. "You are down at the end, Mr. Knighton, with your guest next to you. Do either of you require instruction?"

"No. Thank you. I'll handle any instruction," Knight said, and Day's teeth ground at the condescension, but he kept it to himself and stepped up to his station. He put on his ear guards, but when he felt a tap on his shoulder, he lifted them away from his ears. "Are you okay with this? I can help you if you like."

"I got it, but I can watch if you prefer." Day put on his ear guards and stepped back, watching Knight as he loaded his pistol, cocked it, and then shot a round into the target, just off center. Then he shot an additional five rounds in rapid succession, making a tight pattern in the center of the paper target.

"That's how you should do it. The first is to set the target, and then follow with the others." Knight clearly thought he was helping.

Day lowered his ear guards. "Like this?" He loaded his weapon, set the range, shooting near dead center, and then squeezed off the remaining five shots before pulling in the target for examination.

"Not bad, but you only hit the target once," Knight said once Day had pulled off his ear protection.

"Check again," Day said with a grin. "You'll see a little five-petal flower. I put all six shots through the same hole." He set down the gun, crossing his arms over his chest.

"How? Luck?" Knight stammered.

"You didn't read my file very closely. I came in second two years ago in the National Trap Shooting Finals. Lost by one point." He grinned again. "I've been around guns most of my life. My uncle introduced them to me when I was ten, and he taught me how to shoot. He shot skeet, and I started with that, then moved to pistols and targets. After skeet, this was simple: the target doesn't move."

"You could have said something," Knight told him.

"And miss the chance to wipe the smug look off your face? Are you kidding?" Day grinned again but let it fade quickly.

"But can you…?" Knight let the question trail off. He didn't have to say any more, because Day didn't have the answer to the question of whether he could shoot another person. Day sighed, and Knight nodded once. "I understand," he said in a very low voice. "You don't know until you have to."

They shot another round, and this time Day shot an even tighter round, with very little indication that six bullets had passed though the center of the target. This time he didn't crow. He knew he'd already won the contest he'd suckered Knight into. "Can we go out to the trap range?"

"If you like," Knight said. They asked the range attendant where to go and followed his directions out of the range and into the area behind the building. Manuel met them and made arrangements for them to shoot a round of clay targets each. After gauging the gun, Day easily squeezed off a hundred for a hundred with no difficulty. This was what he did, and Day was as relaxed and cool as he'd felt in years. This was like coming home, and he knew his body well enough to smoothly shoot through the round.

When he was done, he stepped back from the shooter's station to let Knight go. Knight didn't do as well, and Day stopped him partway through. "You're trying to anticipate where the disk will go, and that's throwing you off. Let it come, follow it, get the flow, and then shoot. You have time. This is about flow and balance, letting the weapon become a part of you. Trap shooting is finesse and flow, not muscle." Day stepped back, and Knight did much better with the second half. "See?"

Knight nodded. "I yield to the master," he said with a surprisingly bright smile.

"I've had years of experience." Of course, Knight had as well. His was just very different from Day's.

"We should head into town for some lunch, and then we can go back to the ship." Knight thanked their host, and they stopped on their way out to pay for the shooting time.

"I hope you gentlemen were satisfied," Manuel said as they got ready to leave. Knight nodded and shook Manuel's hand, probably slipping him a tip. They both thanked him and then took a taxi into town, telling the driver they wanted local food. He dropped them at a small restaurant off the main street, and they had a Caribbean curry worth its weight in gold. Once they were full, they walked the main shopping street and finally joined the other cruisers on the way back to the ship.

"Did you have a good time?" Day turned and saw Blain behind him. He groaned to himself and flashed a smile.

"It was great. Knight took me to the shooting club."

"You shoot?" Blain asked, placing his hand dramatically over his heart and then began to snicker.

"Yes. He's one of the best shots I've ever seen," Knight said with such seriousness that the smile faded from Blain's face.

Day remembered his manners. "Knight, this is Blain. He and I went to college together." He hoped like hell Blain would be intimidated enough to keep his mouth shut. He should have known better.

"Dayton and I were close friends back then, but we haven't seen each other in a while." Blain smiled with mock innocence. Day wanted to reach out and strangle him right there. Either Blain was as vindictive as hell, or he just liked playing games. He remembered Blain as self-centered and shallow. But that could be hindsight. Day had been confused and excited enough back then that he'd only seen what he wanted to see, both good and bad.

"That's nice," Knight said without really seeming to care much. "We're heading back. Are you going that way as well?"

Day figured Knight was being nice, but dammit, he didn't need Blain tagging along, blathering about shit the whole way back. He'd be a fucking nervous wreck. "Aren't you with your friends?"

"Yeah, I should find them." Blain smiled. "We should get together and have a drink or something. It would be nice to catch up."

"Sure." What the hell else could he say without letting on that he was as nervous as hell about spending any more time than necessary with him? All he wanted was to get on with this mission. He was starting to think he'd rather take on a nest of terrorists than try to dodge Blain for the next two days. "See you around." He began walking again, and Knight came along with him.

"What was all that about? He was an old friend…." Knight stopped and whispered, "Do you have a problem with gay people? I've felt your tension for most of the time we've been here. Is that why?"

Day rolled his eyes. "No. I don't have any problem with gay people. I just have a problem with him. He acts like we were close friends in college, but we really hardly knew each other."

Knight stared at him, eyebrows furrowed. "You didn't tell me you'd met someone on the ship that you knew. You should have."

"Why? He's a guy I went to college with, and I saw him in the gym on the first day. That's all there is to it." Day began walking. "It's nothing."

Knight caught up to him and grabbed his arm. "Nothing is nothing. This could be a coincidence and then again…."

"What are you thinking?" Day asked.

"When we get back to the ship, I want to ask Dimato to look into something." He picked up speed. "Shit, we need to move."

"What?" Day snapped.

"We need to find out if large numbers of cruise ship passengers have been missing the ship in Costa Maya—more than the usual—you know." Knight walked faster.

"Holy crap. If we're using it to get into the area, then why wouldn't the terrorists?"

"Exactly. Passengers miss ships all the time, and it's their responsibility to get to the next port or back home. I'm sure they track passengers, but the ships keep moving to stay on schedule. So just like we are going to use the ship to sneak into the country, why not them?"

"Records are kept," Day said.

"Yeah. But I doubt they're rigorously checked the way airline records are. It was easy enough for us to get communications equipment and even two handguns on board the ship—all we did was get creative. Do you think the terrorists would be any less creative?" Knight was almost jogging now.

Day kept up with him and got him to slow down. "Don't draw attention, remember?"

They walked back to the ship, boarded, and went right to their cabin. The door stood open, and Day's heart raced for a second until he saw their steward cleaning the room. They stayed out of his way until he was done, and once he'd left, Day set up the communications equipment, and Knight made a secure call. He explained what he needed.

While Knight talked to their boss, Day checked for additional transmissions. There were a lot, and he set about analyzing them. Most were mundane and told him nothing, but one intrigued him, and he spent some time piecing together the parts of it.

Knight hung up from his call. "He's going to see what he can get us. Do you have anything?"

"They're talking about the 'sharing logic' again. Something about populating whatever it is they're building. It's the way the program will move and expand, using what appears to be some existing sharing logic, whatever that is, but they don't say what kind of systems they want to attack."

"Of course they wouldn't. They already know, and they aren't going to spread any information they don't have to. They have to know their conversations could be overheard, so they say as little as possible."

Day put his headphones on, still talking to Knight. "They're talking about deleting things… like a virus, but I think this is different, and I don't know why." He listened some more, rewound the recording, and listened again. Then he took off the headphones. "They're talking about deleting stuff and sharing the program to populate it." Day leaned back in his chair. "Early on, some initial computer viruses moved from computer to computer hidden in files, and on a certain date would delete everything. There are safeguards against those now, and every antivirus program looks for them. There has to be more here, but I can't get it."

"You will," Knight said.

Day paused, not quite knowing what to do with even a partial compliment. He chose to ignore it and began going back through the other transmissions to see if he'd missed anything. He spent a few hours but eventually gave up and put his headphones aside. "Nothing to fucking help."

"You'll figure it out."

He wasn't sure he was going to. Day knew he should be able to and that he wasn't making a connection he should. That was frustrating.

"I called, and we have a dinner reservation for seven, so bring your appetite."

Day checked the time and began listening again. Knight's phone rang, and he half listened to Knight's part of the conversation as his mind continued to churn. There was something else here; he knew it. But he still couldn't put all the pieces together. Finally he gave up, checked his messages again, and closed everything down. “I should be able to get this.”

“Remember that these people don’t want you to hear this conversation. It’s not meant for you. So think about what the person on the other side might know.”

Day shook his head slightly. He was starting to get a headache.

“Everyone brings their own perspective to anything they hear,” Knight said. “When you’re listening to those interceptions, you’re listening as though you’re you. But it isn’t you who’s being spoken to. It’s someone else with different experiences. So try to put yourself in their shoes too. Maybe that will help the messages make more sense.” Knight pulled out his suitcase and placed his dressier clothes on the bed. When he finished, he gathered everything up and went into the bathroom to change.

Day got out some nice clothes as well and changed in the main portion of the cabin. He heard the ship’s whistle blow a few times, and soon the ship rocked slightly as they left port. “You don’t have to do this dinner thing,” Day said when Knight came out of the bathroom. “I did trick you.”

Knight’s expression darkened. “We made a deal, and I intend to stick to it.” Knight grabbed his things, and Day made sure the room looked the way he wanted. Then they left the cabin and walked down the passageway to the elevators. “Do you want to tell me the rest of the story about Blain?”

Day nearly missed a step and almost fell on his face.

“I’m an agent with years of experience. I see a lot of things, and I feel that you’re keeping something else from me. He’s on this ship, and he knows something about you that I don’t. There was a smugness in his eyes and in the curl of his lips. So what’s the deal?” Knight pressed the call button for the elevator. “Whatever it is will remain between us. It won’t end up in some file or report.”

The elevator doors opened, and they stepped inside. Day had no intention of saying anything. “I really don’t want to talk about it. This has nothing to do with our mission, and you’ll have to trust me on that.” His heart pounded in his ears, and he barely noticed the elevator moving. When the doors opened, he stepped out and walked directly toward the onboard steakhouse without looking at Knight. He waited at the door to the restaurant. Knight stopped and simply stared into his eyes for a few seconds and then turned and pulled the door open.

"Let's have dinner." Knight waited for him to step inside and then followed him. The hostess took their name and led them to a table. The server came over almost immediately, filled the water glasses, and took drink orders.

"I'd like a Grey Goose martini, extra olives," Day said, and Knight ordered the same. The server handed them menus, and Day looked it over. The food was covered by the restaurant's thirty-dollar per person cover charge, so there were no prices on the menu. One price and you could eat what you wanted. It was easy deciding what he wanted to eat. When the server returned with the drinks, they ordered, and Day downed half the martini in a gulp. He did not want to talk about Blain—especially not with Knight. Hopefully, he could get a few drinks in him and he'd forget about it altogether. That was his hope and goal, anyway. Something to shoot for. "To success," he said, raising his glass. Knight did the same and took a drink.

He wished he were better at small talk or knew what sort of questions to ask. They couldn't very well talk about the mission. "Do you come from a big family?"

"I have an older sister and a younger brother," Knight answered.

"Any nieces or nephews?" Day asked.

Knight took another drink from his glass. "Bethany and her husband have two daughters. Mary is four, and Martha is six."

The smile told him Knight cared for his nieces very much. But as Day watched, a deep sadness filled Knight's eyes. He resettled in his chair and picked up his glass. He emptied the drink and signaled the waiter, holding the glass up slightly.

"What about your brother?" Day asked quietly.

"He's younger and still playing the field. He has a girlfriend, or at least he had one the last time I spoke with him, but who knows. He seems to go through them like underwear." The server set down Knight's drink and took the empty glass. Knight picked it up and sipped from it.

"What about your family?" Knight asked, and Day got the feeling Knight was trying to shift the conversation away from him.

"I just have an older brother. My parents had both passed away by the time I was sixteen, but my brother was old enough that he took me in and raised me." Day set down his glass. "He worked two jobs to feed us and made sure I did well in school and got scholarships to help pay for college." He was more grateful for his brother than he could possibly say. "He didn't stop nagging me until I graduated, and then his life sort of fell apart. He had a girlfriend, but she left, and now he leads this semihippie life trying to get rich quick."

"Do you get along?"

"Yeah. We always did. What I really think is that he needs to find someone and start a family. He took care of me for all those years, and I think he's at loose ends." Day shrugged. "I'd do anything for him, but I don't know what to do."

"Sometimes the impetus for change has to come from inside, and no one can help, no matter how well-intentioned they are." Knight gulped from his drink and nearly emptied the martini glass. There was most definitely deep pain there, and Day wondered about the source. He'd read what there was in the file. Since there was so little, he began wondering what it didn't tell him. There were no family references whatsoever and almost no history other than a brief outline of Knight's military service. The server brought their salads, and Knight set down his empty glass, ordered a refill, and began to eat.

At least they had the food to talk about, but it seemed not much else. After the salads their steaks and sides were placed in front of them. Knight ate some but seemed more interested in the liquid portion of his dinner. When Knight finished his fourth martini, Day ordered coffee for both of them. He hoped if he stopped drinking, maybe Knight would lay off, and it worked until they were done with the main courses. Then Knight ordered another round. By the time they were finished with dessert, Day was light-headed, giggly, and feeling no pain. Knight mostly seemed like Knight: strong, stalwart, only more talkative. Day was grateful he'd eaten, but it didn't seem to be doing him much good. He was warm and needed some fresh air. The server brought the bill, and Knight handed him his onboard card. Day didn't want to see the amount because the alcohol bill must have been astronomical.

"You're a good man," Knight said when they left the restaurant, throwing an arm over his shoulder. "You tell the truth and don't brag even when you have a right to." Knight stumbled and caught his balance. "I like you. You're a good man."

"You said that already," Day said. It was like the blind leading the blind as they made for the elevator. He pressed the button, and they waited. The sway of the ship seemed magnified, and by the time they reached the cabin, Day was having trouble staying on his feet. He managed to get the door open, and they got inside. Knight leaned against the closet door while Day fumbled to find the light switch.

He found Knight's hand instead, but when he tried to let go, Knight gripped his hand, tugged him closer, and hugged him tight. Then Knight kissed him. This was no fumble, no "oops it's dark and I don't know where my lips are" kiss. This was a full-on, mouth open, "sucking face like there was no tomorrow" kiss.

Day's knees weakened, and he wasn't sure what to do at first. He wanted to kiss back and pull away at the same time. The need to be touched and cared for won out, and he pushed closer, returning Knight's kiss. He wound his arms around Knight's back, pulling them together in a crush of heat that left him dizzy.

"Fuck, Day," Knight groaned when they broke apart to breathe.

Day inhaled quickly, wondering what was coming next. He half expected Knight to realize what was happening and shove him away. Instead Knight moved them toward the bed.

"This.... Fuck, are you sure?" Day held Knight's cheeks in his hand, the day's stubble rough against his palms. His eyes were glassy, and all this was probably because of the alcohol. Hell, what little of his brain was still functioning told him it was likely the booze for both of them, but.... "Fuck it," he cried and pressed his lips to Knight's, tugging at him. He'd been thinking about this for days now, and if Knight was willing, then Day was no way in hell going to say no. Neither of them might remember a fucking thing in the morning, but he'd take what he could get now.

They tumbled in a tangle of arms and legs, using their tongues as implements of war, with lips and teeth as targets. Heat built up fast. Knight fumbled between them, pressing Day down onto the mattress. He tugged at Day's shirt, unable to get anywhere. He gave a low, feral growl, and Day felt him clutch and then pull. The sound of tearing filled the room, and his shirt split. Knight kissed away his protest as he found Day's skin, pressing his hands flat to his chest, heat spreading, scraping his fingers lightly over Day's peaked nipples.

"Yes," Knight hissed.

Day went to work on Knight's shirt, the fabric no match for his strength. Knight sat up and pulled away what was left of his shirt, then tossed it on the floor. He was magnificent, all muscle and sinew that rippled with every movement. Day didn't have much of a chance to look because Knight dropped on top of him again. The next kiss was even more intense, filled with a longing that Day couldn't comprehend. He only recognized it because it reminded him of his own, so he went with it, tapping into the loneliness, yearning, and aching that had built up over years.

"Damn, you taste good," Knight told him, and then he cupped his cheeks and drew their mouths together again.

Day was so hard in his pants he expected his cock to rip through the fabric at any moment. He thrust his hips upward, and Knight sighed into his mouth as Day encountered Knight's fabric-imprisoned dick.

The last of Day's reluctant will fell away, and he slid his hands down Knight's powerful back and over the curve of his ass. He gripped it tight, his fingers meeting firm, hard flesh. Knight grunted, and Day held tighter, pushing forward, needing something so bad he couldn't think.

Knight growled and pulled away. He tugged at Day's belt and then at the top of his pants. He got them open, and Day did the same in return, pushing Knight's pants past his hips. A sigh rumbled in Day's ear the first time their cocks slipped past each other with nothing between them. Knight thrust, and Day did the same. The energy in the room ramped up to rival that produced by the sun. Day sweated up a storm, wet skin sliding, instinct alone driving him. Day jammed his pelvis upward, his hands full of hard, smooth man ass. He grabbed tightly, determined not to let Knight get away.

“Fuck!” Knight yowled, and Day went right along with him. It was primal, passionate, and the heat was intense. He simply held Knight to him with all his might, and they thrust and pressed together as passion grew and built until he couldn’t contain it any longer. His mind was already clouded, and with Knight surrounding him with his weight, scent, and touch, he was happier than he could remember being in a long time.

“Yeah, I’m gonna come,” Day hissed between gritted teeth as the world swam. He closed his eyes, held Knight tighter, and tumbled into sweet oblivion.

Chapter 4

A WEIGHT pressed against him. Knight's cotton-filled head was too stuffed for him to think clearly. This was a dream—it had to be. Flashes of the night before came into his mind, but Knight didn't believe them. He opened his eyes, and the cabin spun as well as rolling from side to side. He clamped his eyes shut again and didn't move an inch. His head ached, and his stomach roiled. But as long as he stayed still, everything stayed where it was supposed to.

The weight next to him shifted and groaned. Slowly Knight's head began to work a little, but he was still afraid to move. A groan from next to him pulled an answering groan from him when the bed shifted. The weight was gone now, and Knight wondered who in the hell was in his bedroom with him, and what had he done last night?

Fast footsteps sounded in the room, and then the door closed, followed by retching that nearly had him doing the same thing. Knight forced himself to sit up. He was naked, his clothing from the night before strewn all over the floor. He leaned forward and instantly regretted it but managed to reach his shirt. He lifted what was left of it from the carpet and dropped it once again. "What the hell did I do?" Knight held his head and tried to get the damned thing to stop turning.

The bathroom door opened, and Knight slowly looked up.

Day came in the room with a towel around his waist. "Do you remember… much from last night?" Day sat on the opposite side of the bed, and Knight turned away. He shook his head and immediately regretted it. "Did anything… happen?"

Knight sighed. Judging by what was dried on his skin, he'd say something did happen, but damn if he could remember what it was right now. "I don't know. I think something might have, but my memory is fuzzy. I dreamed some strange stuff, and if that's what happened, then… yeah." He swallowed hard, and his throat ached like hell. Everything ached.

"I guess we have some explaining to do… to each other at least."

Knight didn't want to think about it. He groaned as he got to his feet and walked to the bathroom. He closed the door as quietly as he could and hunted for something for his head. He found some Tylenol in his kit and took two of them with a glass of water. At least his mouth wasn't as dry now. The ship continued its rolling motion, and a wave of dizziness washed over him. He gripped the counter and held on, waiting for it to pass. Thankfully it did. He grabbed a towel and wound it around his waist. He wanted to take a shower, but he didn't want to turn on the lights or his head would throb again. So he made do with the soft nightlight glow and did what he had to do before leaving the room.

Dayton had managed to partially dress and sat on the edge of the bed, holding his head, groaning softly. Knight got him a glass of water and handed him some Tylenol as well. "This will help."

"I didn't think I drank that much."

"That part I remember. We drank plenty, way too much, and vodka to boot." He groaned and lowered himself to the bed. "After that everything is a blur. I remember reaching the cabin and then…." He groaned loudly as the memory of kissing Day flooded back. What in the hell had he done? He'd betrayed Cheryl and Zachary, that's what he'd done, and now he couldn't undo it. "Nothing…," he lied and groaned. "Everything. We…." There was no way he could lie to Day or anyone. What happened had happened and he needed to Marine up about it. "I don't know why I did it, but as soon as the door closed last night, something in my head went haywire, and I wanted… so I took it." He held his head tighter and hurried back to the bathroom, making it just in time. He knelt on the floor by the toilet and lost what little he had in his stomach.

What in the hell had he done? His memories of the night before were just clear enough for him to remember what he'd wanted and that he'd taken it. He hadn't asked; he'd simply done what he'd wanted. How could he live with himself? Knight began to shake hard. He tried to get up but failed. When he tried again, he got to his feet, pressed the button to flush, and then rinsed his mouth with water before gingerly opening the bathroom door.

He expected a punch, shouts, and maybe a body slam, but he was met with silence. Slowly he stepped into the room. Day lay on his back on the bed, eyes closed.

"There's way too much movement and light."

Knight didn't understand. Well, he agreed with him, but he didn't understand. "Do you remember last night?"

"Most of it now, yes." Day slowly sat up and winced. "I don't know what to say. I didn't mean for any of that to happen, but you kissed me, and I… well…." Day faltered, and Knight didn't know what the hell to do. "I'm sorry."

Knight's legs buckled, and he lunged for the bed rather than hitting the floor. "You're sorry? After what I did."

Day held up his hand. "What do you think you did? Last night things were a little wild and unexpected, but they… God, I don't know what to say. But I think we have some talking to do."

"Talk. You want to talk after I… after I did that to you. If it's any consolation, I only remember parts, but I didn't mean to hurt… to force." God, even the words nearly made him sick. Knight held his head and lay still on top of the covers. "I'll never have another drink as long as I live. I never thought I was capable of doing anything like that to anyone and…."

"Wait a minute. Do you think you forced yourself on me? Is that it?" Day shook his head and groaned. "Come up here, and lie down before both our heads explode. You didn't force yourself on me, if that's what you're worried about."

The relief that washed through him was incredible. Day closed his eyes again, and Knight unwound and lay on the bed, resting his head on a pillow.

"The kiss was a surprise, and I had no idea that… well… like I said, I think we both have things to talk about. Especially after last night."

"I didn't attack you," Knight said.

"Oh, you did that. You were like a long-caged animal that had just been granted its freedom. What I meant was, you didn't force yourself on me. Things were a little energetic, and the whole thing was a big surprise. But there was no forcing. You were kind of bossy and controlling, though. Maybe next time we can change that." Day smiled, and Knight's stomach roiled again.

"We… were together, and I didn't force you."

"No."

"So that means you were okay with what happened." Knight's head pounded.

"Look. If last night was some huge drunken mistake for you, then fine. I can deal with that. But I don't think we do things when we're drunk that we wouldn't do when we're sober. The alcohol lowers our inhibitions so we end up doing what we really want to do. So deny away and hide behind some façade that you were drunk and all that, if you want."

"I didn't say that. God. You jump to the worst conclusions, and for the record, you can stop trying to analyze me. I've had a ton of people do that over the last few years, and they got nowhere, so what makes you think you'll get any further than the professionals? If you want to know something, then ask, and if I don't want to answer, I'll tell you to fuck off."

"Okay. Are you gay?" Day asked.

"Fuck off," Knight answered.

"Why were all kinds of professionals trying to analyze you?"

"Fuck off. Are you gay?"

"Fuck off." Two could play that game.

"Okay. I think we've gotten the picture that neither of us wants to talk about all this shit."

"We sure as hell don't. But one thing we can both agree on is that after last night, whatever we want to call ourselves, there's something about each of us that we both need to figure the hell out."

"Fuck off and amen," Knight answered and closed his eyes. "This fucking conversation is making my head hurt."

"No. I think the fucking conversation actually happened last night, and if I'm remembering correctly, there wasn't a lot of actual conversation going on." Day shifted slightly. "Regardless of what we feel and how uncomfortable we are, we do need to talk this out."

"Fine," Knight breathed. "But not when we're hungover." He put his arm over his eyes, refusing to look at anything. "We need to be sober for that. So lie down, and help me keep the damned room from spinning for a while, and then we can leave this cabin so maybe I can jump over one of the railings, because I think I'm going to die, and that will make the whole damn thing a hell of a lot less painful."

Day smacked his arm. "Fuck off," he said with surprising gentleness, and then he settled, and the room grew quiet.

It took a while, but the room stopped moving, except for the rocking of the ship that he couldn't do anything about, and slowly he felt more and more human. Eventually he got up and went into the bathroom for some more water and decided that taking a shower might make him feel less hungover.

"Better?" Day asked when he came out of the bathroom and began getting dressed.

"Yeah," Knight answered, and Day took his turn. "I don't want to eat anything," he told Day after he'd showered.

"Then let's go lie out on deck for a while and soak in the warmth. We can get some lunch later and do our final preparations for tomorrow."

At least that stuff they could talk about without things getting weird.

KNIGHT ENDED up putting on his bathing suit and doing what Day suggested. An hour later he lay back into a deck chair, breathed deeply, and tried to remember everything that had happened the night before. He couldn't. He remembered that he and Day had had sex; that much he knew. The images that flashed in his mind from nowhere told him it was wild, heated, maybe a little clumsy, and had ended up with two shredded shirts and clothes spread everywhere. He really wished he could remember it.

"Is this chair taken?"

Knight looked up at the handsome man standing near him in the tiniest Speedo he'd ever seen. Nothing at all was left to the imagination, including the man's religion. "No." Knight smiled as best he could and turned away as the man settled on the chair, stretching out so everything was on clear display.

"Where's your… friend?" the man asked in a sultry voice. "I saw the two of you together. You're the hottest couple on this boat." He shifted slightly, and Knight reached to the deck and grabbed his sunglasses, slipping them over his eyes. "Do the two of you play? Because I'd like to be a third for an afternoon."

Knight sat up. "No. We aren't like that."

"Too bad. It would be amazing fun." He flashed a smile, and Knight lay back again and groaned softly to himself. He was still trying to get his head around last night, and this guy wanted to do a three-way. Hell, he wasn't sure if he would ever have a two-way again, and given the way his head felt, even a one-way was probably out of the question for quite some time.

"I think we'll pass," Knight said.

"Pass on what?" Day's rich mellow voice rang out, cutting through the remnants of the alcohol haze.

Knight didn't even want to bring up what had been offered.

"I was just telling your friend here that you two were the best-looking couple on the ship and wondering if you would like to have some fun," the man said.

Knight kept his eyes closed. He didn't want to see Day's reaction, especially if he decided to go with this guy. He was nice-looking. Hell, why should he care? One mistaken night didn't mean he had some hold on Day, after all. It had been a mistake, and they both knew it. Shit, everything was such a mess.

"No, thanks. He and I are exclusive," Day answered and then sat on the deck chair on the other side of him. Knight almost jumped when Day gently ran his fingers along his arm. He managed a smile instead and tried not to turn completely red. Gentle, caring touches had not been part of his life in quite a while.

Knight tried to ignore the man, but it was hard. Eventually he turned his head to the other side, and Day smiled back at him. A jolt of surprise shot through him. A genuine smile greeted him, dressing a face with incredible eyes and those curls that almost covered them. In an instant he forgot about that other guy.

"Feeling better?" Day asked.

"Yeah." The alcohol was leaving his system. His stomach had settled, and his head was clearing. He felt human once again, with the warmth of the southern sun kissing his skin. "You?"

"Yeah. I'm doing pretty well now." Day settled back on the deck chair. "Everything is going to be okay."

Knight wanted to believe that, but he was having a hard time. In a single night, everything had changed. He'd always known he liked men. He was gay, and even though he'd never used that word in reference to himself before, it didn't make it less true. He could live with that. But what he was having a hard time getting his head around was how he'd betrayed Cheryl and Zachary. Well, Cheryl, mostly. He'd somehow cheapened what they'd had together, and he couldn't live with that. And the worst part was he didn't know how to put it into words. Like, sometimes he wondered if he could just say what he was feeling, then everything wouldn't be so jumbled up. But his mind felt like pieces of a jigsaw puzzle, and not a single fucking piece fit with any other one.

He closed his eyes and tried to let the swirl of crappy thoughts settle into a garbage dump of disconnected pieces. He always liked to think he had his stuff together, but he was a mess and had been one for a long time. Knight kept his eyes shut, hidden behind the sunglasses the way he hid the rest of himself, keeping everything closed off. It was easier and safer that way.

"You need some sunscreen," Day said softly from next to him and pressed a tube into his hand. "The sun is very strong, and you'll burn."

"I never burn."

"That doesn't mean you don't need sunscreen," Day insisted. "So put some on, or I'll put it on for you."

As much as he might like that, Knight opened the tube and rubbed some of the cream into his skin. The guy who'd approached him earlier seemed to get the message that he wasn't going to get any more attention and left. Another man arrived, but Knight paid no attention to him or anyone else for that matter. Once he had slathered on sunscreen to Day's apparent satisfaction, he sat back and paid attention to nothing, retreating deeper and deeper into his own thoughts. Eventually basic fatigue took over, and he dozed off listening to a chorus of rough male voices talking over each other, the wind, and the sloshing pool water. It was soothing and warm, and Knight let himself feel safe for a few minutes. He rarely felt safe in any situation, but for now this was what he needed.

He woke to splashes of water on his chest. Knight opened his eyes to a dripping Day standing near him, toweling off. He kept his eyes cracked and just watched. Here it was okay to watch. He and Day had pretty much outed themselves last night, regardless of how much either of them might want to avoid the subject. Granted, Knight wasn't sure how Day would feel about being ogled by his partner, but.... Knight paused. That was the first time he'd thought of Day as his partner. Up till that moment, he considered Day the newbie kid he had to deal with, a millstone stuck around his neck. It still needed to be proven if he could count on Day to have his back, but that he'd definitely see with time.

Knight stretched and sat up, glancing around. The first thing he noticed was that half the men were staring openly at Day and the others were most likely doing their best not to. A pang of jealousy shot through him, but he pushed it away. They'd had one fumbling, awkward... thing... encounter, semifuck—he wasn't sure what to call it— but it sure as hell didn't give him any cause for jealousy. Still, he couldn't help it and stood up, stepping around the lounger to where Day stood. "You seem to be the center of attention."

Day snorted and shrugged. "I've been the center of attention for how I look for a long time. In high school everyone wanted to be around me. The girls hung on me and...." Day paused. "Let's just say I don't see it much anymore. I used to revel in the attention, until I realized it was nothing. They weren't interested in me, just in being seen with me." He leaned forward and used the towel to dry his hair. Then he smoothed it down with his fingers in a vain attempt to tame that riot of curls. It wasn't going to happen, and Knight smiled.

"We should get some lunch." He was getting hungry, which was a good sign he'd recovered from his overindulgence.

"What prompted all that last night? You didn't drink like that the other nights," Day said.

Knight wasn't going to talk about that here… or at all. "Fuck off," he said gently.

"Okay, but you're severely limiting the avenues of conversation."

"You're welcome to tell me your life's story anytime you like, but I get the feeling you aren't interested in doing that any more than I am." Knight grabbed his towel and slipped his feet into his rubber deck shoes. "Let's go change, and then we can eat. Maybe we'll both feel better after some food." He didn't mention making plans for tomorrow. They needed to do that as well, but he couldn't bring that up with so many ears around. He motioned for Day to lead. They left the pool deck and took the stairs down to their cabin. "Let's eat and then plan," he said as soon as the door was closed. "We're going to have to figure out what we can take, and leave the rest. So…." He looked out toward the balcony. "Anything sensitive cannot be found."

"I'm aware of that," Day said. He grabbed some clothes and went into the bathroom. Knight took the chance to pull on a T-shirt and pair of shorts over his suit. "We'll need the communication equipment, and it's portable enough that I should be able to put it in my backpack. We'll also need my laptop. It's small, and I can put that in my pack as well."

"All right." Knight started making lists in his head. "We'll be able to get a few supplies once we separate from the ship. I'm hoping it won't take too long to find them and put this group out of business. We aren't here to infiltrate or try to become part of them or anything. What we need to do is shut them down and make sure they can't execute what they're planning."

"I understand. But we also need to know what they know so precautions can be taken to ward off future attacks." Day was already at his computer. "We're intercepting a lot more transmissions, so after we eat, I'm going to need to sift through them."

Knight was no help at all on that front. "Then I'll put everything together for tomorrow, and we can review the plan once you're done."

"All right. I'll follow you when we hit the field."

Knight pulled out the desk chair and sat down. "I know you have skills and the drive to do what needs to be done. There's no doubt about that. But fieldwork is about contingencies and thinking on your feet, as well as contacts. I have one a few miles outside of Costa Maya who'll be able to help us with some additional supplies."

"Then why isn't he supplying the guns? Why did you have to bring them?"

"Miguel is watched. He's known to the Mexican authorities, so if we were to try to send him anything, it would raise suspicion. And while he has connections, he couldn't guarantee to have what we needed, so I made it happen. He would have put himself in danger if I'd asked him. But another rule of fieldwork is never put your friends at risk if you can avoid it in any way. Miguel still needs to live and work in the area long after we're gone, so any help he gives us will never be spoken about under any circumstances."

Day nodded. "Let's go eat. You and I need nourishment, and then we need to get to work."

Knight would have loved to spend the day up on deck in the sun, but they had a task to do, and nothing could interfere with that. He and Day had to be ready to go come hell or high water. "Let's go."

They left the cabin and went down the passage to the back of the ship, then took the elevator up to the buffet. They ended up waiting in line for a few minutes. Knight was very hungry, and as soon as they got a table, he headed to the buffet while Day agreed to stay and order soft drinks. He heaped his plate, and when he returned there were cups of coffee and water, along with a Coke, waiting. He sat and dug into his chicken, beef, rice, and potatoes. Some of the dishes he'd taken were unfamiliar, but they were good, so he ate it all happily.

Day returned. "I had to fight for the fried chicken." He sat down and dug in.

"Eat plenty. We'll have limited resources tomorrow. I have things set for us, but they're minimal." He didn't want to say much more, and Day seemed to understand.

"What are your parents like?" Day asked.

Knight was ready to say he didn't want to talk about it, but the question was easier to answer than others. "My father is a Baptist minister. Very old school. My mother is the choir director, and my father's ministry permeated all aspects of our lives growing up. The list of things we weren't allowed to do was longer than you could possibly imagine." Knight picked up his piece of chicken and began pulling it apart, taking a bite. Mostly he was using it as cover so he could decide how he wanted to explain things. "Most ministers are different at home than they are at church. At least that's what I've been told. My father wasn't. He was pious at church and even more so at home."

"What do you mean?"

"Dad genuinely felt responsible for the spiritual lives of his congregation and their ability to secure a place in heaven. He truly believed, and still does, that he's saving souls for Jesus. The problem was that as kids we wanted and needed a father, not a minister or someone more worried about our immortal souls than if we were confused about who we were. My father knew who we were—we were his children, and we were going to be the perfect models of how a Baptist minister's children should act at all times." It was so hard to explain without points of reference.

"Is that why you became a Marine?"

"Yup. Don't get me wrong. I adored the Corps. Those years were some of the best of my life. I joined up before the ink on my high school diploma was dry. My father was livid and prayed for my soul for days because I was most likely going to take life. He couldn't abide that." Knight put down his chicken and wiped his fingers on his napkin. "I have to give my father credit—he wasn't a hypocrite. He preached the Ten Commandments from his pulpit and did his best to live them each and every day. But I was thrilled because the Corps has its own set of commandments: honor, duty, loyalty, honesty, brotherhood, as well as instilling a sense of purpose and self. They say they want a few good men in the ads, but what they develop are men who are beyond good."

"Can I ask why you left?" Day set his fork down as well.

"That was really complicated and more than I think I can go into right now." So much of his life was wrapped up in what he wasn't ready to talk about. He kept thinking he'd dealt with those feelings and had put them in the box where they belonged. "I'll say that I mustered out for my family. I thought I was doing the right thing." Looking back, he wasn't so sure it had been the right choice. Hell, so many of his choices had turned to crap that he was no longer sure he was capable of choosing, so he'd drifted for months.

"The rumor around the office is that you… fell apart. I asked people what happened, and they said if I wanted to know that I had to ask you."

"Did you ask a lot of people?"

"No. I asked a friend who knows everything and is a bit of a gossip, but he refused to tell me what he knew, so I figured he didn't know anything. After that I decided if it was important and I needed to know, you'd tell me."

Knight nodded. "If you need to know, I promise I'll definitely tell you."

Day nodded and went back to his lunch. Knight hadn't expected that kind of easy acceptance from Day. Most people were curious and kept asking questions. That Day was willing not to probe and let him open up in his own time added to the respect he was developing for him.

"What is your brother like?" he asked Day.

Day chuckled. "You'd hate him."

"Why?"

"He's the exact opposite of you in a lot of ways. He worked all kinds of jobs to help raise me, and then once he was done, he went hippie, I guess. He took off and travels the country, working odd jobs and living off the land. Stephen has always had a wanderlust that he denied until I was on my own, but then he just left and never looked back. I see him a few times a year but never know when he'll show up. I usually see him around the holidays when the need for family becomes more important. He'll stay a few days and then be gone again."

"Do you miss him and wish he'd stay?"

"Yeah, I miss him. He was mom, dad, and brother all rolled into one. I owe him everything, and yet…." Day sighed. "I've told him he always has a place with me if he needs one, and if I said I needed him he'd get here in a heartbeat, but I won't. It would be mean of me to deny him the life he obviously loves. He gave up a lot to help me, so the least I can do now is support his decision." Day picked up his glass and drank the last of the water. "Come to think of it, you and my brother have more in common than I thought."

Knight didn't really see that, but he remained quiet.

"Stephen was always fiercely loyal and gave of himself to take care of me," Day said. "He did what he needed to do without a single complaint, and he was young… too young to have to raise a teenager, but he did it. He's also intensely independent, and sometimes he can be a real pain in the ass." Day let the last part dangle.

"He sounds like a decent enough guy," Knight said as he finished the last of his food and tried to decide if he should go back for more. He settled for another cup of coffee and just sat while Day finished his lunch. He didn't want to overdo it after the workout he'd given his system.

"My brother is pretty cool."

Knight nodded absently. "How do you think your brother would react if he knew about… last night?" That was as close to talking about what happened as he thought he could come.

"He'd probably be fine with it. Stephen is really cool that way. Very liberal and accepting." Day pushed his plate away. "And no, I've never told him. Haven't told anyone except, well, you, and Blain, of course."

"Ah, I was wondering about that. Was he your first?"

"Yes. Such as it was. The affairette we had is best left unspoken. I didn't know much, and he was the kind of guy who didn't stick around for breakfast." Day smiled. "Sort of a come and go. I thought it was more, and I got hurt. He maintains that it was because I was in the closet, but he wasn't interested in anything beyond sex. Not really." Day scratched his head slightly, mussing his floppy hair. Knight loved the way it fell and wanted to run his fingers through it. "God, I was so stupid back then."

"If you think your family would support you, then why keep the secret?" Knight asked. He knew his own reasons but really wanted to know Day's.

"Work, mostly. People can be cruel, and I wanted to be judged on my merit rather than on that aspect of my life. I was also told that guys could get pigeonholed if they came out, so I figured it was easier to keep it to myself. It wasn't like I dated other guys. I work, come home, fall into bed most of the time, and then go to work again. I live for my job pretty much most of the time, and if I have free time, I go shooting."

"Seems pretty lonely," Knight commented.

"And you haven't exactly been a social butterfly," Day countered.

"That's true, but I did have people in my life. I haven't spent all that much time alone." The more he thought about it, Knight realized he had been alone a lot since Cheryl and Zachary's death, and it had taken its toll. The drinking was one sign of it, and the fact he had little desire to spend time with people. He had gotten to the point that going out was too much trouble, so he just stayed home. "Okay, you have a point." He'd denied who he was for so long he'd actually begun to believe the delusion was real.

"I've been pretty much alone since Stephen took to the road. I had friends in college, but mostly they've gone their own ways. It's what happens." Day set down his coffee mug. "Let's go so others can eat and we can get done what we need to."

Knight agreed, and they left the buffet and strode along the pool deck to the forward elevators. The breeze was nice, and the water was enticing, but they had things to do, so no matter how much Knight wanted to chuck it and have fun, he kept walking and took the elevator down to their deck.

In the room, Day got his equipment set up and went right to work analyzing the transmissions while Knight began packing the things they would need. They weren't expected to get into port until midmorning, but it was best to be ready.

"Do you have something?" Knight asked when he saw Day grinning.

"I figured it out. I'm not sure what we're going to do about it, but this transmission mentions One Drive. As soon as I heard that, it all fell into place. They're planning to attack cloud storage providers." Day motioned, and Knight came around to look at his screen. "People sign up to purchase space on the cloud to store backup copies of documents and stuff. Some businesses store all their data on the cloud. That way it can be accessed from anywhere by any system."

Knight nodded. "I have a Dropbox account so I don't lose my stuff if the computer crashes."

"Exactly, and one of the functions that's available is the ability to share files with others. So what I think they've done is develop a program that will share itself across accounts and then, at a prearranged time, delete the contents of the account."

"Okay, but wouldn't that just delete the backup? What good would that do?"

"Well, it would, except what if the program was set to tell the system that the backup on the cloud was the primary, and if the primary was then deleted by the terrorists…."

"It would delete the files on the host computer when they came online because the agent on their computers would think it was supposed to in order to keep them in sync." Knight was beginning to see the issue. "And if that happened, then it wouldn't just be pictures that got deleted…."

"No, entire business file systems could be wiped out. Also, the increased traffic on the Internet would be enormous with all those files and messages being sent all at once from every user. It would overload the communications backbone in some areas, causing additional issues. There is so much commerce being done online now that any long-term interruption would cost billions, tens of billions, maybe, and undermine confidence in the systems." Day swallowed hard as he looked at him.

"How sure are you of this?" Knight watched over Day's shoulders.

"Very sure," he said and pointed to a map. "Think about it. If they timed it right, say at the height of trading, they could bring the stock markets to their knees. Transactions are completed over the Internet. Hell, most transactions have an Internet component. Even if it's a secure VPN tunnel, it still uses the bandwidth. If these guys are successful in getting this to spread, it could be a lot more catastrophic than just data loss. The ramifications could ripple through the infrastructure and the economy for months."

"Okay. So how do we stop it?" Knight asked.

"I'm not sure. The easiest way is to get to them before they can deploy. It isn't like we can defuse it. Once the program is unleashed, it's out there doing its thing, and it will be hard to get in front of."

"What would the system look like?"

Day shrugged. "It would be a computer. Now, they would probably need to open multiple accounts as well as hack some in order to get this to permeate quickly. If it's slow, the companies can react to protect themselves." Day continued typing. "I suspect they've already done their hacking and have taken over a number of accounts without the owners knowing. The one bright spot is that they're still having trouble with the sharing logic. The program needs to move itself as if it's being shared from account to account. That isn't working for them. We need to get our hands on their equipment as well as the people behind this, and especially the brains."

"Okay. Could this be done by one person?"

"I doubt it. There's real expertise at work here. I think we need to contact Dimato and let him know what we've found. Have you heard back about people missing cruise ships in the area?"

Knight shook his head and dialed their boss using the secure line.

"We may have a line on what we're up against," he said when Dimato answered. "You were right—it appears to be an attack on data, but they seem to be using cloud storage systems to make the attack. Dayton is currently analyzing how that could be done."

"Very good," Dimato said. "Excellent. I'll have some friends contact the cloud-storage companies and make sure they know we've detected a potential threat so they can be ready." Knight heard papers shuffling and then the soft clicks of a keyboard. "You two were also right about people missing cruise ships in Costa Maya. There were seven reported incidents over the past six months with various cruise lines. And those are only the ones reported. There are probably more that weren't reported. Two seem to be legit, and five appear to be aliases. We're trying to get what we can."

"All right. Thank you. We're getting ready and will leave the ship as planned tomorrow. We're taking what we can and leaving the rest."

"Don't worry. Your family will be there when the ships docks back in port to claim your luggage and get it back to you. Just stick to the plan and take these guys out. Do it as fast as possible, and get the hell out of the country."

"How do you suggest we do that? You planned out how we were going to get in, but you haven't helped us with the details to get us out.

I was planning to hike back into town, claiming we got separated from our group. Then hopefully we can get a ride to an airport." He waited to see if Dimato had any other suggestions. He didn't seem to, so Knight continued with his plan, knowing things could change on a dime.

"Stay in touch, and call if you need backup." That was Dimato code for "call if you need military support, and I'll call in some favors to get you out."

"We will. We're going to go silent starting tomorrow once we leave the ship and will only call for help. However, if you don't hear from us in forty-eight hours…." He didn't have to spell it out. If they weren't back out within two days, something had gone very wrong. "You can decide what you think is best at that point."

Dimato huffed. "I understand, but I have a reputation for bringing my men home, and I'm not going to let that go easily. So listen up. Come hell or high water, you communicate back, no matter what."

"We will if at all possible," Knight promised and then disconnected. He relayed what he and Dimato had talked about.

"Are you sure about us getting out?" Day asked.

"No. But we'll figure it out. If we're successful, we won't need to use as much stealth as we did getting in. We just need to get out in one piece." He returned to making the necessary preparations, and Day returned to his analysis. "Have you been able to narrow down the source of the transmissions?"

"Five miles west and a mile north of Costa Maya. We're going to need to figure out transportation. There's a road through that general area, but there must be a track or something back." Day turned his computer so Knight could see the screen. "I think this is a track that will take us back there, but I suspect it will be watched."

"Yeah. So we'll have to figure out how to get back there without being seen." Knight stared at the screen. "There are ways. We just need to be creative." He'd done things like that as a Marine, so he thought along those lines. "The road isn't too long, and they aren't going to be expecting anyone. Though they may be taking security precautions." He'd have to scout ahead to see what they were up against. "How recent is the photograph?"

"It doesn't have a date stamp."

"Send a note to Dimato and request a recent image with as much resolution as we can get. That should tell us a lot." He hoped. The more they knew going in, the better their chances of getting in quickly and making it out again in one piece.

Day got busy, and Knight continued running through options and scenarios. Getting to the location should be relatively easy. He could see that in his mind. "I think we should look like tourists who got lost," Knight said, thinking out loud. "At least for as long as we can. That way no one will pay much attention to us. They'll think we're a pair of gringos and probably laugh at us behind our backs, but they won't give us a second thought. When we get close, I have camo ponchos we can wear. They will make us harder to see." He took the small packages out of his bag and dropped them in the pack he would carry. He also made sure they had water and food. He'd already backed up the data he needed from his laptop, so just before they left, he'd wipe the machine and leave it behind. "Do we really need to take all the communications equipment?"

Day looked up from where he was working. "We do if we want to talk to anyone securely, or if we want to track any signals."

"Well, we know where they're working from, and we could make a regular cell call if we're cautious about what we say. I'm concerned about the weight with taking all that." Knight pointed to the case that housed the comms equipment.

Day went over, pulled a lever, and removed part of the system. "The rest is battery and power. This is all we need to take. At full charge, the battery is enough for about two hours of use. So as long as we're careful, we can only take this. That will save us a lot of room."

"Good. But what do we do with the rest?"

"I was planning to dump it overboard before we get into port, unless you have other ideas."

Knight didn't at the moment. He hated to waste an asset that they might need at some point in the future, but leaving it in the cabin wasn't an option. "We could take it all with us and then see about finding a place to hide the base unit in port. It would be off the ship, so if we need it, we could retrieve it later."

"It fits in the case, but that will mean we have less room for other things."

Knight grinned. "Don't worry. Once we dump it, we can buy water and things in port." A plan was coming together. "We won't take anything with us that we can replace in one of the shops. That way we'll have room for what's vital and buy the rest using the room made by hiding the base unit. That should get us where we need to be."

"Okay." Day began typing again. "That was fast. Dimato sent the images we requested."

Knight stood behind Day and peered down at his screen, doing his best not to inhale his scent. He failed and stifled a groan. He needed to keep his mind and attention on the task at hand.

"This is the most recent photograph of those he sent." Day enlarged the area near the road.

"See that?" Knight asked, pointing. "There's something just off the road. I'd guess a guard and probably a vehicle. They're trying to keep a low profile and keep people away at the same time." He took control and slowly moved the image, scanning it. "There's where they're working. See the tracks leading in? They're using the foliage for cover, but they aren't doing a good job of hiding their tracks, and if I'm not mistaken, that's a small hill, probably an overgrown building or temple. They must be using it for cover." He continued looking and grinned.

"What?" Day asked.

"See the rectangle that's partially obscured? I suspect that's a generator they're trying to disguise. They probably have branches or something over it, but they didn't bother to change the shape."

"How did you see that?" Day asked, turning his head to the side. "I just see jungle."

"Look at the line right there. Jungles don't have straight lines. I bet if we take out their power, they'll be crippled. At least their equipment and computers will be. That should buy us some time and cause confusion."

"They may have batteries."

"But they don't last long in most cases. Equipment and computers pull a lot of power, and the batteries will drain quickly, correct?" Day nodded. "So what we need to do is take out the generator, not shut it off. If they can't restart it, they're done." Knight smiled, and Day nodded. They looked through the rest of the aerial photographs for any other clues, but he had difficulty picking out other things. Anything else that was there was either well hidden or inside something else.

"We know what we're taking, and we have a plan to get away and make it over there. What about getting back?" Day asked.

"I'm thinking we'll hide the vehicle we'll try to liberate at some point a little ways away and walk in. That way we can use it to get back and leave it where it can be easily found so the owners aren't permanently harmed. Once we get in, we take out the generator, destroy whatever else they have, and get out." He turned to Day. "That is probably going to mean taking out the men as well." He knew Day could shoot, but could he kill? "Remember, once we start, any men who are there are going to try to kill us. So you've got to be prepared to do what's required."

Day took a deep breath. "I will. Don't worry about that. I'll have your back the way you'll have mine." Knight wasn't sure. Day said the right things, but Knight knew some men could kill, and some couldn't. "What?"

"It's not that easy." Knight turned and walked toward the sliding doors. "When I was in boot camp, there was a guy, Howie. He was as gung ho as they came, and he excelled during training. He could shoot, run, fight—all of it. The guy was a machine—big as a house and the first person you'd want on your side in a fight. Well, at least that's what we all thought." Knight pulled the curtain back and stared out at the water. "He was shipped overseas and ended up in Afghanistan. Then everything changed. I wasn't there, but apparently he was on patrol, and his unit was ambushed. One of my buddies was there and said that Howie pulled his rifle, aimed, and stared. He couldn't pull the trigger. When it came down to it, he hesitated."

"What happened?"

"Howie died right there. The guy shot him in his moment of hesitation. We'll never know if in the end Howie could have done it because he didn't get the chance. The enemy got him first." Knight turned around. "So I want you to get it through your head right now: don't hesitate or stop to think. You shoot to protect yourself, me, and the mission. The others aren't going to have a crisis of conscience.

They'll just shoot, so you do the same." He was as harsh as he could possibly be. "I don't want you to end up like that, and it could happen. I don't care if you have to detach yourself or anything else. Just do what you have to. Do you understand me?" Knight snapped a lot more venomously than he intended.

"I'll do what I have to."

"And you'll feel like shit about it. We all do the first time we have to kill. That comes with the territory too. But in the heat of it, just do what you have to. After it's over, I'll be there and so will others who have gone through the same thing." Knight wished someone had explained all this to him the first time he'd gone into battle and had to shoot a kid barely into adulthood. That had hurt, and he could still see his face, the surprise. The kid couldn't have been more than fifteen, but he carried a machine gun and was getting ready to use it on Knight's buddies. Knight had had no choice, but he would never forget it nonetheless.

"You'd really be there?"

Knight nodded. "Of course I would. You're my partner." He turned and stared at the sunshine bouncing off the water. It was nearly blinding and yet one of the most tranquilly beautiful sights he'd ever seen.

"Knight," Day whispered from right behind him. "I'm scared."

"Good. I'd know you were lying if you said you weren't. Use the fear, and let it keep you on your toes. Everyone is afraid. The successful ones use that to help them stay alert and at the top of their game."

Day didn't move, and Knight could feel his heat right behind him. He was afraid to move. Day rested his hand on his shoulder. "We really need to talk about last night. I know you don't want to. You'll talk about going in to blow people up, shooting, and God knows what else we're going to have to do. Yet you won't talk about what happened between us last night."

"I can't. Not yet. I need to keep focused on the task at hand."

"Fuck the task at hand," Day told him.

Knight turned around and locked his gaze on to Day's deep brown eyes and the worried curve to his lips. Knight stepped closer, and Day slid one hand around his neck and then to the back of his head, pulling him closer. "What are you doing?"

"Well, I thought that if you didn't want to talk about last night, then maybe you were a man of action." Day pulled him closer and kissed him hard. Knight hesitated and then wrapped his arms around Day's waist, pulling the sweet, intoxicating-tasting man to him.

"Fuck," Knight whispered when they broke apart.

"I intend to," Day said before he could miss a beat, and then Day pressed to him once again, kissing the life out of him. He cradled Knight's head, kissing and fucking his mouth with his tongue. Day took two seconds to breathe and then sucked on his lower lip hard enough to almost draw blood. "No hiding behind alcohol or anything else. You want me—I can feel it." Day thrust his hips forward. "Now you can feel it too. So if you don't want to talk it out, then we'll fuck it out." Day propelled him over to the bed. The mattress hit him at the backs of his knees, and Knight went down. He ended up sprawled on the bed, and Day hurried away.

"Where the hell are you going?"

"Condoms. They were in the cruise welcome pack. I guess they wanted to send a message." He dropped them on the bed and crawled on top of him. Day tugged at the hem of his shirt, and Knight lifted his arms. He wanted this just as badly as Day did, maybe more. His conscience pricked at him, but he batted it away as Day dropped his T-shirt on the floor and caressed his chest with warm hands.

"Fuck."

"You better believe it," Day countered, and before Knight could correct him, he was groaning at the way Day pinched his nipple and then leaned forward, licking and sucking.

"What makes you think you're…."

Day stopped and glared at him. "If you think that because you're bigger and, I don't know, older, that I'm somehow the woman, you'd better think again. You gotta give to get, and don't you forget it." Day didn't give him a chance to respond before he licked his chest and then down his abs. The protest that formed in his mind evaporated like morning fog. He gasped and ran his fingers through Day's soft hair as he explored his stomach, teasing at the band of his shorts with his tongue and fingers before popping open the button holding them closed.

Day pulled the fabric apart and slid his hand from Knight's belly button lower and lower before slipping under the band of his swimsuit. "Jesus…," Knight growled as Day cupped his balls in one hand, using the other to work the shorts and suit down his hips.

"Screw it." Day pulled his hand away and climbed off the bed. He yanked Knight's shoes off forcefully and then tugged his shorts and swimsuit down his legs and dropped them on the floor with a little flourish. Then Day grabbed the hem of his own T-shirt and pulled it up and over his head. Knight's mouth went desert dry as all that honey-gold skin came into view. He hadn't shaved, and damn if he didn't want to ask Day to never shave again—he was even hotter with his slight beard. "You want to see the rest?"

"Fuck yes!" Knight answered gutturally. Day turned around and slid his pants down, asscheeks shifting in front of him. Once everything was off, Day turned, and Knight stared. He'd felt Day's cock, but seeing it… fuck. He sat up and wrapped his fingers around the thick length. Day beat in Knight's hand with each thrum of his heart.

Knight stroked slowly, and Day gasped and moaned softly before pressing Knight back. He went willingly and stared as Day climbed onto the bed. Chest met chest as Day's skin met his. Hips came together, followed by lips, and then Day's cock nestled next to his, sliding alongside. His world exploded in a burst of light, and Knight held Day tightly, groaning as they began moving together. He ran his hands down Day's muscular lats and paused at the small of his back before pressing upward, cupping the cheeks of his firm ass. "Fuck," Knight whispered between breath-stealing kisses, and he pressed Day closer.

"Yeah," Day agreed and kissed him harder. Knight rolled them on the bed, smiling down at Day when their roles reversed. He kissed him, and Day rolled him right back, eliciting a groan combined with openmouthed surprise. "I get to be in control." Day slammed his lips against Knight's, and Knight held him closer. Day's weight felt good.

Day broke their kiss and licked down Knight's neck to the base of his throat. "Damn, you taste good. I never expected another guy to taste like this, like you."

"What did you expect?" Knight's words trailed off into a groan.

"Don't know. Doesn't matter." He sucked at a nipple and then continued his explorations. Knight hadn't thought much about what sex would be like with Day, but he'd expected someone reticent. He wasn't. Not in the least. Day seemed to be going for it, and when Day slid his tongue up the length of his cock, Knight thought he would never breathe again.

"Damn," he groaned.

"Yeah," Day mumbled and sucked the head of Knight's cock into his mouth.

"Fucking hell," Knight groaned and pressed forward, wanting more. Day backed away and then took him once again, gripping his cock and sucking deeper. The wet heat was awesome. Hell, it was the best thing he'd felt around his cock in like… ever. Day took more and then bobbed his head. The movements were tentative and sometimes hesitant, but Knight could care less. He loved every second of it.

He stilled when Day lifted one of his legs before pressing a finger to his opening. He wasn't sure about that, but as soon as Day swallowed him deep, Knight forgot all about that… until Day slipped a finger inside him and touched something that sent electric shocks all through him. "What the hell was that?" he breathed. "Do it again!"

Day pulled off and said, "I read that there's a spot with some men and—"

"That was rhetorical. Talk less… suck more."

"Bossy," Day countered and sucked him in again. Knight felt as though he wasn't in control of his body any longer. Day had him doing things he never thought he could or would do. He'd long felt that he'd given up this part of his life. He'd done it for his family, but now….

"Stop thinking, and let it go," Day told him and added a second slick finger. Knight took a second to wonder where the lube had come from, but he didn't freakin' care. All he knew was that Day was somehow playing him like an instrument, and he wanted it… hell, he needed it as badly as he needed air to breathe.

Day's fingers slipped away, and Knight groaned loud when Day left his cock too. He'd been starting down the road to heaven, and he hadn't wanted to stop.

Day opened one of the condom packs. It took him a few seconds to get the condom on, and then he lubed it and stepped forward. "Is this really okay?"

"Fucking hell. Yes. If you're going to fuck me, then do it now." The growl barely sounded like words to him, but Day lifted Knight's legs, settled his ankles on his shoulders, and then moved forward. Knight had only been on Day's end of the equation before. He gritted his teeth and then blew out his breath as Day breached him. "Damn…."

Day stopped, and Knight breathed as though he'd just run a marathon. His head spun, and he already felt full, but Day pressed deeper, sliding his thick cock into him. God, how was he going to take more? Knight was seconds from asking him to stop when he felt Day's hips against his ass.

"Jesus, fuck…," Day ground out.

"No kidding," Knight countered. Day stroked his chest, and Knight felt gentle hands on his chin. When he turned Day's gaze burned into him, hot and intense. Neither of them moved. Fuck, Knight was afraid to breathe, and then the most amazing thing happened: Day slowly began to shift his hips back and forth. Knight knew what fucking was—he'd done that before— but this…. God. The movements were slow and even. Hell, Day hardly moved at all, and Knight's breath would whoosh from his lungs.

"What the hell are you doing to me?" Knight asked through a haze of lustful confusion.

Day smiled and moved faster without shifting his gaze. Knight released some of the tension he'd been holding in his body, and pleasure instantly bloomed from deep inside. Day caressed him and held him in his gaze, in his hands. It was as if Day really cared for him. That notion was hard for him to accept. It went against everything Knight had had drilled into his head for years. He'd known he was gay and that he preferred men to women—he'd accepted that. But he'd always thought that sex between men was just sex, nothing more than animal urges. But this was something more. Day was making it something more… or was it him?

"Let it go," Day whispered and leaned forward, kissing him hard as he picked up the pace. "Let everything go and soar."

How Day understood what he was thinking puzzled him, unless he was thinking the same thing. That had to be it. Both of them were equally confused. He could understand that and did as Day commanded, losing himself in those chocolate eyes and musky-scented skin. Day's movements quickly became more frantic, and soon the bed rocked in time to the motion of the ship. Knight wouldn't be able to hold off his explosion much longer. He spit on his hand, gripped himself, and stroked for all he was worth.

"Open your eyes. I want to see you," Day said. Knight hadn't even realized he'd closed them, but as soon as he slid them open, Day's passion-filled gaze met his again. Knight gasped, and Day thrust deep and hard, then pulled away and nearly out before slamming back into him. "I know what you want. I can see it in the way your breath hitches when I touch you and the way your eyes shine." Day pulled out again and then slid back into him, rolling his hips in rhythmic action that pulled his release from him.

Knight could hold off no longer. Catching his breath, he cried out as his release slammed into him. Day thrust deep and held, throbbing inside him.

They both held still. Knight was afraid to move and damn near wrung out. He hugged Day to him and languished in the skin-to-skin warmth. Day breathed heavily into his ear and after a few seconds, sucked on it lightly. "You're… wow."

Knight smiled. "It's been a long time."

"For both of us."

"I suppose, but how did you know how to… if you haven't done this very much, how did you get so good?" Knight cracked his eyes open.

"Natural talent combined with… well, porn." Day grinned like a little boy who'd been caught with his hand in the cookie jar.

"That must be some porn," Knight quipped, and Day lightly smacked his arm. Knight tightened his hold and closed his eyes once again.

"Smartass," Day murmured. "I'd like to see what talent you have."

"You would?" Knight asked and rolled them on the bed. Day grinned up at him. "We'll have to see what we can do about that."

Day wrapped his arms around Knight's neck, pulled him down, and kissed him. Whereas the ones earlier had been filled with fire, heat, and searing passion, this was slow, languid, and filled with warmth and pleasure. It was so different and yet the same. It was Day.

Knight returned the kiss and slowly let the heat build. Day felt so damn good in his arms, like he belonged there. But Knight could not allow that feeling to take root. They were on a mission together, and it seemed both of them had long-repressed passions bubbling to the surface. That didn't mean it meant anything other than what it was right now.

Energy and heat returned to Knight's body, fueled by Day's touches.

"I love your ass," Day told him, sliding his hands down to grip Knight's butt.

He never thought he'd enjoy that, but from Day it was hot, tender, and intimate all at the same time. He thrust his hips lightly, and Day responded by doing the same. "Are you usually so eager?"

Day shrugged. "Don't know. I'd like to think it's you."

Knight captured Day's lips. "I'd like to think it's me too." The thought that he could turn Day on so quickly after such intensity was enough to wake Knight's own body. He pressed closer to Day and slowly flexed his hips, sliding his hardening cock along Day's. "Where's the lube and that other condom?"

Day looked at the table beside the bed, and Knight reached for the lube packet and slicked his fingers. He slowly teased the skin of Day's opening before pressing a single digit into him.

"You don't have to treat me like I'm fragile."

"I won't hurt you."

"I know you won't," Day said.

Knight pressed deeper. He curled his finger slightly, and Day gasped and held him as though he were going to fly apart. Knight centered him by holding his gaze. He tore open the condom packet. There was no graceful way to do get the damn thing rolled on, as Knight found out, but he managed it and pulled Day to the edge of the bed. Knight stood on the floor and pressed Day's legs upward to his chest. Then he locked his gaze to Day's, listening to his breathing, and slowly pressed into him.

He'd had sex before, but nothing prepared him for the heat and pressure that surrounded his cock as Day's body opened to him. Knight's legs shook with excitement so great it had to get out somehow. He didn't want to go too fast, but every instinct he possessed told him to bury himself in Day and ride like the wind.

"That's it," Day ground out and pressed to him, forcing him deeper.

Knight lost the battle for control, snapping his hips forward. Day cried out, and they both stilled.

"Fuck, you feel good on my cock," Knight whispered.

"So did you."

Knight moved closer, the way Day had begun moving with him. The wisdom was that you gave what you wanted. Day gripped his arm. "Am I hurting you?"

"Hell no." Day pushed back hard, driving Knight deep. "Fuck me like you mean it."

Knight pulled back and slammed into Day, hips slapping against his ass. "Is that what you want?"

"Fuck yeah."

Knight gripped Day's ankles, spreading his legs and letting go of the last of his control. He snapped his hips, driving deep into Day. Everything was instinct now. Sweat poured down his chest, and he pistoned his hips like a machine. Day rolled his head back and forth on the bed, eyes wide, chanting "fuck yeah" over and over again. Knight released Day's ankles and grabbed his hips, using the leverage to slam their bodies together. The heat, the right grip, and the sounds Day made all combined to nearly drive him out of his mind.

Beads of sweat ran down his forehead and chest. He stroked Day's chest and then grabbed his cock, stroking him as fast and hard as he could. "Grab the bed, and hold on for dear life," Knight warned him, and Day gripped the bedding as Knight threw all his weight and intensity behind his thrusts.

Good Lord, he had no idea where this passion and intensity came from. He'd always been a careful lover, but Day drove him wild, and his inhibitions fell quickly by the wayside. "You're fucking hot with my cock inside you."

"Yeah? Prove it!" Day gasped and held tighter to the bed, and Knight let go of everything. His head was light as a feather, and his heart pounded in his ears. Sweat continued rolling off him. "Jesus Christ," Day cried loud enough to alert half the ship to what they were doing. Somehow that pleased him no end. Day tightened around him, gripping his cock like a vise.

Tingling began at the base of his spine and spread throughout the rest of him. Knight's knees wanted to buckle, and he only remained upright through sheer will. His legs shook, and Knight gasped and moaned through Day's release. What an amazing sensation that was, feeling and watching Day come unglued around him, that sheer joy and intensity he knew would stay with him. Knight whimpered as he slammed into Day, holding still as his orgasm overtook him. He came hard, filling the condom, his body shutting down in the aftermath of two powerful releases in less than an hour.

He collapsed forward into Day's arms, unable to remain upright. He gasped when their bodies separated. Every touch seemed heightened and out of proportion. He didn't want to move, and yet he was afraid of crushing Day. He managed to settle on the bed next to him, breathing like he'd just run a race. "I'm sorry."

Day stilled. "What for?"

"Hurting you. I had to have hurt you. I was so out of control."

Day stroked his arm. "You didn't, and yeah, you were out of control in the best way there is. It was awesome that I could make you let yourself go so completely. I always want that." Day shifted on the mattress. "Scoot up so you're all the way on the bed."

He did as Day said. He had no energy left to argue. Once he was settled, Day removed the condom and left the room. He returned with a cloth and placed it on Knight's head.

"I'm okay," Knight said.

"Just lie there, and for once don't argue."

Knight stayed where he was, letting the cool air dry his skin. "God. Are you sure I didn't hurt you?"

“No. I promise I’ll tell you if there’s something I don’t like or want. I have a voice, and I’m big enough to make what I want known. You don’t have to worry about things like that.” Day scooted closer and placed an arm over his chest. “Just rest awhile, and you’ll feel more like your cranky, bossy self.”

“You really know how to poke the bear, don’t you?” Knight warned.

“See, you’re doing better already.”

Knight heard a smile in Day’s voice. He couldn’t see it, but he definitely heard it.

“Now, do you want to tell me why you’re so afraid of hurting me?”

“You really are nosy enough to be a shrink.” Knight moved his arm and opened his eyes, turning to Day. “Fuck off.”

“After what we’ve just done, I’m afraid that’s a complete impossibility. So now you have to tell me. I’m not asking you to tell me all your secrets, but I think this is one that’s pertinent. Maybe not to the mission, but to me.” Day lay back down. “I’m waiting.”

Knight groaned. “Aw, hell.” Just what he fucking wanted to talk about right now.

Chapter 5

DAY LAY naked against Knight. This should feel strange as hell, lying naked next to his work partner. But it didn't. Granted, if the powers that be at work found out what they'd been doing on this "work" cruise, the whole partner thing would probably change fast, along with their employment status. Dammit, he needed to focus and pull away from his stupid worries for the moment. "You don't have to tell me."

Knight moaned softly. "You can knock off the passive-aggressive shit. It's annoying." Knight turned toward Day.

Day had already noticed that when Knight wanted to hide from the world, he played ostrich with the whole "arm over his eyes" thing. He pulled the arm away and turned toward Knight.

"If I hear a sigh or see any signs of it or some other nonsense, I'll…," Knight said.

"You'll what?"

"I'll heave you over the railing and tell everyone you could no longer live with your assholeness." He sounded serious. "Either that or I'll say you were a spy and I dumped you over to keep you from spilling government secrets."

Day rolled his eyes. "You're the ass, not me."

"They don't know that."

"Okay, as long as we agree who's the ass, I got it. No pity or feeling sorry for you." He wanted to smile but kept it off his face. Knight was being serious in his own mock-threatening way. Whatever had happened had affected him deeply. Day quieted and lay on the bed, the ship rocking gently, the sun shining in the open curtains. He should have been relaxed and drifting off to sleep in such an otherwise peaceful atmosphere, but instead he was on edge.

"I was nineteen. I had left home and was on leave after boot camp," Knight said. "I got two weeks. The other guys were going home to see their families. But I wasn't going to do that. I had gotten away and didn't see any need to return to my father's scrutiny. So I stayed in San Diego with one of the other guys. Mark and I had been friends of a sort, and he found himself in a similar situation to me. So we got a small place and figured we'd spend a couple weeks doing nothing on the beach." Knight didn't look at him, and Day kept quiet. He didn't want to interrupt the flow of the story.

"Mark was a great guy." Knight rolled his head on the pillow. "He was injured in Iraq five years ago and lost his legs. I went to see him after that, and he wasn't the same. No one knew what to do for him, and his parents were beside themselves. He took his own life a few weeks later because he could never see himself as a complete man after that."

Knight returned to looking at the ceiling. It must have been easier for him not to make eye contact, even though Day wished he would.

"He had an old car, so one morning, we took a buzz up the coast to Venice. Muscle Beach. He and I were both bulky and strong, so we figured we'd put on a show. Of course, compared to those guys we weren't much, but it was fun. Mark wandered off on the boardwalk to have some fun, and I went into one of the gyms and then back outside to take in the beach itself. God, there were guys everywhere, and I'd had weeks of intense physical training locked away with guys who talked about almost nothing but girls and fucking. I ended up hanging around with some of them, and I got noticed. I was young, good-looking, and what some of the guys seemed to be looking for. I got invited to a bar, and it didn't take me long to notice there were only guys there."

"Your first gay bar?" Day asked.

"Yeah. Guys were buying me drinks, and I downed most of them because, hell, I was young, stupid, and horny. A lethal combination. Anyway, this guy approached me after I'd had a few, and he came on strong. Said he loved Marine types and wondered if I'd like to have some fun with him. He was cute and nice-looking, dressed, well, for fucking. Everything about him said sex. He had an apartment in the area, so we went there, and things got going really fast."

Day was following the story, but up till now didn't see a problem. "Doesn't sound like an issue."

"There wasn't one. The guy said his name was Jimmy, probably a fake name, but it didn't matter. He said he liked strong guys, so I manhandled him a little. I didn't really hurt him, and he seemed to get off on it. I kind of liked it too. I was strong, and we were having a good time." Knight cleared his throat. "Anyway, we got down to the highlight of the evening, and we were really going at it. Jimmy was screaming for me to fuck him, and I was giving it to him like there was no tomorrow. Suddenly there was this pop, and Jimmy starts to moan. It sounded different. Not happy, but I didn't understand that right away. I was in the zone." Knight paused, and Day turned to look over at him. "I stopped eventually and his jaw was set, face contorted in pain. I pulled out and settled him gently on the bed."

"What happened?"

"I don't know. He said it was all right, but I knew he wasn't. I asked if he needed help, but he said that I should probably just go. He started moving toward the side of the bed, and I helped him." Knight was becoming more and more agitated. "All I kept thinking about was what if I got caught here? I'd be out of the Corps, no family, disgraced, and I'd have no place to go."

"What did you do?" Day asked, trying not to let the worry show in his voice.

"I helped him up, and he stumbled and then made his way to the bathroom."

"He was walking on his own," Day said.

"Yeah, but I could tell there was something wrong. I mean, he wasn't walking right, and he was all hunched over. I heard him in the bathroom, and I thought maybe he was getting sick. I asked if he was okay, and all I heard was him say that I'd better go. So I gathered my clothes and stuff. When I was dressed and ready to leave, I said good-bye and asked one more time if he needed help."

"Did he respond?"

"Yeah. He said he was fine, so I left and found Mark. He was talking up some girls on the beach, and I went along with him. We got something to eat and had some drinks, but I was all out of sorts and kept looking around. I expected people to come looking for me at any time. Of course no one did, and at the end of the day, Mark and I went back to San Diego. He'd gotten laid, and I drank a little more and ended up sick in the bathroom at the restaurant before laying off. By the time he came back, I had gotten most of the crap out of my system, and we drove home. Probably a stupid thing to do, but we were the kings of stupid."

"I don't think I understand."

"I didn't think anything of it until… well, you know how things have a way of coming back around? Well, it did a week later. The people next door got the newspaper, and they were gone so I picked it up so folks wouldn't know they weren't home, and I saw Jimmy's face. There were people trying to raise money for him because he'd injured his spine and couldn't walk anymore. His parents were from the San Diego area so it made the papers there."

"How do you know it was your fault? Did anyone try to contact you?"

"No. And what was Jimmy supposed to say? He got hurt fucking with some random guy from a bar? No. He made up some story about falling down stairs and getting hurt, but it was him. I heard the pop. We were just fucking, but I must have been doing it too hard or something. I know I hurt him. And I haven't been with another guy… until you."

Day didn't know what to say. So many things popped into his mind. He wanted to say that fucking someone into paralysis required something else to be wrong. That didn't just happen, but Knight seemed to think it could. He wanted to comfort or at the very least soothe. But he wasn't sure how to do that without it sounding like pity or any of the other things he knew would send Knight over the edge. Knight had confided a story that Day suspected he had never told anyone before… ever. How could he? Day turned toward him. Knight was still staring at the ceiling, eyes unblinking.

What the fuck could he say that would make a difference? There wasn't anything, not really. Knight had to come to the realization himself that he wasn't responsible. Words were too easy, too quickly thrown about so much of the time. So Day did the only thing he thought he could do. He reached between them and took Knight's hand in his. Entwining their fingers, he simply held it and stayed where he was. Eventually he felt Knight squeeze his hand in return and he knew his message had been received. No pity, no sympathy or platitudes, just support. That was all he wanted to convey.

IT WAS quite a while before either of them moved. Their palms had sweated together, but Day didn't mind. He held Knight's hand for as long as he let him. When Knight finally shifted, their hands separated, and Knight got off the bed with a small groan. Day said nothing about what he'd been told. He simply watched as Knight padded naked toward the bathroom.

Once Knight was out of earshot, he sighed and lifted himself off the majorly rumpled bedding. His entire body ached but in a way that sent a little rush of heat through him. He liked the reason for the aches. Water ran in the bathroom, and then the shower started. Day thought about asking if Knight wanted some company but thought better of it. He needed time to deal with memories he had probably thought were locked away tight and had now been exposed to the harsh light of day once again.

In a way, Day was honored that Knight had shared his story and had trusted him enough to tell him what had happened. Not that it mattered to him. He knew Knight hadn't meant to hurt anyone. Day needed his turn in the bathroom, so he pulled on the pair of shorts he'd been wearing earlier and sat at his computer to see if any additional information had come in. Not that he was able to concentrate at the moment, but it gave him something to do. There was more chatter, and he began running it through his programs to see if there was anything meaningful. Something caught his eye, and he scrolled back.

"Knight," Day said when he heard the water stop. "Knight."

The bathroom door opened. "They've solved the sharing issue. That seems to be their last impediment to implementation as far as I can tell. They're still talking, so I hope that means we still have a little time."

"Me too," Knight said without a lot of energy. He looked drawn and tired, not that Day was a bundle of energy. Between their athletic sex and then Knight's story, Day was drained. However, there was still work to do and preparations to make. "What time do we dock in the morning?'

"Ten," Day answered after glancing at the schedule. "I've been thinking. I know the original plan was to use the excursion to take us inland, but since the group is so close to town, they're going to take us farther away from the area we need to see."

"I agree. I think we need to cancel the excursion. It will only raise suspicion if we don't show up. Dimato's idea for that didn't strike me as well thought out. Disappearing from a smaller group would be more noticeable than simply getting off the ship, melding into the area, and not returning. Besides, Dimato doesn't know everything I know."

"What does that mean?"

"We all have contacts, and some of them you don't share with anyone. My friend Miguel is my contact. Dimato doesn't know he exists, and that's the way I plan to keep it." Knight's hard expression held a warning.

"So how do we get there?" The tour was supposed to be their transportation, but if it wasn't needed, then it had to be replaced. They could walk, but that wasn't the most pleasant idea and didn't provide for a fast getaway if necessary.

"Leave that to me," Knight answered. Day nodded and decided to trust that Knight knew what he was doing. "Sometimes you get by with a little help from your friends." Knight flashed him a quick smile. "I'll be back. You finish up what you need to, and when I come back I'll lay out my plan, and we can go from there." Knight left the room, and Day tried not to get his feathers ruffled about the whole "my plan" thing.

Day's sigh rumbled in his throat. He pushed back the chair and decided a shower was probably in order. He needed time to get his head around the fact that his first field mission was actually going to happen. He'd figured that at some point it would get called off or the location would change and they wouldn't be in the right spot or something. So many things could go wrong or change at a moment's notice that he'd been sure something would mess this up. But it appeared to be happening, and they were in the right spot at what could be just the right time. It was exciting and frightening at the same time.

Day went into the bathroom and started the water before stepping into the small tub. He washed his hair and body quickly, the remnants of what he and Knight had done washing down the drain. When he was done, he rinsed off and got out, drying quickly before fussing a little with his hair to make sure it didn't clump and look stringy. Then he left the bathroom and dressed before returning to work.

"I think it's approaching the point where I can't do much more," Day told Knight as soon as he'd returned and closed the cabin door. "We've pretty much pinpointed the location and confirmed it with satellite pictures."

"The only thing I'd really like to know is, how many people are there? And can you tell who they're communicating with? The signals we're intercepting are from this area, but who are they talking to? Where are they located?"

"That's the hard part," Day explained. "We're only getting what's originating from here because they're using sat phones, not standard cells, and it's a flaw in their design that we're exploiting. If they were using newer equipment, we'd be getting almost nothing at all. Based on what's being said, I believe the other side is somewhere in Colombia. Medellín has been mentioned, but that doesn't mean much. They don't speak a lot about locations. They aren't dumb and seem to be aware that they could be intercepted, so they say only what they need to."

"Then why all the chatter in the first place?" Knight asked almost to himself.

"I think the boss, whoever he is, required status reports," Day explained, and Knight chuckled. "What?"

"That means he doesn't fully trust these guys. That's good. We might be able to use that to our advantage at some point. Not sure how, but it's good to know."

"Why?"

"Because any fact or impression can be valuable. You don't know when a piece of information will be key to getting you in or out when the time comes. Assets can come at any time. So I suggest you store all the information you can glean from these conversations and lock it away. We might need it." Knight turned away, and Day saw him yawn. "Other than that I think we're as ready as we'll ever be."

"You wanted to review the plan," Day prompted.

"Yeah." Knight sat on the edge of the bed and laid out what he saw happening and when. "This is an outline, and we'll make adjustments as we go, but we need to have an overall plan. If we get separated, we'll designate a place in Costa Maya to meet back up. One other thing. Equipment is expendable, so dump it if you need to. Make sure it's not operable, so water works for anything electronic and there should be enough of it around. Same goes for weapons. Don't get caught with anything on you that could be used against you. If the police or the army show up, be wary. They could well be on the take or even part of the plot."

"Okay. It's a lot to take in."

"Yes, it is. We need to look like tourists at all times except when we're making our last incursion. If anyone sees us, we'll say we're exploring the Yucatan looking for ruins. There are plenty of them, so that should work for us. Just keep your wits about you and think. Don't just react. Sometimes instinct is good, but sometimes what it screams at us to do is the exact opposite of what we should do."

"Okay. I'll try."

"Are you nervous?" Day nodded. "Excited?" Day nodded again. "Scared enough to wet yourself?"

"Almost."

"Great. If you weren't scared, I'd wonder what was wrong with you and suggest that maybe you stay here so you don't get both of us killed. Use the fear, but don't let it run you. The fear isn't in control. You are."

"Do you think there's a possibility that we could take these guys out without destroying all their equipment? It would be amazing to see what they're doing and how they planned to pull this off. The information on the programs they developed would be valuable to the storage companies as well as the government."

"We'll have to see. Our main goal is to stop this attack. If we can procure additional assets in the process, sure, that would be good. The last thing we want is to neutralize this group and have another spring up using the same methods and programs. We'll destroy everything if we have to. That's most important: take away the enemy's ability to wage war."

"Okay." Day continued looking through what he had but gave up after a while. There were no more connections he could make. "I've requested fresh photographs. A satellite is expected to pass over the area first thing tomorrow morning. It will be an hour after sunrise, but it should show if anything has changed."

"Good idea," Knight told him with a smile.

"So now what?"

"Dinner is in a few hours. I say we relax and make the most of the evening we have. Tomorrow will be a long day, so we need to get plenty of sleep tonight."

Day wondered if that was an allusion to what they'd done this afternoon but didn't ask. "I was thinking I'd go up, swim, maybe bubble a little in the whirlpools. See what's happening." It sounded like a good way to relax and keep from obsessing about what they were going to be doing tomorrow. He'd thought about going to the gym, but he'd already had his workout and needed relaxation. Day hunted up his bathing suit and changed out of his shorts. When he came out of the bathroom, Knight had changed as well. He had his back to him, so Day took a few minutes to enjoy the tree-trunk legs and beefy ass view. "I'm ready when you are." Knight turned and grabbed a towel and his key card. Day made sure he had his, and they left the cabin.

The pool deck was hopping. A live reggae band was on tap. The whirlpools were crammed, but a little space appeared in one of them, and as Day climbed in, with Knight behind him, it didn't take him long to realize why. The other men watched him openly, a few licking their lips. He wasn't sure what to make of it and decided to ignore it.

"Having a good time?" he asked instead.

"Yeah," one of the men answered, and the others nodded their agreement.

Day settled back and relaxed, closing his eyes. Knight sat next to him, but the tension didn't seem to leave him. "You'd think after earlier…." It wasn't necessary to finish the whispered thought. "Just relax." Day patted his hand under the water.

Knight turned toward him, scowled, and then turned away. Day wasn't sure what he was upset about and closed his eyes again. A foot brushed against his, but Day ignored it. It happened a second time, and he slid his eyes open. One of the men from across the tub caught his eye, and the foot brushed him a third time. Day pulled his legs back and realized that all the guys were still watching him. The scowl remained etched on Knight's face. Day leaned closer and gently touched Knight's chin. When he turned to him, Day gave him a hard, but relatively quick kiss and then pulled away and sat back. Before he closed his eyes once again, he noticed that Knight's scowl was gone, and a few of the guys fanned themselves dramatically while another chuckled.

"Tough luck, Rudy," one guy said.

"Smartass," Mr. Footsie retorted. Water splashed.

"I hope you're happy," Knight whispered.

"I am, actually. Thank you." He smiled without opening his eyes. Let them be jealous. Or envious. Whatever. They could look if they wanted, although Day wasn't sure how comfortable he felt about being the object of other men's attention. He'd spent so much time denying who he was that it would take time and a lot more soul searching for him to be comfortable in his own skin. However, he felt like he might finally be getting there.

"How long have you been together?" one of the men asked Knight. Day paid no attention.

"Well, we've been friends for a while, but…."

"The sea worked her magic on you? How lovely. A real onboard romance." He sounded giddy, and Day cracked his eyes open to get a look at him and then closed them again. The guy was most likely nearing fifty, sitting next to a man of the same age. They appeared to be together and happy, sitting close to each other.

"I guess you could call it that." Knight didn't sound comfortable.

"He never likes to talk about himself," Day added, nudging Knight lightly with his arm. "And relationships…." Day smiled. "Feelings…." He placed his hand over his chest and tried to look shocked.

"Fuck off," Knight deadpanned.

"That's Knight-speak for 'I don't want to talk about it.'"

"Aww, that's so cute. See, you know you're hitting it off when you've developed your own code for things," one of the older men said.

Knight said nothing, and Day could not suppress a chuckle. "In this case, it means that Knight here is a closemouthed ass." He turned to him. "It's one of the things we agree on." Knight huffed but didn't refute it. Day closed his eyes once again and let the sun, the warmth from the water, and the happy jumble of conversation wash over him. He let go of the worry and simply relaxed. Tomorrow would bring whatever it would. They had a plan and had prepared as much as they could. All they needed now was to get in, complete the mission, and get out again.

Some of the guys got out of the tub, which made more room. Day shifted a little and extended his legs once more now that Mr. Footsie had left. It was nice, and eventually he opened his eyes, and one of the other men engaged him in conversation.

"So how did you two meet?"

Day glanced at Knight, who remained quiet. Asshole. "We work together, and I'd seen him around but would never say anything because it's work. Anyway, I was out at a club and there he was, a tall, quiet wallflower. So I walked over and asked him to dance." Day figured if he was going to make up a story, it might as well be a good one. "But he turned me down, saying he couldn't dance. I also think he was a little surprised to see someone from work. I managed to get him on the dance floor, and he was right. The man dances like a duck with broken wings. I had to get him off the floor before he hurt someone." Day smiled, and Knight humphed. "After that, he excused himself and must have left, probably intimidated by me."

"Yeah, right," Knight scoffed.

Day had figured that would get a rise out of him. "So at work, I was cool but arranged to bump into him on a regular basis, and eventually I wore the big lug down until he agreed to see me."

"Yeah. That is *so* not how it happened. You chased me, and I finally went out with you to stop the kicked-puppy-dog looks. It was pathetic. He hung around my office, shooting me these wounded looks. I took pity on him and agreed to drinks if he'd stop with the hound-dog expression." Knight flashed him a "two can play this game" look.

"Didn't matter—I still wore him down, and we've been dating now for a few months, and when he asked me to come on the cruise with him, I reluctantly agreed so he wouldn't be lonely." Day did his best to look innocent.

"That's bullshit, and you know it." Knight looked pissed, and Day cracked up. He couldn't help it. Knight was getting upset over a fake story about a fake relationship that was a cover for an undercover mission. That was priceless and a story he could never tell anyone. Sometimes life wasn't fair.

"It's okay, honey. You're a catch. I'm just the only one who sees it."

"What did I say about poking the bear?" Knight growled.

"You're not a bear." Day reached over and rubbed Knight's chest. "You're not hairy enough, although you are growly enough. You can be a bear light or a bearette." He was having way too much fun with this. "You're definitely no cub."

"Thank God you caught that. I was starting to worry." Knight was still growly, and Day figured it was time to back off.

"So what will you do when you get home?" the older man asked.

Day shrugged and glanced at Knight, who shrugged as well. "Probably see what happens." Knight put an arm around him and tugged Day closer. He didn't want to read too much into it, but he liked the idea of seeing where things went with Knight after all this was over. However, he figured the mission would be over and they'd both go back to their lives. It was likely that Knight would sink back into his solitary lifestyle. Day already knew that things were different for him. This trip had already opened his eyes to a world where people were open about who they were. He liked that and was tired of denying a large part of himself. Maybe he'd actually date. "The office can be old-fashioned."

"Lots of 'phobes?"

"Yeah," Knight answered. "Plenty of them, including our boss. I think he's the worst." Day wondered if that was a word of warning. "He doesn't understand anything that will get in the way of the job, and in his view, something like this would definitely interfere. He can be a real prick."

Day nodded. The guys probably saw it as agreement, and he hoped Knight understood that his message was received. "Do you all have plans for tomorrow?" It seemed like a good time to change the subject.

The men talked about the excursions they had planned. Most were heading to the ruins on one tour or another. He and Knight said little about their plans other than that they intended to explore a little and see what they could find.

He was starting to get warm, so Day got up and sat on the edge of the tub for a minute. He tapped Knight on the shoulder and then got out and walked over to the nearest pool. He slid into the cooler water, paddling a little. The pools weren't really large enough to swim in, but cooling off felt good. Day did notice that a number of guys became interested in swimming about the same time he did. It was nice for his ego, being the center of attention. He knew he was good-looking, there was no doubt about that, but it seemed there was only one man whose attention he wanted. Day climbed out of the pool and went to find a deck chair, drying off before lying down to enjoy the late-afternoon sun.

Knight came over eventually and sat silently in the deck chair next to him. Day could feel his presence more than hear or see him. He didn't look away from the sky, but he knew by the sound of Knight's breathing and the scent that wafted over to him who it was. Their little encounter in the hot tub puzzled him. The story had been as fake as they came. The basics he'd made up on the fly, kind of. He'd thrown in some elements that were true to keep it believable. But had Knight done the same? Day mentally slapped himself for thinking like an angsty teenage girl. Things were the way they were. He and Knight weren't a couple. They were playing the role of a couple to maintain a cover that would no longer be needed in a few days.

He needed to let it all go—Day kept telling himself that. But fuck, he didn't have to see the guy to know he was there. He could feel him, smell him. He was letting his emotions run away with him. He'd spent a long time alone, and he was latching on to the first person who came along. Granted, Knight was a stand-up guy, powerful, hot, intense… well, an intense asshole, but he could deal with that. Day knew how to counter assness with a little stubborn humor.

"The sun is going down," Knight commented, stating the obvious. Day had watched the shadows lengthen on the deck and groups of guys pick up their towels to head inside. The number of inhabitants of the deck had thinned greatly. Even the music had stopped. Now the waves and wind made their own melody to the rhythmic rocking of the ship.

"Do you want to leave?" Day mumbled. He wasn't in the mood to move, but he wanted to check on things one last time tonight. He'd also do it again first thing in the morning so they would have the most up-to-date information.

"Don't know. Seems silly to lay out when there's no sun." However Knight didn't move at all.

"What was your family like… before…?" Knight asked. "Was it happy?"

"Yeah," Day answered with a smile. "We used to go camping as a family. Dad was a huge hiker, and Mom was a huge 'stay back at camp, read, and make dinner' kind of lady. Stephen and I used to go with Dad. We'd leave after lunch and get home late in the afternoon. Mom would send along things like marshmallows and stuff like that." Day chuckled to himself. "I remember this one time when we were out for this hike in one of the state parks. It was a trail that Dad said had a shelter with a fireplace at the end. I must have been eight, and it was a long walk. Dad put me in charge of the marshmallows."

Knight chuckled, soft but deep, like fine, rich music.

"I was a young kid, and we walked, like, forever. So when we reached the shelter, Dad had us hunt for sticks while he started a fire. Once everything was ready, he turned and asked for the marshmallows.

"'I was hungry,' I told him. There was one left in the bag, and I was reaching for it as I answered. Stephen snatched the bag away, and I ran, figuring Stephen was going to punch me or Dad was going to spank my heinie." Day laughed when he thought about it. "Needless to say, Dad did come get me, after letting Stephen roast the last marshmallow. He didn't spank me. In fact, I think he was trying not to laugh."

"Oh God. You must have been something else as a kid."

Day shrugged. "They gave me the bag, and I thought they were mine, so I ate them as I walked. Dad had a pack with him, so I thought he had other food for us to eat. All he had was water and granola bars, which don't roast well." Day let the warm memories of the family he no longer had wash over him. "After a little while, we put out the fire and walked back. Of course, Dad told Mom what happened, and she glared at me for two seconds and then laughed her butt off, telling Dad he should have known better. After that, I was never allowed to carry any of the food on the hikes." Sadness washed over him. "My dad was so patient. He was really smart, but my grandparents didn't believe in education. They believed in work, so he got a job right after high school. He always did his best for us." Day paused.

"You said they were gone," Knight prompted.

"Yeah. Mom died about two years later, I guess, when I was ten. She got breast cancer, and they couldn't save her. Dad lasted six more years, and then he was killed in an accident at work." Day stopped. "He worked in a warehouse, and a section of full shelving collapsed. It hadn't been put together right or something. After that Stephen raised me until I was old enough to be on my own."

"How old was he when your dad died?"

"Twenty-one. He had hoped to go to college but couldn't afford it. The company Dad worked for provided some life insurance and a small settlement for the accident, but it wasn't enough for college. I was able to go because of scholarships. I told him he should go, but by then he had other plans. After I finished school, there was still a little money left, and we split it. I still have most of my share." Day paused and then turned onto his side. "It's going to sound dumb, but as long as I have it, I feel like I have part of them still. It's stupid, I know."

"Family isn't stupid, and wanting to still have one… well, that's what we all want." Knight's chair creaked as he stood and then pulled on his T-shirt. "I think we've shared enough sad stories for one day." Knight inhaled deeply. "Sometimes life sucks. We do the best we can and then move on." He strode off without another word, and Day lay still, needing a few minutes to himself. God, this had been one hell of a day for baring hurt and pain.

He needed to push all that from his mind. He and Knight had a mission to pull off, and that was where his mind needed to be, not on his parents, who had been gone for more than a decade. His dad would have told him to get his head in the game, and that was what he intended to do. Day steeled his resolve and stood up. He grabbed his shirt and pulled it over his head before picking up the rest of his things.

After checking that he had everything, he left the deck and headed down to the cabin.

Knight had already changed and sat behind his computer. "There's a message from Dimato wishing us well and saying that from their end the chatter seems to have stopped. He says the last message they intercepted was three hours ago, and there's been nothing since."

Day dropped his towel and the rest of his crap. He could change later. He logged on and checked his own equipment. "I have a single message from about an hour ago." Day slipped on his phones and listened. "It's short. *Ir mañana.* It literally means go tomorrow." Day's stomach clenched. "However it could also mean soon." Day checked further but found nothing more. "I'll check later, but I think they've gone silent. Whatever they're planning could happen tomorrow or the day after. If they're truly ready, I doubt they'll wait long unless there's something significant they want to coincide with. But I don't know what that could be, if anything."

"When would an attack like this have the greatest impact?"

"I'm not sure. I suspect they would want to do it during off-business hours. Companies tend to staff less at those times so they would be slower to respond, and this kind of attack would require a chance to build. If it were caught and neutralized early...."

"Okay, so either first thing tomorrow morning, or late afternoon or early evening. I suppose they could do it late at night as well." Knight was quiet for a few seconds, then said, "If they do it early in the morning, then we'll be too late. We can try to mop up and take them out, but the damage will have been done." Knight began pacing. "Can you call Dimato and make sure he knows what you've found? He can alert the companies to the threat. They can be aware and try to minimize the impact to their systems, and we have to hope like hell they wait until we can crash their little party."

"Already on it. I'm sending him a message right now." Day typed an instant message and sent it. Dimato replied immediately that he understood and was forwarding the information to the proper people. "He's passing on the message through channels."

"Good."

"But won't that take longer?"

"That's just code in case anyone is listening to us. No worries." Knight began pacing. "I hate this point in the mission. There's nothing we can do but wait and then be ready to go."

"Well, that's a twist on 'hurry up and wait,' I guess," Day said.

"Yeah. Still sucks."

Day could believe that. Knight was most definitely a man of action. "Let's button things up here and get ready for dinner. I know we have some time, but if we get dressed, we can stroll the promenade and see if there's any shopping we need to do." He stood. "There could be something there we can't live without."

"Good God. Did you get the gay shopping gene?" Knight's tone was derisive.

"Not really. But it will give us something to do, and sitting here in the cabin waiting for something that isn't likely to happen isn't going to do either of us any good. We've gathered the information we can. We know where they are. If necessary, we'll mop up, and then the brains can figure out how to fix the mess. Hopefully we'll be able to head this off. But pacing like a caged tiger isn't going to help."

"Fine," Knight agreed. "But you're the one who needs to get changed. I don't think they'd want you dressed like that on the promenade. You'd start a stampede." Knight grinned at him. "Mind you, the view is quite spectacular."

"So you do like me?" Day teased.

"Go change," Knight said and turned away.

He was the most frustrating person Day had ever met. He wanted to slap him up the back of the head to get him to say what he felt, just once. Not that it would do any good. Knight's head was too damn thick for the message to really sink in. He opened the closet door and pulled out his hanging bag and carried it into the bathroom. "You know tonight is one of the dressy evenings." Day smiled at the swearing he heard from the other side of the door. He hung up the bag and got to work cleaning up. Then he dressed and stepped out of the bathroom, carrying his jacket over his arm.

"How dressy are you going to get?" Knight turned and stopped dead. "Holy hell," he breathed. "You…." Day looking down at the tuxedo he was wearing to make sure nothing was wrong. "Dang, boy, you look good enough to—" Knight paused. "Well, we did that earlier, but damn. There's still going to be a stampede. Those boys are going to be following you around like the pied piper." Knight went to the closet and pulled out a suit bag and took his turn in the bathroom.

Day finished dressing and put his dark socks and black shoes on. When he slipped on his jacket and checked himself in the mirror, he had to admit that he looked good. He smiled and straightened his tie before stepping away from the mirror. He made sure all the equipment was stowed out of sight and then sat down on the small sofa. Knight joined him a few minutes later, looking dashing in his dark suit.

He was definitely made for clothes like that. Broad shoulders filled out the tapered coat that highlighted Knight's trim waist. "I think we'd both better stay out of the stampede." Day grinned and helped Knight straighten his tie.

"I hate wearing this thing," Knight grumbled.

"You look dashing," Day teased. "Finish up, and we can wander around." Tonight was the last bit of fun they would be able to have. After dinner they needed to work, sleep, and then be up early to make final preparations for the job they had come here to do.

Knight finished, and they made sure they had everything. Then they left the cabin, heading toward the elevators.

"My, don't you like nice." It was Blain, commenting as they entered the elevator lobby. "Almost good enough to eat. Well… been there… done that."

"He certainly does, and I like it when he dresses up for me," Knight broke in before Day could say anything, puffing up to look as big as possible. Blain's eyes widened, and he took a step back. "The bitchy talk isn't cool. It only makes you sound stupid," Knight continued. The elevator doors slid open, and Knight guided them inside the empty car. "You can wait for the next one," he said, glaring until the doors slid closed. "What a huge ass."

"Well, something on him has to be huge," Day quipped before he could stop himself. Knight turned toward him, and they shared a laugh as they went down. The doors slid open, and the two of them stepped out into a sea of commotion. People milled around, talking and laughing as they made their way down the center atrium of the ship.

Some of the shops were having sales on the promenade, and there were crowds milling and jockeying to get a look.

"I've seen schools of piranhas that were less voracious," Knight commented as they made their way around a table where people were picking through piles of ten-dollar scarves. "You'd think it was the bargain of a lifetime, but those same scarves are probably offered on each cruise, and they have bales of them in the back somewhere," he whispered. "They probably buy them for a buck apiece at one of their ports."

Day figured he was right, and they passed the frenzy only to encounter another. This one was twenty-dollar watches with brand names he'd never heard of before. People were trying to squeeze in so they could grab up the supposed bargain. One guy had eight of them and announced to everyone who'd listen that he'd finished his Christmas shopping. "Ho ho ho," Day whispered softly to Knight, and they shared a smile.

They went into the shops to get out of the hubbub and looked through what was for sale: jewelry, clothing, souvenirs, booze, cigarettes—all the usual duty-free items. There was nothing either of them needed, but they continued to wander, and at one point Knight threaded his arm through Day's, and they walked together until it was time for dinner.

THE FOOD was good, and so was the conversation. However, as soon as dinner was over, they went back to the cabin, changed clothes, and got to work. "They're quiet," Day told Knight when he checked for chatter. "I even checked other frequencies coming from the same area to see if they had changed. There's nothing."

"All right. We'll wait for the final satellite flyover in the morning, adjust plans as necessary, and then get to work. I need to wipe all sensitive data from my computer. I've backed it up so nothing will be lost, but I don't want to leave any of it here."

Day reached for the system and installed a program on Knight's computer. "You've deleted it all?"

"Yeah, but deleted doesn't mean gone."

"It will now." Day started the program. "This will go though and reset all deleted space so it will be like factory new. It doesn't touch what's there but truly cleans the empty space. If anyone tries to recover anything, they'll get zilch." Day passed him back the laptop. "It's going to take a while to run, so leave it alone, and then you can put it in your luggage."

They had planned to leave everything else. The room had to look like they had missed the ship rather than planned to take off. So their things were left spread out in the bathroom, and clothes hung in the closet. Day did put his tux back in the hanging bag, but he left it in the closet. He hated to do it, but that was what he'd signed up for.

"I'm going to take a walk," Knight said and grabbed his key card. "I need to clear my head so I can make sure there's nothing we forgot. I won't be too long."

Day kept working. "Okay." He thought about offering to go with him but held back. If Knight needed time to think, then he probably wanted time alone. Day returned to getting his equipment ready to go and making sure he had everything he might need. Now that the group had gone silent, he was second-guessing whether they needed the communication equipment but finally decided being able to communicate out if they needed to was just as important as listening in.

Knight still hadn't returned by the time he finished up. It was getting late, so he set everything aside, closed the closet door, and tidied the room before cleaning up and getting ready for bed. He thought about pulling on underwear but decided against it. He turned out the lights and lay on his belly on the bed. The cabin was dark and slightly warm. He slid his arms beneath the pillow, rested his head, and closed his eyes. He knew he wasn't going to sleep. He was way too keyed up and worried about tomorrow. He and Knight were under the gun. Something was most definitely going to happen, and they had to be successful.

The cabin door opened, light shining in the room, and then it closed again. "Day?"

"Hmmm," he answered without lifting his head. "Are you okay?"

"Just spent some time thinking and going over things."

Day heard Knight undressing and then stepping into the bathroom. Day closed his eyes once again and waited for him to come out. Light briefly filled the room, then he heard a soft click, and the room went dark. Knight came closer and sat on the edge of the bed. Day remained where he was.

Knight touched his back. Day hummed softly and felt Knight shift his hand. He slowly caressed downward and over the curve of his ass. Day stilled as Knight stroked him. "You're incredible," Knight said through the darkness.

"You can't see me."

"I don't have to." He moved closer, and Day felt him straddle his legs, Knight's bare butt resting on his thighs. "I can feel you."

Day kept his eyes closed, surrendering to and reveling in Knight's attention. He needed this right now. His mind had been going in a million different directions, but with a single touch, it centered on Knight. Day hummed his pleasure softly. The last few times they'd been intimate, it had been frantic, energetic, and almost a battle. Day didn't want that this time. There would be plenty of fighting tomorrow. There could be combat of some sort. He might even have to decide if he could shoot someone.

"Just relax, and stop worrying about everything," Knight whispered. "I can almost hear your mind running through all your concerns. Stop it. I'll have your back. Never doubt that. Just like I know you'll have mine." Knight gripped his shoulders and then worked his thumbs along the base of Day's neck.

"Damn, that's good," Day moaned softy. He couldn't see anything in the darkness, so he kept his eyes closed and put himself in Knight's hands. There were so many questions he wanted to ask, but now was not the time, and…. He needed to face it: he and Knight had been thrown together in a situation that neither of them would have been able to resist for long, given the circumstances. As soon as the mission was over, they would both most likely go back to their own lives and let this interlude fade to happy memory.

For now he intended to add to those memories. He knew he was acting like a schoolgirl. He and Knight had been having sex and getting to know one another, that was all. He highly doubted there would ever be anything more to it. A few times when Knight's guard fell, if only for a few seconds, Day saw pain that went deep. That kind of pain wouldn't heal or go away in a few days. It was permanent.

"Do you like this?" Knight made long strokes up and down his back, shifting his entire body. When he leaned forward, Day felt Knight's cock press to his butt, sometimes nestling between his cheeks. Then he'd straighten up again, and the pressure would dissipate and then disappear, only to make itself known again.

"Yes," Day whispered. "After my dad… passed," he began, "I never wanted to let anyone tell me what to do or have control over me. Stephen was always very good about that. He guided without ordering. But I want to…."

"I know. Men like us don't give up control very well." Knight leaned forward and kissed his ear. "After…." Knight paused. "Well, let's just say I always want control of everything. It makes me feel like I can't be hurt. After what you told me, I see that same thing in you." Knight held still.

"Yes, but there are times when letting someone else have control—" Day was unable to finish his thought. He wasn't sure what he meant or where his thought was going, so he let it trail off.

"Will you let me have it now?" Knight sucked on his ear, and Day hummed his approval. Knight wound his arms around his chest, holding him while at the same time lightly stroking over his pecs, bumping his nipples with his fingers as they passed.

"Yes."

Knight released him, and Day heard him fumble with the nightstand. Knight must have found what he was looking for because he slipped his arms back around him, pressing his chest to Day's back. They shared their heat, and Day turned his head to the side. Knight kissed him. It wasn't elegant or graceful, but it was nice, and Day found he liked being held. Knight surrounded him, and nothing could harm them. They were alone and safe. He could give up the control, nerves, worry, and everything else he'd held on to for a very long time and just be. At least for a little while.

Knight pulled back and kissed his shoulder, then along his neck. He slid down Day's back, his weight lessening as he trailed kisses along Day's spine. When he reached the small of his back, Knight licked a trail up his side. Day squirmed and tried not to giggle. Thankfully Knight only did it once, and Day settled once again as Knight slowly gripped his legs and ran his hands over his calves and up his thighs. Damn, that was leg-quivering good. Day held the edge of the mattress. He wanted to stretch his legs out farther, but Knight was in the way, so all he could do was stay still and hope like hell Knight continued. "What, are you teasing me?"

"No," Knight answered.

He felt Knight shift, and then both hands continued up to his ass, spreading him. "Holy fucking God," Day swore as wet heat slid up his crack. He tightened his grip on the mattress and hissed between his teeth.

"You're the porn guy. I'm sure you saw this," Knight said in a deep rumble.

"Yeah, but I never expected you... expected anyone...." Day gasped again as Knight cut him off, licking him hard. Day arched his back, pushing up with his hands, head falling back. Nothing he had ever imagined felt as fucking amazing as Knight's tongue on his ultrasensitive skin. He wanted more so bad he could taste it, and when Knight parted his cheeks, probing him with a firm tongue, he got it. He quivered from head to toe, and the tiniest movement of his hips scraped his cock against the sheets, sending additional sensation through him. He wasn't ready to come, but the tingling had already started. He held still, doing his best not to move while Knight did his very best to blow the top of his head off.

Day hardly knew what day it was or where he was. By the time Knight stopped, he could barely put a thought together. He quivered and breathed deeply, trying to figure out what the hell was coming next. Knight shifted on the bed, his warmth disappearing. Day heard a small rip and then waited a few more seconds. "I need you," Knight whispered, and Day nodded in the dark. Forming words was out of the question, so he groaned instead, still clutching the mattress.

His arms shook with anticipation. Knight pressed fingers into him and then slipped them out. Then Knight pressed to his opening and sank into him. Day hissed and did his best to breathe while he was stretched damn near to the limit. Knight was big. He'd found that out already, but it seemed like the fucker had gotten bigger. A wisecrack flittered around the edges of his mind. It didn't stay long. Knight pressed further, and Day couldn't stop the steady stream of obscenity from crossing his lips. "Fricking son of a bitch." Knight stopped. "Don't you dare!"

Knight continued until he was pressing his hips to Day's ass. Then he stretched out on top of him, sandwiching Day between the mattress and Knight's intense heat. They didn't move. Knight held him close, licking his ear and throbbing inside him. Damn, that felt good.

Day pressed back against him just to let Knight know he liked it. Knight stayed where he was, but when Day clenched, he felt and heard Knight sigh. As close as they were, sound wasn't necessary. He could feel Knight's excitement and hear the way his breath hitched when he clenched his ass around him as tight as he could.

"Oh God," Knight moaned softly into Day's ear.

Day smiled and did it again. Knight moved his hips slightly, and Day gripped him again while he moved. The shudder that went through Knight started in his chest and ripped through his entire body. Then Knight pulled away and pressed into him, and it was Day's turn to shudder.

"That's it," Knight whispered, and Day felt him kiss his shoulder as he slowly withdrew and then entered his body again. Day splayed his arms and gave himself over to Knight. It felt weird and right at the same time. Weird because part of him rankled at being so completely under someone else's control and right because he knew in his heart that Knight would do the same for him if asked.

When Knight pulled away, Day started in surprise. Knight patted him lightly on the side, and Day rolled onto his back. Knight waited for him to get comfortable and then entered him once again. In the darkness Day couldn't see Knight's face, but he knew where it was from Knight's breathing, and he locked on to the source of the sound. It surprised him how completely dark it got aboard ship and how wonderfully concealing and liberating the dark could be. In the dark, Day could let go of his inhibitions, opening himself up without feeling as though he was giving up anything.

The two of them moved together, Day breathing along with Knight as he sent shocks of passion through him. There was nothing tentative about Knight. He moved with power—demanding, taking, and giving at the same time. They had started out gentle, but within seconds, passion transformed their time together into heat, fire, and energy. Knight pulled completely away from him and then pressed back into his body, disconnecting and reconnecting within seconds.

"Knight," Day whispered over and over. He wondered about Knight's first name. At times like this he wished he knew it so he could use it and tell the man just how deeply he touched him. Everyone called him Knight. He wanted something special he could use, but he had nothing. "Give me all you have."

Knight hesitated and then picked up speed, driving into him with each breath. Day reached for himself, stroking to the timing of Knight's thrusts. The pressure building inside him was nearly overwhelming, and he needed release more frantically than he'd needed anything in his life before. Knight shifted slightly above him, and Day howled to the ceiling as a jolt of pleasure shot through him. He stroked two more times and then shook as he came apart, crying, whimpering, and moaning so loudly he nearly drowned out Knight's moan as they joined together in sweet release.

Chapter 6

KNIGHT SLEPT like a baby with Day pressed to him and didn't wake once all night. They ate breakfast and then with surprising ease left the ship and headed into the port area of Costa Maya. A few old cars that served as taxis were waiting. Knight led the way toward one, and he and Day climbed in. Knight gave the driver Miguel's address and sat in the backseat, silently hoping the car remained in one piece long enough for them to get where they needed to go.

The drive only took a few harrowing minutes, and both of them damn near had whiplash from the erratic driving before the driver finally pulled to a stop. Knight paid him in US dollars and got out of the car, grateful to be on solid ground once again. "You call when ready to go back?" the driver asked and passed Knight a card with a phone number on it. Knight smiled and took it, shoving the card in his pocket after the man drove away.

"Not likely," he muttered. The house they stood in front of looked like the other houses they'd passed: rough, weather-beaten, ten years away from its last paint job. He pushed open the gate on the metal fence. It protested loudly as he pushed it open and walked through the once nice yard, which now looked like the jungle was trying to reclaim it. Knight knocked on the front door, and it opened.

"¿Qué quieres?" a man asked in rapid Spanish.

Day translated in Knight's ear.

"Knighton," he said and waited. A few seconds later, Miguel appeared behind the man.

"Come in, my friend," he said brightly, pushing the other man out of the way and opening the door farther. "This is my useless brother-in-law, José," Miguel said with a smile. "He speaks no English."

"This is my partner, Dayton."

"Good to meet you." Miguel closed the door to a very nice home, the inside comfort not even hinted at from the outside. "I know why you are here, and I have things ready for you." Miguel walked through the house, and they followed. His brother-in-law made to do the same, but Miguel spoke sharply to him, and he fell behind. "I keep him out of my business as much as possible. Mostly he comes here to get away from my sister and their six kids." Miguel laughed. "He complains about the kids but never leaves my sister alone. I think he's trying for a world fucking record. At least that's what Ana says. When they fight he comes here to drink my beer and then goes home, and they make up and make another kid." He laughed and showed bright teeth. "They are both stupid, so perfect for each other."

They passed through the house and out to a courtyard, crossing to another building. Inside was what Knight had been hoping for.

"I have C4 and detonators," Miguel said.

"Excellent. We have some communication equipment we would like to leave. If anyone comes after us, destroy it."

"Sí, Knight. I understand. Like we did in Panama?"

"Yes, exactly. We will come back to get it." Knight figured it would be safer here than hidden at the port. "If we don't return for it in two days, destroy it and call this number." Knight held out a card with just a phone number on it. "That will alert the right people. Do not put yourself in danger or call attention."

"Sí, I understand. You need weapons too? I have a rocket launcher and grenades."

Knight took what he thought they might need but declined the rocket launcher. He paid Miguel in dollars and packed up their purchases, and then emptied Day's pack of all excess equipment.

"Where you go?"

Knight told him the general direction they were heading but no more. It was better he didn't know.

"The ruins, huh?" Miguel said. "I thought so. There have been reports of dead bodies and ghosts. People have gone out there and have not returned, which started rumors. I thought someone was up to something and using fear to keep people away. You must be careful."

"We will." Knight hoisted his pack onto his back while Day did the same. "What is the best way to get out there?"

"You walk?"

"If we have to."

"I tell my brother-in-law that you are doctors looking to study the ruins. He will take you there and not ask questions. Just pay him, and he keep his mouth shut, if I tell him. It will make Ana happy." Miguel smiled. "It will also get him out of my house and refrigerator."

"So two for one?" Knight asked.

Miguel grinned. "Sí, two for one. Maybe you take him and they use him for target practice?" Miguel teased, and Knight laughed. "No, Ana no have anyone to yell at and then she turn to me." Miguel shook his head. "Let her yell at him. It what he good for."

"Sí," Knight said and smiled back. He and Miguel shared a laugh. Knight had met Ana, and he didn't want to get on her bad side. When she was angry, which he'd seen just once, after Panama, when he'd brought Miguel back wounded, she was a one-person army. Never again.

"Come, we get you on your way. Be careful."

"I'm always careful," Knight retorted.

"Not in Panama," Miguel teased, and they shared another laugh. Knight glanced at Day and realized he would have to fill him in at some point, but not right now. There would be time to tell stories if they got out of this in one piece. "José," Miguel called and then spoke to him rapidly as they stepped back into the courtyard. Knighton definitely needed to improve his Spanish.

Miguel led them up to the front of the house. "Thanks."

"Think nothing of it. Just don't get him killed or we'll both incur the wrath of Ana. He'll take you within a mile or so of the ruins, and then you'll be on your own. There are trails that lead to it. We used to explore them as kids. They existed up till a few years ago. Things grow over fast here, but it should be passable. I asked José to drop you at the head of one of them."

"What does he think?"

"That you're archaeologists, like Indiana Jones. He loves those movies." Miguel laughed, and they waited while José pulled up in a car even older than the damned cab. They got in, and José began talking a mile a minute. Knight turned to Day, who smiled and nodded.

"He's talking about movies. Just grin and nod until we get where we need to be."

Knight followed Day's lead, and José took off. Why in the hell did everyone here drive like a demented race car driver? At least they wouldn't raise any suspicion if anyone noticed them. The car they were in looked like all the other ones he saw. José prattled on, and Day answered him every few minutes. They seemed to have developed a rapport, which pleased Knight.

They quickly left the town and drove down a nearly empty road. José slowed and pulled off. He said something to Day, who handed him some cash and then motioned to Knight to get out. José and Day continued talking, with José laughing before pulling away. "What did he say?"

"Not to pick up any golden idols. It's a reference from the Indiana Jones movies. He also asked where your whip was. He says you look like Indiana Jones."

"So he bought it?"

"Seemed to. It was all he talked about. He even said if we find something interesting, we should bring him pictures so he can say he met the real Indiana Jones."

Knight looked up, and José waved as he passed them after turning around. "Miguel said there was a path."

"I think that's it," Day said, pointing.

It wasn't much of a path, but Knight could see people had walked that way. They headed down and pushed aside the undergrowth. Thankfully it wasn't as bad a little ways in, and they started walking. Some leaves and branches covered the path, but it was fairly clear for most of the way. In the distance Knight could see a slight rise. It wasn't much, but it had to be where they were heading. He ignored the bugs that buzzed around him and turned back to Day.

"It's all right. You have to ignore them and keep moving," Knight said in a whisper. "Think of the mission and nothing else. Everything is about that right now. It will make it easier."

Day nodded, and Knight had to give him credit. Day was doing his best. He knew he wasn't trained for this the way he was. But Day stopped fanning his face and kept up with him in the brutal sun. After a few minutes, Knight stopped and opened his pack, then handed Day a poncho. "We're going to need to put these on soon." He looked up at the sky. Clouds were building, and he was sure rain would start in a few minutes. "When it rains, it will come hard and heavy. Just do your best to keep everything dry."

"I'll try."

"We left the truly sensitive stuff at Miguel's, but as for the rest, it's best if we try to keep it dry."

"Okay." Day put on the poncho over his pack. He looked like a hunchback, but it would do. Knight did the same thing, and they began moving again as the rain arrived. One of the good things about it was that the insects left them alone.

They trudged on as the rain continued. Knight ignored his wet pants and picked up the pace. Thankfully the clouds appeared content to stay around, which would help cover them. The hill got larger as they approached, and Knight slowed their pace until they were walking in near silence. The foliage thickened as they neared, the hum of a generator mixing with the rain, and Knight had to move carefully, climbing around and over the trees and brush so they wouldn't disturb their potential cover. Finally they reached the edge of the cleared area and followed the sound to the generator. It was then that voices could be heard. He crouched down and motioned for Day to do the same, straining to hear the two men standing under a small awning. "What are they saying?"

"Mostly they're talking about women," Day said. "Crudely." Knight looked at the two men who stood near a rough doorway in the stone. "Mayan pyramids aren't hollow."

"This isn't a pyramid," Knight said. "It looks more like the remains of a building of some type." He pointed to fresh wood. "They shored it up and are using it for cover. It shouldn't take much to bring it down."

"Why here?" Day asked. "They could do this just about anywhere."

"They needed cover and neighbors who wouldn't pry. Out here they can do whatever they want." Knight put his fingers to his lips as one of the men came closer.

Another man exited the building and said something that Knight didn't understand. He turned to Day, who had paled.

"He says in five minutes the gringos will pay."

Knight nodded and began looking around.

"You need to take out the generator," Day told him. "And fast."

Knight opened the pack and pulled out some C4. He got it primed and shoved it beneath the generator. The explosion should send it sky-high and create quite a show. It would have been better to make it look like the generator had malfunctioned, but he didn't have time, and the access panel was on the side facing the compound. This would have to do. "It will blow in three minutes. We need to get the hell away." Knight began to back up, and Day went along. "Let's see if we can circle around to the other side. That way when everyone rushes to see what happened, we can take them by surprise." He pointed to a tree set apart from the others. "Let's use that as a reference."

Knight made his way away from the generator. The undergrowth was thick, but he made it through. He'd been trained in all kinds of warfare and could get around in just about any terrain. The problem was that Day couldn't. Knight realized that as soon as he turned back and didn't see Day any longer. He stopped and waited for a few seconds, listening for any indication of where he was but heard nothing. Knight thought about going back to look for him, but time was running out. They had a meeting point, and it was best they both get there without fumbling blindly through the undergrowth.

He continued forward, winding around areas that were impassable, going as quickly as he could. He needed to find Day and make sure he was okay. All hell was going to break loose any minute now, and they needed to be together if they were going to be effective. Knight swore under his breath at Day and himself. He should have kept a better eye on him. Day had been doing so fucking well that Knight had forgotten just how little experience he had.

A crack a short distance away caught his attention. Knight crouched low and waited. He hoped like hell it was Day, but if it was one of the terrorists, then he certainly didn't want to be spotted. He saw movement and a flash of honey skin. Knight hurried forward and nearly tumbled into Day before pulling him down. "Stay low." Knight checked his watch. "We're out of time. You take one of the guards, and I'll take the other." Day nodded.

The explosion sent out shock waves and knocked them to the ground. The generator shot into the air like a rocket and then fell back to the ground fifty feet from where it had once sat. Knight recovered and took out his guard. Day was still scrambling to get to his gun, which he'd dropped during the explosion. Knight aimed for the second guard, but he screamed at the top of his lungs just before Knight squeezed off a shot that silenced him.

Other men came running out of the doorway, guns leveled. Knight went down on the ground and stayed still. He knew as long as they didn't move they weren't likely to be seen. One of the men started shooting into the brush with automatic weapon fire, but he was way off, and the bullets ripped the foliage apart near where the generator had been. The others joined in.

"Stop," someone yelled, and they ceased. Knight couldn't see who it was. The man remained just out of sight in the doorway, but then the men nodded and took cover. Knight saw some of them take off for the brush and he knew he and Day needed to move or they would be quickly surrounded. Knight lobbed a grenade after them, and it exploded at the edge of the jungle. Men screamed. He lobbed another, and a quick glance told him Day had found his gun. Knight took out another of the men.

"That's enough, gringos." A click from behind him brought Knight to a complete stop. He turned and stared as a man in fatigues pointed a gun at Day's head. Day dropped his gun, and Knight released the grenade he had been reaching for to throw through the doorway. It rolled away into the brush. "Stand up slowly, and don't make any fast moves."

Knight stood, the leaves near him moving back into place. "I got them," the man yelled in English with a heavy accent. "Do exactly as I say or I blow his brains out." He carefully lifted Day's pack and slung it over his shoulder.

Knight nodded.

The man let Day stand and then motioned with his head toward the doorway.

"Do as he says," Knight told Day.

"Smart advice, Mr. Knighton," the man with the gun said. Knight stopped in surprise. "I know who you are. You don't know me, but I know you." He turned to the side, displaying a nasty scar on his cheek. "This was a gift from you in Panama."

Fuck. Why did that operation always come back to haunt him? He moved toward the clearing, hands out at his sides, with Day next to him and the man behind him, the gun still pointed at his head. Knight glanced all around. He saw little movement.

"You're very good," the man said. "My men didn't know what hit them, but then they were mostly dumb villagers who wanted to make some extra money. Expendable." He smiled and shouted some orders in loud Spanish. A few men stepped out of the undergrowth, guns trained on them. Knight braced for the impact of bullets. But the man shouted more orders. Knight really wished he knew what was being said. He glanced at Day, who understood and mouthed, "Looking for others."

Good. If they thought there were more, that would keep them busy for a little while, and it might keep them alive a little longer. They were better off alive and under control to be used to neutralize anyone else they thought they might find.

"No fast moves." He pressed the gun right to Day's head. Knight nodded. He wished he could get a message to Day. They were being directed toward the doorway, and once they were inside, they had a lot fewer options. He caught Day's eye again and mouthed the word "trip." He hoped Day understood. Knight might be able to gain an advantage if Day were out of harm's way even for a second.

As they approached the doorway, Day's foot caught on something on the ground. He went down hard and fast. Knight whirled around, grabbing the gun from the man's hand. He got his hand on it as a single shot rang out. Knight stopped dead and let go, the gun dropping to the ground.

"That's enough, Vasquez," another man said. "Bring him inside and kill him if he so much as moves again."

Knight turned to Day, expecting him to slowly get up. He didn't. Knight saw red on the ground around Day, and he wasn't moving. One of the men began to walk over. "Leave him," the new man with a thick black beard said. "Get that backup generator hooked up and ready to go!" he barked and then waited for Knight at the doorway.

Knight took a last look at Day and hoped like hell he was still alive. He didn't see movement of any kind, and he feared the worst. Fuck, he'd killed another person he—

"Well," the man said as soon as Knight stepped into the near darkness of the building. "It isn't much, but it's home." He laughed. "At least it's our home for a few more hours. Then we'll be gone, and all anyone is going to find is what's left of you and your friend."

"We should kill him now," the man with the scar said. *Vasquez*, Knight remembered. "I know this man. He is dangerous and has nothing to live for." Vasquez peered in Day's pack and then tossed it aside.

"How the hell do you know that?" the other man, who seemed to be the leader, asked.

"I take away what he live for, just like he take from me, and I got paid for it too." Vasquez laughed, the gun in his hand not wavering for a second. Knight saw red and shook with rage before bring it under control. He wanted to rip Vasquez apart, but he had to keep his wits if he was going to have any chance at getting out of this.

An engine started, and the man in charge began slowly moving around the space, which for now was lit with battery lamps. One of the men brought in a cord and unplugged a power strip and plugged it into the extension cord.

"Your little stunt was only a minor delay," the bearded man said. He turned on a light, and the man in charge with almost black eyes stared back at him. "Allah provides." He grinned as a pair of computer monitors powered up. "All I really need is these to finish this."

"Who the hell are you?" Knight asked as he surveyed the room. The black stone walls appeared old, very old, but the wood-beamed ceiling was still light in color, like it hadn't been there too long. Crude furniture lined the walls, including a small table, chairs, and a few beds set just off the floor.

"A freedom fighter," he answered. "I fight to get your imperialist country out of my homeland. In a few hours, they will be very busy trying to save their businesses, and they will know that we can reach them anywhere and at any time." His accent was flawless, and Knight wondered if this guy was some homegrown terrorist. From his appearance he was definitely Middle Eastern, but the speech pattern didn't fit at all. In fact, Knight detected a hint of Boston, possibly.

The power went out again, and the man pulled over a chair. "Tie him up, and then go see what those idiots are doing. I need power for twenty minutes and then we're done and gone. After that we don't need any of them any longer." The implication was clear. None of them were going to live much longer, including the men who'd been helping this bastard.

Knight was shoved onto the chair and quickly bound—hands and ankles, tightly. He tried all the tricks he knew, but the ropes were pulled tight, and he figured he was lucky he still had circulation in his legs. Then Vasquez—the man who'd killed his family—stepped away from him. Knight seethed with anger. He tried to keep his head about him, but it was fucking hard for him to do. The man who'd killed his wife and son was right here, and the asshole said he'd gotten paid for it. Knight wanted to leap out of his chair and strangle him with his bare hands until he told him who'd paid him. He clenched and unclenched his fists, seeing red.

"I know it's killing you. You want to know everything. If you're good, I might just tell you before I put a bullet in your head."

"Stop it, Vasquez. Just see to the generator so we can bring an end to this and get the hell out of here. We don't want anyone else dropping in on us, so move." The man in charge turned back to his computers, half watching him. "I need power."

Vasquez left, and Knight tried to figure a way out of this mess. He had to stop this. He was so damned close, and he had to see if Day was alive. If so, for how long? He'd been shot and could be bleeding to death. Knight's mind moved from problem to problem.

The lights came back on, and the computers began going through their startup processes. The man placed his cell phone on the desk next to him. Then, as the monitors came up, shots rang out outside. "That's Vasquez tying up loose ends."

"Do you really trust him not to kill you too?" Knight asked.

He scoffed without turning away from his keyboard. "He hasn't been paid yet, and he won't do anything to me until he is. And by then I'll be gone and so will all this. There's nothing you can say to get to me, so just sit quiet and watch."

More shots rang out, and then Vasquez returned. "Everything is all taken care of. No one is left to tell anyone anything. All we need to do is take care of him." Vasquez was clearly relishing the thought.

"Good. We'll finish up in a few minutes, and then you can put a bullet in his head, and we'll blow this place to pieces. Those archaeologists will return to nothing but blocks and rubble. They can piece this place back together if they want. Hell, they might even think he was some sort of sacrifice if they wait long enough." He quieted and muttered in Arabic just loud enough for Knight to recognize the language. "Just a few more minutes."

Fuck, he had really stepped in it on this one. There wasn't much chance that either of them would get out of this, and the attack they had tried to foil was going ahead regardless of what they'd done. Knight kept trying to find an angle, but there wasn't one. He was at their mercy… and they didn't seem to have any.

Then a shot ran out, and Vasquez fell to the floor. A second shot followed, and the man at the computer keyboard slumped forward, blood and brain matter spattering across the monitors.

Knight turned toward the doorway and saw Day leaning against the stones. "Can you untie me?"

"I'm not sure I can walk that far," Day said, his breathing labored. He continued using the door to hold him up. Knight bounced up and down to get closer, inching toward Day. As he got close, Day released the doorframe and half collapsed against him.

"Just get one hand. I can do the rest," Knight said.

Day was weak as hell, but he managed to loosen Knight's right hand, and he got it free. Knight got his left hand out and then untied the binds at his ankles. He stood and helped Day to his feet. Then he righted the old chair and sat Day down in it. Knight wasn't sure how much, if any, of the attack had started, so he yanked on the computer cords, and all the equipment went dark. He left the light plugged in, so he could see, and returned to Day, who looked pale. "Where did he get you?"

"Left shoulder."

Knight looked around for something he could use as a bandage. He found a pack on one of the beds. He opened it and pulled out what appeared to be a clean T-shirt. It would have to do. "Thanks, asshole," Knight said to the dead guy still slumped over the keyboard.

He hurried back to Day. He ripped the poncho apart and pulled open his shirt. He found both an entry and exit wound. Knight tore the shirt into two large pieces and a strip of cloth. He bandaged both sides as gently as he could and used the strip of cloth to tie the bandages in place. It was crude, but hopefully it would help stop the bleeding.

Knight looked for where Vasquez had dropped Day's pack and found it just off to the side of the door. He pulled out a bottle of water, opened it while he returned to Day, and helped him drink some.

"I see you both in hell," Vasquez said. He had a small gun pointed at them as he got unsteadily to his feet. Blood covered the front of his shirt. Knight had been so concerned about getting free and helping Day that he'd forgotten one of the basics: make sure the enemy is disarmed, even one who's down.

Knight straightened up and placed himself between Day and the gunman. He needed Day out of the possible line of fire. Vasquez was unsteady on his feet, and Knight saw blood dripping down the leg of Vasquez's pants. He wouldn't last long at this rate. He had to be bleeding out. "Why did you kill my family?" Knight demanded.

"Revenge for my family," Vasquez answered, his face contorting in pain. Knight wanted to rush him, but he couldn't get an opening. "You kill my father, and I kill your wife and son."

Knight heard Day gasp, and he did his best to ignore it, his attention instead focused on Vasquez and the gun. "Who paid you to do it?"

Vasquez teetered, and Knight struck. He crouched, and with a roundhouse kick, he knocked Vasquez's legs out from under him. Vasquez went down, the gun flying away. A shot rang out, the sound bouncing off the stone walls, ringing in Knight's ears. He wasn't hit and lunged at Vasquez, who lay on the ground. Knight rolled him over. "Who paid you?" he asked frantically.

Vasquez breathed wetly, and Knight knew he didn't have much time left.

"Who paid you to kill my family?" he yelled at the top of his lungs. Knight reached for the knife at Vasquez's belt and pulled it out. "Tell me or I'll send you to hell in more pain that you can imagine." Vasquez's eyes were open, and Knight brought he knife to one of them, knowing he could see it. "Tell me, and you'll die quickly. Otherwise I'll cut you to pieces a little at a time." He pressed the knife to Vasquez's face as his eyes closed, and he exhaled, blood oozing from the corners of his mouth.

"*Fuck*!" Knight yelled, throwing the knife against the wall, shaking from head to toe. He'd been so fucking close to getting answers. Two years he'd searched, and this was the only lead he'd ever had. He stood and kicked the dead man in the side and then went through his pockets. He found a cell phone and shoved it in his pocket.

"Knight," Day whispered from behind him. "He's dead, and we need to get out of here. I need help. I don't know how much longer I'm going to last."

Knight still shook as he got to his feet and helped Day to his. Together they went out into the late-day sunshine. "How did you get the gun?" Knight asked.

"They thought I was dead when Vasquez had finished." Day pointed at the bodies near the door. "Poor suckers didn't know what was happening and then they were all dead. I got one of their guns as soon as he went back inside. Then I lay back down on the ground. You know I'm a good shot."

"You're the best I've ever seen." Knight sighed. "I need to put an end to this. Stay here." Knight settled him gently on the ground. "There's water and food. You need both." Knight handed him the pack and hurried away. He turned off the generator and carried it inside. He opened the fuel cap and turned the piece of equipment on its side. Gasoline leaked out onto the floor, pooling and then soaking the stones. He went back out and found a single half-full gas can. He carried it inside as well, leaving the top open. Once that was done, he gathered the weapons and threw them inside with the rest.

Given the number of beds inside, there had to be a camp nearby. Knight wished he had time to search for it, but Day was getting weaker. He retraced his steps and found his pack hidden under the foliage. He pulled out the last of the C4, set the detonator for ten minutes, and placed the explosive near the gas can.

"Let's get the hell out of here." Knight took the pack and helped Day to his feet. "Shit. Can you stand a minute?"

Day nodded, and Knight ran back inside. He grabbed the blood-spattered cell phone off the desk and hurried back out. Bracing Day as best he could, they started walking up the dirt road. They passed a truck, and Knight peered inside. It was empty, and the passenger door was unlocked. Someone had been careless, which was a boon for them. Knight pulled open the door and helped Day inside. Then he hurried around to the driver's side.

"What are you doing?"

"Starting the car," Knight answered. It was an old truck, and getting to the starter wires was easy enough. He sparked them, and the engine started. Then he put the stick shift in first gear, gunned the engine, and took off like a bat out of hell. Knight handed Day the phone he'd taken off the desk. "Can you call Miguel?"

Day fidgeted with the phone. "It's locked."

"Fuck," Knight said. "Hold on to it anyway. It belonged to the fucker behind all this. The tech guys may be able to get something off it when we get back." He was hoping the same thing about the other phone as well. "Why would they need the satellite phone if they had cell phones too?"

"No towers to ping off of, and I suspect service out there was spotty. Why?"

"He was fiddling with his cell phone as he was about to send the program. I thought he was going to use the Bluetooth and an Internet connection to send it. But if he didn't have good reception, why bother?"

"Who knows? Maybe the technical guys can figure it out once we get everything back." Day sighed. "He could have a special application he developed for the phone. I don't know. My head feels light, and I can't really think very well."

"I know." Knight fished in his pack and pulled out his phone. "Use this one. The unlock code is 5793. Once you have it up, I'll tell you the number."

"Okay," Day said, and Knight rattled off the number from memory. Knight never kept any sort of phone book or history in his phone. That would make it harder to get anything off it if he were captured. Day handed him the phone.

"We're on our way back," Knight said when Miguel answered. "We'll be there soon. Hold your ears. It's going to be a whopper." He checked the time and hung up.

He managed to keep the truck on the road as the sound reached their ears. Knight pulled off and turned to watch as a fireball went up in the air, followed by a cloud of black smoke. He pulled back onto the road, only slowing down as they reached the outskirts of the town. He drove to Miguel's and parked the truck in front of the house next door. Miguel came right out and looked up and down the street. "Come inside. The police are up in arms, and they're heading to your aftermath. Did you do what you needed to?"

"Yes. But it wasn't easy." Knight helped Day out of the truck and inside the house. They had to be careful not to draw attention to themselves, and as soon as Miguel closed the door, Day collapsed onto the sofa. "He was shot in the shoulder. The bullet went all the way through, but he lost a lot of blood." Knight knelt next to the sofa. "Can you talk to me?"

"Hurts," Day mumbled.

Miguel checked the bandages. The bleeding seemed to have stopped. "He need more help than either of us can give him." Miguel hurried away and returned with fresh shirts. "You need to put these on so you don't look like you been walking in the jungle. Then I get you back into town and onto the ship. It leave in two hours, and that the closest doctor."

Knight helped Day out of his current bloodstained shirt and into the fresh one. He knew it hurt, but it couldn't be helped. The miracle was that he was able to get him into it without moving his arm much. "What do you want me to do with the weapons?"

"Leave them with me. I'll make sure they completely disappear." Miguel left the room and returned with a bottle of tequila. "Take a sip of this," he told Day, who complied. "Good. Now rinse your mouth with it." Miguel put a little on his fingers and sprinkled some on both of them. "Now they'll think he had a little too much fun when he looks like hell getting back on board."

"Thank you," Knight said and hurried outside. He retrieved their backpacks from the truck and followed Miguel out back. He handed him the guns, and Miguel wiped them down. Then he grabbed a blowtorch and heated them before smashing the barrels with a hammer.

"Now they can't be test fired by anyone." Miguel made short work of the rest of the weapons. Knight handed over the remaining explosives and everything else he needed to get rid of. "You need to dump those bags and any of the clothes you've worn."

"I know. We have to make sure there's no residue on anything we have with us before we arrive back in the US." They were going to have to fly home, and the last thing they needed was to get all that way only to call attention to themselves. Knight pulled Miguel into a hug. "Thank you for everything."

"No. Thank you. I owe you and I always will. You get me out of Panama when I expect to die." Miguel hugged him back and then they parted. "Go get him back to the ship, and call your people to get him some help. I don't think he die, but he needs help or his arm may not heal." Miguel handed him the equipment they had left with him. They returned to the main house, where Knight packed everything. Miguel took anything they didn't need. "I will take you back to the port. Just leave the truck. My brother-in-law will change whatever he needs to and will be grateful for a new vehicle."

"Can you stand?" Knight asked Day. He got to his feet but was very wobbly.

"I ate something and feel a little better."

"Okay. Then let's get back to the ship, and we can be on our way." Knight helped Day out of the house and to Miguel's truck. They got in, and he drove them toward the port. Miguel handed Day a bottle of juice. The sugar would do him good and should last long enough for them to get on board.

"I can't take you all the way to the port. I tend to be watched, so I don't want to put either of us in any danger." Miguel pulled off just outside the entrance to the port area, and Knight helped Day out of the truck, then slid an arm around his waist as they walked back to the ship. They showed their ship passes and were allowed to enter.

"Are you going to make it?" Knight whispered as Day's steps began to falter. Knight was carrying both packs and doing his best not to look as though he was propping Day up. If he looked too sick, they wouldn't let him on the ship, and then they'd be right back where they started from and no closer to getting Day the help he needed.

"Yes. I'm going to be fine," Day said, tension increasing in his body even as he kept it off his face. "Let's just get this done." They reached the gangway, and Knight let Day go ahead. Day must have found some internal strength, because he strode up toward the ship and handed the attendant his card. He was scanned on and walked through the metal detectors without stopping. Knight put their bags on the belt, hoping he'd set the comms equipment upright so it would be disguised. The bags went through, and no one tried to stop him as he stepped through the detectors, which beeped like crazy.

"Did you empty your pockets?" the attendant asked, and Knight reached into his pants pocket and felt one of the detonators. He must have shoved it in his pocket when he set the final explosives. Now he needed to dump the damn thing, but everyone was looking at him. There was no way in hell he could let them see what he had.

"It must be the belt," Knight said and pulled it off. He hoped the reduction in the amount of metal he had on would be enough to let him pass. Knight placed the belt to go through the scanner and walked through the detector once again. It stayed quiet, and he gathered his things on the other side.

"Sir."

Knight tensed. What could they need now? He was so close. Knight turned slowly, and the attendant handed him his belt. "Thank you." Knight put it back on, grabbed their bags, and joined Day where he waited. He helped Day to the elevator, and when the doors opened, they got in, and Day leaned against the wall. He looked seconds from collapse as they rode farther up into the mammoth ship. People got on and off until they finally reached their deck. Knight helped Day down the passageway and used his key card to open the door. As soon as it closed, he helped Day down onto the bed. "Let me look at your shoulder."

"No. Call Dimato, and let him know we were successful and neutralized the threat. Then see if he can help us. The doctor on board ship is not going to treat a gunshot wound without asking a million questions. So…." Day's breathing was labored. "Just call him."

Knight took out the equipment and set it up as best he could. He'd seen Day do it and hoped he did it right. When he made his call, it went through, so he was pretty pleased. This was not a call he wanted going through the ship systems.

"The light is green. You're good," Day told him.

"Yes," Dimato said when he answered.

"We're out, and the threat is neutralized. As soon as the ship gets underway we'll be out of reach of the authorities."

"Very good."

"We do have an issue. Day was injured and needs a doctor. There is one on board ship, but…." Knight's throat tightened. "Day was shot through the left shoulder. He also saved my life." Knight glanced over at where Day lay on the bed with his eyes closed. "The bullet went through, and we've stopped the bleeding, but it needs to be looked at."

"I'll make a few calls. You two relax and get back here. Make sure to write up your report of the operation before you get back. This isn't a vacation."

"Actually, it is, now. He's going to relax and needs to be taken care of." The ship's whistle blasted. "And for the next few days we'll be at sea. So we'll get done what we can. The rest will have to wait until we arrive."

"Knighton," Dimato said warningly.

"Don't fucking mess with me right now," Knight snapped. "I'm not in the fucking mood. Just handle the medical care for Day." He disconnected.

"Do you think you should have pissed off the one guy who can help?" Day asked. "You know, you tend to piss off everyone at some point or other. Did Miguel get the same treatment?" Knight's breath rumbled in his throat. "I'll take that as a yes. So what did you do to change his mind?" Day had his eyes closed.

"I saved both his and Ana's lives."

"Did you put them in danger first?" Day asked.

"We were working together," Knight protested.

"So yes." Day smiled and shifted slightly on the bed with a groan. "Hurts like hell."

"I know. I've been shot a few times."

"Probably by your friends," Day quipped, and some of the knot in Knight's chest and stomach loosened.

"You can't be too bad off if you're picking on me," Knight told him. Day still didn't open his eyes. "I know you're tired and need to rest. But we need to get this shoulder looked at." Knight was tempted to just go down to the doctor and threaten him within an inch of his life until he did what Knight wanted him to. He wasn't above using anything he had to, including physical intimidation, to get what he needed. "I can give you something for pain," Knight offered.

"Why didn't you say that before?" Day groused, opening his eyes and glaring at him.

"Now who's pissy?" Knight asked.

"I'm entitled. I was shot on this little clambake."

"And you saved my life." Knight opened this kit. "It's just ibuprofen, but strong ones." He filled a glass with water and handed Day the pill, then helped him drink the water. Then he set the glass on the stand beside the bed and sat down. Day closed his eyes once again, and soon his breathing evened out, and some of the lines on his face disappeared. The medication must have been doing its job. Now he just needed to hear something.

The cabin phone rang, and Knight snatched it up. "Yeah." He had no time to be pleasant.

"This is Dr. Forester, ship's physician. I received an unusual call and… I'm not sure if… well, I will try to help Mr. Ingram. Can you please bring him to sick bay?"

"As long as we'll be alone."

"Uh—yeah. I think I'll need to come see you," Dr. Forester said uncomfortably.

"We'll be waiting." Knight hung up and turned to Day. "The doctor is on his way. I honestly don't know how much he can do for you while we're at sea, but at least he can make sure the wound is clean and there isn't any infection. He can probably give you something better for the pain."

"And use bandages made from something other than some deranged man's T-shirt." Day forced a quick smile.

There was that. He'd done the best he could with what had been at hand. "Just relax as best you can." Knight stood, and when a knock sounded on their door, he opened it and let the doctor inside. He also checked that the passage was empty.

"I've never gotten a call like that before," the doctor said as soon as the door was closed.

"You were instructed to tell no one," Knight said seriously.

"The man I spoke with sounded like he could bring the weight of the world down on me if I said a word about anything, and I don't know anything… so." He seemed very flustered.

"All you need to do is treat Day, say nothing, and you'll be fine. We'll pay you for whatever you need, so no one should ask too many questions. Were you told anything?" Knight asked, keeping the doctor in the entry area so he couldn't see Day.

"Just that someone needed help, and that I was to treat them without questions of any kind." Dr. Forester had blond hair, blue eyes, and would have looked more at home on the pool deck than in a hospital. Maybe that was why he was here onboard ship. "Now, can I get a look at the patient?"

"Yes." Knight stepped back and let the doctor farther into the cabin. Knight stayed out of the way but watched as the doctor spread out a pad on the bed and then helped Day onto it. He cut off the shirt Day was wearing and then began undoing the makeshift bandages. Dr. Forester turned to Knight with raised eyebrows once he saw the wound.

"We'll give you no details, but the bullet went clean through. There appeared to be little spatter or flattening as it went." Thank God. A different kind of bullet could have messed Day up very badly.

"I won't ask how or where this happened because… I don't want to know."

"That's best for everyone," Knight answered. He kept his voice soft. They hadn't heard anyone in the other cabins, but it would be problematic to say the least if they were overheard.

"There isn't a lot I can do." Dr. Forester looked at Day. "You were indeed lucky, and it must hurt like hell, but I'm going to clean the wounds, bandage them, and give you a sling to immobilize the arm. You're going to be sore for some time, but I don't think anything vital was hit. You just lost a lot of blood." He went to work and didn't speak much. "I'll give you something for the pain, and I suggest ordering room service and remaining here as much as you can. You're going to need all the rest you can get, and once you get back to the States, you might need to see a surgeon about repairing the muscle. There isn't anything I can do for you in that regard."

"Thank you, Doctor," Day whispered softly. "I know this is confusing and difficult. But we're the good guys. You don't need to worry about whether you're doing the right thing. It's just safer for you if you say nothing to anyone." Day winced as the doctor cleaned his shoulder and then bandaged each side until his skin was covered with gauze and tape. Once the doctor was done, Day settled in the bed and closed his eyes.

Knight explained what he'd given Day for pain, and the doctor nodded and handed him a small pill bottle. "Good. I'll leave these with you. They're stronger and should be used sparingly. I suspect the pain will begin to subside in the next day or so. The number-one thing he's going to need is rest." Dr. Forester gathered his things. "I'll come back tomorrow to check on him. Because of the way he was injured, I want to ensure no infection gets a chance to take hold." He handed Knight a second bottle. "These are antibiotics. Give him one now and then one every eight hours." The doctor stepped to the door, obviously anxious to be on his way.

"Thank you for everything," Day said, but Knight didn't think the doctor heard him in his haste to get out. He'd seen reactions like that before, and it didn't surprise him. Whoever had talked to the good doctor had put the fear of God in him, and he wanted to be as far away as he could get. Knight knew that would help ensure he never told anyone anything, which was the most important thing.

"Tell me what happened to your family," Day said. "I heard what Vasquez said to you about killing them."

"Fuck off," Knight said, without heat, and Day smiled. "You need to get some rest."

"Okay." Day was already fading fast. "But I'm not going to let you off the hook. Either you tell me or I'll start looking through every system and archive until I find it, and then I'll be mad at you for making me hunt for it." Day shifted slightly, winced, and then settled to sleep.

Knight sighed and got out his computer. He hooked it up, logged on to a secure connection, and got to work tracing Vasquez and his family back to Panama and earlier. It was clear that Knight had harmed his family in some way and that was the source of his personal hatred. Maybe that held the key to him figuring out who would be willing to pay to destroy his family—and, by extension, him.

Chapter 7

DAY SLEPT for much of the rest of the evening. His shoulder ached like hell, and he took the pills when Knight offered them to him and ate some, but he wasn't really hungry. That night he managed a trip to the bathroom and washed up as best he could with one hand. He needed to feel clean, and he got most of the way there.

"Do you need help?" Knight asked as he stepped out of the bathroom. He didn't look up from his computer screen and hadn't for hours. Next to him rested the plates he'd brought back from the buffet earlier, with the remains of their dinners.

"I did, but I managed," Day said without heat. It wasn't as though Knight was even listening or paying attention. Whatever he was hunting, it trumped everything else in the world. And that was fine. Day had always known or strongly suspected that what had happened between the two of them had been little more than a fling, at least from Knight's perspective. Besides, his first field mission had been a success, by and large. Yeah, he'd gotten hurt, but he and Knight had arrived in time and neutralized the threat. It hadn't been pretty, and there were bound to be questions, but it was a success by most measures. The world was safer, and they had been able to bring back equipment that might help lead to other avenues of inquiry. With that success would come other field missions, which was what he'd wanted.

"I could have helped."

"You can't take your eyes off that computer screen for more than the time it takes you to shove food in your mouth. So how are you going to help me?" Day walked to the dresser and grabbed a pair of briefs. He managed to get them on one-handed without falling and then went back to the bed. He climbed under the covers and turned out the lights, leaving only the computer screen to glow in the dark. "I suggest you go take a shower—you stink. And then if you want to come to bed, you can join me." Day closed his eyes.

Knight grunted, and the chair creaked slightly as he got up. Day heard him grumble under his breath as he closed the laptop.

"I suggest you get rid of the dishes as well. The food will smell by morning."

Knight grumbled again, but the plates clinked as he grabbed the dishes and then left the cabin. Day waited for him to return. He heard the key card slide into the lock, and the door clicked. It opened slowly, and light from the hallway shone in the dark room. Day opened his eyes, instantly alert. Something wasn't right. Knight would have come right in. The door began to close, the room darkening once more. Day's heart raced, and he wondered what he could use as a weapon.

The door burst open, light flooding the room once again. "Move and I'll break your fucking neck and throw your ass overboard," Knight growled. Day turned on the light and got out of bed as the cabin door banged closed.

He pulled on shorts as Knight brought their visitor into the room. "What the hell are you doing here?" Day asked. The man didn't move or say anything. Knight turned, and Day saw Blain in Knight's grip. "What the fuck, Blain?"

"You?" Blain sneered.

Day walked over to where Knight held Blain. "What the fuck are you doing? Why were you coming in my room, and where did you get a key?"

"I was told to make contact with the people in this cabin. If you'll check my pocket—" Blain's usual mincing speech pattern was gone. He sounded very confident and authoritative now.

Knight didn't let him go, so Day reached into his pocket and pulled out a case. He opened it and showed the shield to Knight.

"You can let me go now," Blain said.

"I don't think so. Explain yourself," Knight said.

"I'll ask you again," Day said. "What the hell are you doing here?"

"As you can see, I'm with ATF. I was sent on this little cruise because we'd had reports that this particular run was being used to move people into Mexico. We thought it was for the purpose of moving drugs and weapons in and out of the country. That area of Mexico is a key part of the drug trade. After a call came in that a friendly needed help, I was sent to make contact." Blain looked him over, and Day suddenly felt exposed. He was also a little light-headed, so he sat on the edge of the bed and pulled the covers up to his waist. "I take it you're the friendly who needed medical care."

"Yeah, and it's possible that your problem was also our problem, but it wasn't weapons or drugs. It was a cyberattack," Day said. "Although they may have been doing other things to finance their operation. We didn't really stick around, and they weren't talking."

"So the explosion?" Blain asked. "That was you?" He appeared impressed. "I'll tell no one, so if anything comes around, everyone can deny knowledge. The powers that be will claim it's a local problem. That is, if the Mexicans bring it up, which I doubt they will."

"Just clearing up loose ends," Knight said. Day noticed he wasn't giving a lot of information, so he made a note to be more circumspect. Day saw the way Knight's gaze bored into Blain. He wasn't telling him anything he didn't have to. "Is there anything further you need?"

"No. I was simply told to make contact and ensure that any help you needed was given."

"Your timing was perfect… after all the excitement is over."

"I couldn't break cover any more than you could," Blain said sternly to Knight and then turned to him. "I'm glad you're going to be all right. I was informed that you weren't attached to a particular agency, but if there's something that needs to go up official channels, I can help."

"We'll let you know." Knight walked Blain to the door. "Thanks," Day heard Knight say, and then the door closed again. "That fucker is lucky I didn't break his neck. Wonder why he was sneaking in? Did he knock?"

"No, he had a key card," Day answered. "Shit."

Knight called Dimato and explained what had happened. "Just check to see if this guy is real. He can't go anywhere while we're out at sea." Knight paused. "I need to know if he's a threat, an ally, or a bureaucrat out to make his career." Another pause. "Thanks. I appreciate it. … No, I didn't get hit in the head. … Maybe the baby agent you saddled me with is rubbing off on me. … You can only hope." Knight walked over to the bed after he'd disconnected. "The cabin door is locked. There isn't much I can do about the balcony door. But it doesn't open quietly, and the change in air pressure would alert me."

He pulled back the covers, and Day pushed him away with his good hand. "I saved your life, you asshole. You can go sleep on the couch, old man."

Knight stopped. "What'd I do?"

"Baby agent," Day scoffed softly. He was really too tired to fight, but he'd had enough of that shit.

"I was just…."

Day shifted to the one side of the bed and closed his eyes. He'd proven himself in a lot of ways. What shocked him was how much that name bothered him. "I'm a better fucking shot than you are, thank God. Otherwise you'd be dead. Hell, we'd both be dead, because as soon as they discovered me, they'd have put a bullet through my skull." He was all churned up inside, out of control, and he hated feeling that way. Maybe it was all that shit from last night. He'd given himself to Knight like some wanton slut and…. Fuck, it was just a fuck. It had always been about fucking. Day needed to forget about everything else and accept shit for what it was. A fuck was a fuck, and that was it.

"I never said otherwise," Knight told him sharply. Then he yanked a pillow from the bed.

"Stop," Day said. "You can sleep here." He knew he was being an ass, but he still moved farther away from Knight's side of the bed. He wanted to be left alone. The mission was over, other than getting back to port and then home in one piece. Then he and Knight would go their separate ways. Hell, he'd probably never work with him again, which was fine with him. This trip had brought up feelings and crap he needed to deal with and that was best done away from Knight.

"Thanks," Knight said without emotion and carefully got into bed.

Day's arm and shoulder ached like a son of a bitch. The pills only lasted a few hours and then the pain increased from the dull ache it seemed to be at the best of times. He got up and managed to find the bottle of pills on the edge of the desk. Thank God the ship wasn't rolling, because he was damned unsteady enough on his feet.

If it had been really moving, Day knew he'd be flat on his ass. He opened the bottle and got a glass of water. "How many of these am I supposed to take?"

Knight groaned. "What?"

"How many of these pain pills am I supposed to take?"

"Up to two," Knight answered, and Day got two of the goddamned things out of the bottle and swallowed them with some water. He drank more because he felt dry and then climbed back into bed, hoping like hell the medication would take the edge off and allow him to sleep.

They sent him to blessed oblivion for a few hours. With the pain masked, he was able to sleep for a while. He woke to a bone-dry mouth, light peeking around the edge of the curtains, and Knight's arm around him. Day wanted to move away, but it felt good to be held, so he stayed where he was and closed his eyes once again. Knight would most likely wake soon and pull his arm away on his own. Day was too settled, and if he moved a muscle, the pain would start again, and he'd never get fucking comfortable.

He must have fallen asleep again, because when he woke, his shoulder throbbed. He also had to pee, so he carefully moved Knight's arm and got out of the bed, then walked to the bathroom. He used the facilities and drank some water. He thought about taking more pain pills, but they would put him out, and he needed to eat and move around a little before that happened again.

"What are you doing?"

"Trying to get dressed so I can get something to eat." He pulled open the closet and found a pair of shorts. He returned to the bed and managed to get them on, but fastening the damn things was impossible, and moving his arm at all only made the pain scream at him like an opera diva at full belt.

Knight pushed back the covers. "Get back in bed. You can clean up if you want. I'll go up to the buffet and grab a plate for both of us. That way you can stay still, and it will be easier than trying to get you dressed. Maybe tomorrow you'll feel better." Knight grumped his way through getting dressed and then left the cabin.

Day was too tired and hurt too much to care. It seemed they were both prickly, and there wasn't much he could do about it. He closed his eyes and let the slow motion of the ship lull him back into a doze. He couldn't do much more than that with the pain, but at least it wasn't as sharp as it had been the day before. A knock sounded on the door, and Day groaned as he got up and answered it. Their cabin steward stood outside.

"I'm sorry," he said immediately. "I thought you had left."

"It's all right. Could you come back in ten minutes?" The steward agreed, and Day closed the door. He then looked around and did his best to gather the comms equipment and stash it under the bed. He found a loose shirt that he managed to get over his head and his one arm into. Then he pulled open the balcony door and settled into one of the lounge chairs.

Knight returned and brought in the food. "What's going on?"

"The room needs to be cleaned. It smells like a hospital, and I figured we could eat out here." Day wasn't interested in moving. "I also thought that once the steward was done, I could take something for the pain and go back to sleep. You can go to the gym or go have some fun." Day wasn't interested in having Knight schlumping around the cabin while he slept. "There's no need for you to watch me sleep."

He took the plate Knight offered and set it on the small table next to him. Then he sat up and slowly started to eat the eggs, bacon, and hash browns.

"I got what I saw you eat before. I hope it's okay?"

"It's good. Thank you."

Knight noticed what he ate—that was a small surprise. At least some of it could be finger food, which helped.

Day continued eating as Knight got up at the steward's knock and let him into the room. Then he settled back on the balcony with the door closed. Day enjoyed the sea air. It was soothing and fresh. Once he'd finished eating, he lay back, and Knight left once again, returning a couple minutes later with two pills and a glass of juice.

"The steward will be done soon, and then you can go back to sleep," Knight said.

Day popped the pills into his mouth and took the glass of juice, drinking most of it before lying back and closing his eyes. They were on the shady side of the ship, and as far as he was concerned, he didn't need to move an inch for the rest of the day.

A pillow was slipped behind his head, and Day lay back against its softness and bade farewell to consciousness without a care. He was comfortable, and the pills had him floating on pillows of happiness. This was the life—no cares, only floatiness and warm breezes.

The light shifted, and he tried to get out of the sun. It was at just the wrong angle, however if he could shift just so, maybe he could go back to sleep. It didn't work. Day cracked his eyes open. He was alone on the balcony. He turned his head away from the sun, but he was getting too warm and uncomfortable. With a soft sigh, he carefully got up and went inside the cabin.

It was empty. Knight had obviously gone somewhere. Day checked the clock. It was after noon. He'd slept for hours. His shoulder ached, but he wasn't ready for more medication, and he was hungry. The thought of trying to get something to eat felt like too much work, so he settled on the bed and turned on the television. The room-service menu was next to the bed, so he opened it and made a call. He ordered food that would be easy to eat with his fingers and was breathing hard by the time he hung up. How could he hope to do anything at all if that small amount of activity exhausted him? Maybe something to eat would help.

The cabin door opened a few minutes later, and Knight came inside, wearing his bathing suit. Day did his best to ignore the sight of all that rich skin accented with dark hair. "Feeling better?"

"A little. Still very tired." He concentrated on the television. "I ordered room service for lunch. If I'd have known you were coming back, I'd have gotten something for you too. I can call them back and add to the order." Day picked up the phone and made a call, handing the menu to Knight. He added what Knight wanted to the order and then hung up. "I hope it gets here soon."

"Damn, you're impatient," Knight commented.

"I'm hungry and injured. I'm entitled to be impatient." Day yawned. He tried to stop it but couldn't. "Did you have a good time?"

"Yeah. I soaked away some of my own aches and pains." Knight did look relaxed. "I think this evening, once the pool deck thins out, I'll help you get a suit on, and you can soak in one of the tubs. Hopefully it will help you feel better, and as long as you keep your bandages dry and are awake enough, you should be fine."

"That would be nice." Day turned back to the television and did his best to relax. "Tomorrow we're in port, aren't we?"

"Yeah, Jamaica tomorrow, and then we'll head back to Canaveral. I'm ready to go home. I didn't have anything planned for tomorrow because I wasn't expecting to be on the ship."

"I know, and I'm not going anywhere. I might go up and sit on deck if I feel up to it, but otherwise I plan to rest. You feel free to do whatever you like, though."

Knight got some clothes and went into the bathroom. When he came out, he settled in the blue upholstered chair near the balcony door and seemed to get comfortable.

"It really isn't necessary for you to wait around for me all the time," Day said. "I know you'll only get bored."

"I'm not. I'm waiting for lunch to arrive." He leafed through one of the cruise magazines that came with the cabin. Day turned his attention to the television until a knock on the cabin door announced that their food had arrived. Knight went to get it, and Day moved to the small sofa.

They ate at the coffee table. Day was hungry and ate his chicken fingers and fries like he was half starved.

"Damn, don't eat your fingers while you're at it," Knight quipped, setting down his burger.

"I was hungry."

"That's a good sign. I remember the last time I was shot—I don't think I ate for days." Knight looked shocked and then he turned away, looking miserable. He sighed, and the expression was gone, but he sat back and no longer seemed interested in his lunch.

"Is this about what happened to your family?" Day asked.

"Fuck off," Knight said.

"It might help to talk about it," Day suggested.

"Fuck off!"

"You know you can't keep everything bottled up inside you all the time," Day pressed.

"I said fuck. Off. And I meant it. You don't know shit about crap, so leave it alone!" Knight picked up his plate and carried it over to the room-service tray. He set it down none too gently and then strode to the door. It slammed closed after him, and Day stared at his plate in the now empty cabin. Well, he'd certainly messed that up.

He finished his soda and then took the dishes to the tray. He knew he should put it out in the hallway. He tried to pick it up one-handed but quickly realized he was going to make a hell of a mess, so he left it where it was and went to the bathroom. He washed up, took some more pills, and returned to the room. He climbed into the empty bed and watched whatever was on television. He had nothing else to do. He thought about calling the doctor to have him come look at his shoulder, but sleep seemed like a much better idea. Eventually the medication caught up with him, and he turned off the television, got comfortable, and closed his eyes.

The next thing he knew, the light outside had faded. He was still alone, needed the bathroom, and his shoulder was killing him once again. He got up and took care of business before deciding that he needed to get the hell out of this cabin. He was damned tired of sitting in the room all alone. He should try to get some work done, but he had no energy for it. All he wanted was some dinner and maybe to soak in a hot tub for a little while.

Day checked in the mirror that he didn't look like too huge a mess and found he looked awful. So he shaved and brushed his teeth, because his mouth tasted like death, and then changed into decent pants and sucked in his belly far enough that he managed to get them fastened with a single hand. He did forego nice shoes and wore what he could slip on his feet. Then he grabbed his card and left the cabin. He'd had enough of buffet food and wanted to be waited on, so he walked to the elevators and went down to the dining room. There would be people there—people who talked and actually said something. Deep down he was hoping Knight would show up, but he knew that wasn't likely. Day had pushed, sure, but God, it hadn't warranted this kind of reaction.

The dining room doors were opening for his late seating. Thank God he didn't have to stand around and wait, and it wasn't one of the dress-up nights. There was no way he could have managed that. He got to the table and sat down.

"Well, look what the cat dragged in," Willy commented as he and Bobby pulled out their chairs to sit down. "We were starting to think you'd abandoned us altogether."

Bobby gasped. "What happened to you? Did that huge grumpy thing you were with the other night get a little too energetic?"

Willy smacked Bobby on the shoulder. "Don't be catty."

"I had a little accident in Costa Maya. It isn't serious, but the doctor thought it best that I keep my arm immobilized." He figured it best to make light of his injury, especially at dinner. Although he had no doubt the true story would have kept everyone riveted, it was a story he would never be able to tell.

"Where's your other half?" Kevin, the bottle blond, asked as he took his seat.

"I'm not really sure right now."

"Did you two fight?" Willy asked, and Day nodded. It was the easiest explanation. "Then find him after dinner." He leaned closer to Bobby. "Makeup sex is the best kind. Sometimes I swear Bobby picks a fight just so we can get to the good stuff." They both laughed as the others joined them at the table. The only empty seat, now quite conspicuous, was Knight's, and Day doubted makeup sex was in the cards. Hell, sex of any kind was pretty much off the table as far as he was concerned. Yeah, it had been great, but sex was obviously all it had been, and he was coming to the realization that he could get that just about anywhere without all the drama and pain-in-the-ass prickliness that came along with Knight.

"Sorry I'm late," Knight said as he pulled out his chair and took his seat. He leaned close and added in a whisper, "You could have left a note. I looked for you when you weren't in the room."

"You could have been less of a dick earlier," Day retorted, and then he forced a smile and turned back to their dinner partners, ignoring Knight. Yeah, it was a cheap shot and even a little childish, but he'd offered to listen and try to help, and all Knight had done was take his head off.

“So, Day here says he had an accident in Costa Maya,” Willy said to Knight. “What happened?”

“He was getting on one of the tour buses and fell forward. Jammed his shoulder when he went down. He dislocated it slightly. I was able to put it back in place, and the doctor wrapped it and checked it over when we got back to the ship. I know it hurts like a son of a bitch, and he’s been in the room on pain meds since we got back. Thankfully he was feeling well enough that we could come to dinner.” Knight was laying it on a little thick, but Day went along with it. The explanation made sense even if it made him look clumsy.

The efficient waiter brought menus, and Day looked his over and set it aside. There were limited things he could eat one-handed. Drinks were ordered and brought, and then orders for dinner were taken. When the waiter got to him, he clicked his teeth gently. “I need something I don’t have to cut, but I’m hungry for beef.”

“No problem,” the waiter said and began writing. “I take care of you.” Day ended up with a fruit appetizer and a Caesar salad to go with the “no problem” beef. He stifled a yawn and did his best to ignore the ache in his shoulder. The others’ orders were taken. Thankfully, the conversation shifted away from him, and Day sat back and listened.

“That explosion the other day?” Kevin began. “I heard on the pool deck that it was the military blowing up some terrorist weapon cache.” He turned to them. “Did you see it? We were on our way back to the ship from our excursion to the ruins and had just passed that area about a mile or so back when we heard and felt the explosion. It was something. The bus rocked with the force of it, and the fireball must have gone a mile into the air.”

“We saw it too,” Knight said, letting the exaggeration stand. “We were wondering if there might have been issues getting out of port after that.”

“It was far enough away that it didn’t affect anything. Thank goodness,” Kevin said. Their salads arrived, and Kevin barely stopped talking to eat. “Some of the guys are having a dance party on the pool deck tonight. Apparently it’s an impromptu thing and supposed to be wild.” He leaned closer. “I also heard that there were guys getting it on in the hot tubs early this morning. They were putting on a show for anyone up there."

"Too bad you missed it," one of the other men said. Day couldn't remember his name, but his hair was as fiery as his tongue was sharp. "Apparently the real fun was in the sauna this afternoon. It was a regular orgy in there at one point."

"Were you there?" Kevin asked snarkily.

"No, dang it. I was a few minutes too late. You know how it is with those things. If you get there too late, everyone's come and gone, but the place smelled like the world's most active sperm bank. And the guys leaving all had that happy 'just blew a load' look. I hope they hosed the placed down overnight."

Day smiled at the comment. It was a funny image whether it was true or not. He mostly concentrated on getting his melon to his mouth without gnawing on it like he was an animal. "Here," Knight said softly and cut it for him. Day thanked him and finished his cool, sweet portion. Just what he needed.

The Caesar salad was easier, and when the main course arrived, he wasn't sure what he was going to get, but his steak had been cut into small pieces and drizzled with a nice amount of sauce. It looked wonderful and tasted amazing. "Thank you," Day said to the server.

"You're very welcome," the waiter said softly and continued around the table, making sure everyone was happy and had what they wanted. As soon as he was done with his entrée, Day excused himself. He was already feeling tired, and his shoulder ached all to hell.

He left the dining room and headed for the elevators. He'd just pushed the button to go up when he felt a hand lightly touch his back. "You don't have to come with me," Day said when he turned to Knight. He wasn't sure how he felt about being touched that way.

"I was done, and I wanted to make sure you got back to the cabin. You seemed about ready to fall over."

"I'm tired, and my shoulder hurts like hell," Day groused as the elevator doors opened. They stepped in, and he stayed quiet as they rode up in the full car. When they finally reached their deck after stopping at every single one in between, they stepped out. Day managed to get back to the cabin, and once inside he lay down on the bed, too tired to undress.

"I'm going to give you something for pain and then see if the doctor can check your bandages before you go to sleep." Knight handed him some pills, and Day popped them in his mouth and swallowed, then closed his eyes, letting Knight do what he wanted. "He'll be right up."

Day hummed that he'd heard. Knight opened the door at the knock, and the doctor came in. He changed the bandages and cleaned the wound once more.

"It looks good so far. Are you taking the antibiotics?"

"Yes," Day answered. The doctor redressed the wound, then Knight took care of payment once the doctor explained that all medical services on board ship must be paid in full. "Thank you," Day added as the doctor got ready to leave. Once he was gone, Day undressed and cleaned up before climbing under the covers. He usually liked to sleep on the side with his hurt shoulder, so getting comfortable was difficult. He finally settled, though, and closed his eyes.

Knight turned off the lights, and then the room was quiet. Day wondered where Knight was. Then the bed dipped next to him.

"I was married. Her name was Cheryl, and we had a son, Zachary. I had joined the Marines and was on leave when I met her. Cheryl was kind and thoughtful, beautiful, and she understood about military stuff. Her dad was career Army. We started off as friends, and I expected that was all it would ever be, but we… experimented, and she got pregnant."

Day rolled onto his back, Knight's dark form unmoving from where he sat. He kept quiet and let Knight say what he wanted to say.

"I didn't know what to do at first. I cared about Cheryl. She was an amazing friend, and she was going to have my child." The words came fast. "I wasn't going to let her do that alone. We were close, so I did the right thing and married her. I grew to love her very much." Knight turned slightly, but Day could see very little in the dark cabin. "Both our families were thrilled, and my father held the wedding in his church and had a friend officiate. Cheryl being pregnant wasn't mentioned, but that didn't really matter."

"Were you happy?" Day asked.

"Yes. She wasn't the grand passion of my life, but I figured I wasn't going to have one. And then Zachary was born, and I realized he was my grand passion. He was my son, and we did everything we could together. I took him to the park, we went to games, camped—all the stuff fathers and sons do." Knight wiped his eyes. "Like I said, we were happy. Cheryl got a job at Zachary's school, and I completed my years in the service. I thought about enlisting again, but with the military, there's no say in where you're posted, and when Scorpion approached me, I agreed. I had the training and skills they wanted, and my family could settle in one place. I was paid well and could afford to take good care of them and provide the life I thought they deserved. Everything was going well. I was gone a lot, but I always had been, and they had a home they could count on."

Day pushed back the covers, the sleepiness from the medication vanishing. "What happened to them? I heard what Vasquez said."

"I came home one evening. I'd been working on a job in Europe, trying to capture a fugitive who'd decided that he was safer outside the country. It was my job to convince him to come back. And I'm good at my job, or at least I was then. Anyway, I came home to find both of them dead. They'd been shot while they were sleeping." Knight's voice broke. "I found Cheryl first. I'd gotten home late and went to our room. As soon as I approached, I knew something was wrong. I could smell it, and the panic rose in my throat. I'd even pulled my weapon, but all I found was her motionless on the bed. I took one look and ran to Zachary's room. I found him too, still in the dinosaur pajamas I'd gotten him the last time I was home. They'd both been shot in the head."

Knight inhaled deeply. "I ran to the bathroom and threw up. Me, a Marine who had seen bodies blown to bits, and all I could do was throw up and then collapse into a pile on the bathroom floor. I don't know how long I just sat there before I made the call to the office. At the time I was working directly for Mark Cale, and he swung into action. The locals were bypassed in favor of the feds, but try as they might, they agreed on one thing: whoever had done this was a professional and left no trace. Mark went back through my cases, and other than people I'd pissed off, they found absolutely nothing. They never even figured out how he got in the house. I knew it was a challenge. Whoever did this was testing and taunting me."

"So nothing happened?"

"No. But I fell apart. For weeks I didn't function at all. Mark eventually came by and talked some sense into me. I said I couldn't go back into the field. I didn't trust myself not to just walk in front of a bullet. So I went into Research and Records. I kept hoping something would cross my desk that would give me a clue who did this so I could track them down and make them suffer as much as I have." Knight's breath faltered a little. "And don't get me wrong, I will track them down, and they will suffer at my hands."

His voice sent a shudder through Day.

"Then I got the very first clue, and the bastard who actually killed them is dead. You shot him. But he said there was someone else involved. He was getting his own revenge, but he said he got paid to do it. So I took a step forward, and I have an avenue of inquiry, but I missed the really big prize. The asshole died before he could tell me who hired him."

Day didn't correct him. He doubted Knight would have gotten anything from him. Day had placed a well-aimed shot, and the fucker couldn't have lived for very long after that. Even if he had, the hate Day had seen in Vasquez's eyes had said that he would have taken his secret to the grave. He decided to try another tack. "Do you think he could have been lying just to get to you?"

"I suppose it's possible. But at the time I was in his control, and he had every reason to believe I was going to die at his hand." Knight shook his head. "He wanted me to know he'd done it and that I wasn't going to get all the answers."

Day could understand that. "All this happened about two years ago, didn't it?"

"Yeah. Most people know I went pretty nuts for a while and then retreated. I couldn't handle anything for a long time. I crawled in a bottle and stayed there when I wasn't working. It was deliciously numbing, and I could forget what happened, at least for as long as the booze held out."

"How long did you do that?"

"Until about a week ago? I didn't do so well. My resolve lasted what, five days, and then I was drunk off my ass again." His self-flagellation was obvious in his voice.

"I'm guessing you were drinking to forget that night." Day touched Knight's shoulder. "I've been there. There were a lot of times I wanted to drink after my dad died. I did it once too. Stole a bottle from Stephen and hid in the shed behind the house. Dad had been gone a week, and Stephen found me after I'd had about three gulps."

"What did he do?"

"Joined me. We were both miserable. After that, I didn't touch the stuff again until I was legal. I was so sick, and all Stephen did was make fun of me for being a lightweight. That was Stephen—he let me discover things for myself, and then made sure I was safe and didn't get hurt. I think that was the last time I got drunk before that night with you. And I don't ever want to do it again. When Miguel gave me that shot of tequila, I'm surprised I kept it down." Day closed his eyes and debated saying anything more but then figured what the hell—all Knight could do was get angry with him.

"I used to think I had it so bad. I'd lost my mom and dad, so I figured everyone should be nice to me and cut me some slack. Some people did, and others didn't. But… there are people worse off than us. Like those people who live near Miguel. I bet their houses aren't like his."

"No. The insides are like the outsides, and they're scraping to put food on the table. I know we didn't see it, but up the road a few miles toward the ruins is this little town. It's not much more than a wide spot in the road with maybe six or seven houses. The town exists on people who pass by. The women cut pineapple and papaya and sell dollar bags to tourists. That's how they sustain themselves. A few dollars a day per family is all they have, if they're lucky." Knight turned and sat facing him on the edge of the bed. "I know I'm lucky. I live in a country where I have everything I want at my fingertips. I know I should let go of what I feel sometimes. But the only thing that kept me from killing myself in those darkest hours was the thought of revenge. I will get the people responsible for the deaths of my wife and child. After that I'll figure out what else I want to do with my life."

"That's a hollow existence. You know once you get the guy responsible, you'll feel just as empty. It won't bring them back." He knew that well. "I spent months bargaining with God to make my mother get well. I promised I'd be good and that I'd like girls. I made every promise in the book, but she still died."

"It's all I have," Knight said. "They deserve justice for what happened to them."

Day was too tired to argue, and he knew Knight wouldn't change his mind. Not with a belief he'd held so close to the core of his being for so long. He could understand Knight wanting revenge. Hell, Day's hands clenched when he thought about it, his own sense of right and wrong kicking into high gear. "They do." Day tapped Knight on the shoulder. "But it isn't going to happen in the next two days."

"Yeah, I know," Knight admitted.

"And the guy who actually pulled the trigger is dead."

"Yeah."

"So there is some justice there. Also, the guy who paid for this doesn't know that you know what happened. He thinks he got away with it. Nothing has happened, and the killer hasn't surfaced. Now that he's dead, they're going to feel even safer."

"What's your point?"

Day scoffed. "I'm tired and hopped up on drugs. I don't know if I have a point." He lay back down. "Sorry. I'm not thinking very clearly. Let's go to sleep, and we can start to work in the morning. I'll hook up the comms equipment, and instead of going into Montego Bay, we'll see what information we can dig up."

Knight stood and huffed softly. "No. You're right. I need to keep this quiet for now. Besides, I don't want anyone listening in or looking over my shoulder. I'll handle this when I get back. There are too many potential eyes and ears here." He walked away, and the bathroom door opened and closed. Day pulled the covers up around him, shivering as Knight's pain and loss washed over him. Day had promised once before that he wouldn't show pity or sympathy. He knew Knight hadn't wanted it then, and he wouldn't want it now. So when Knight came out once again and got into bed, all he said was good night and then closed his eyes.

Day probably would have lain awake for hours had it not been for the pain medication, and soon he was asleep, lulled by the rocking of the ship, which ceased at some point during the night, most likely when they came into port. He tried to go back to sleep, but was wide-awake as the sun lit the very edges of the curtains. It was early in the morning, but he knew he couldn't back to sleep, so he got up, dressed, and left the room.

He rode an empty elevator up through a mostly deserted ship to the pool deck and wandered around in the early morning air. A few people sat in the whirlpools, but he had the deck pretty much to himself. The quiet combined with the surrounding island view gave him a chance to collect his thoughts. He leaned against the railing and watched as the ship came into the dock. If he expected the answers to what was bothering him to simply come to him in a flash of understanding, he was mistaken. He ended up watching the whole docking procedure and then, as more and more people came up on deck for their morning run or a dip in the pools before heading to shore, he left the pool area and took the stairs down to their deck.

He walked down the passage and was just making the slight curve when he saw someone going into a cabin up ahead. He could have sworn that was their door. He'd come this way enough times to know that was about where their cabin was located. His first reaction was anger. If Blain was pulling his little trick again, Day would beat the shit out of him.

He was just about to insert his card in the lock when he stopped, hearing muffled voices from inside. Because of the kind of cabin they had, the door was angled slightly in the hallway. Day pressed into the angled area and placed his ear to the door.

"Where is your friend? The one with the wounded flipper?"

"What do you want?" he heard in Knight's deep tone. The response was muffled. "You would have been better off to have stayed away and just gotten off the ship."

"Family is family" was the response. At least Day thought that's what he heard. Good God, this was a clusterfuck. What was with these people? "Your friend better get back here soon."

Jesus Christ. They should have thought of this. Dimato had reported that an unusual number of people had not returned to the ship at Costa Maya. He and Knight should definitely have considered that the terrorist group might have someone on the ship. Day remembered the peephole in the door and moved away out of sight, hoping like hell he hadn't already been seen. He needed to figure out what to do and fast. He couldn't just walk in or leave Knight alone.

Day looked up and down the passageway. A few doors down, a tray sat on the carpet. Day hurried down to it and cleared off the trash, leaving it on the floor. Then he took the dirty plate, placed the cover on it, and added whatever was left that didn't look like trash. Carefully he lifted it and managed to balance it on his good arm. Then he approached the door, standing just off to the side. He gently knocked on the door, which was all he could manage with his wounded arm. "Room service." Day hoped like hell Knight would realize it was him.

"What is it?" The voice definitely wasn't Knight's.

"Room service. I have your breakfast, sir," Day said adding a slight accent and hoping it wasn't too much. Day rapped again to add a sense of urgency and waited.

"Leave it outside the door."

"I can't do that, sir. It must be signed for." Day was intent on keeping up the pressure. It was all he could do. Day heard shuffling and then heard the metallic sound of the door latch. It opened slightly, and as soon as he saw Knight standing farther back, he rushed the door, pressing all his weight into it. The tray began to fall forward, and Day did his best to push it toward the stranger, who tried to catch it out of instinct.

Knight rushed forward, grabbing the intruder by the arm and flinging him inside the room. A gun went skidding along the carpet, and they were lucky the damn thing didn't go off. Knight lost hold of the intruder, and he spun away, unfortunately in the direction of the gun. Knight went after him, but it was clear the intruder was going the reach the gun first.

"Watch out," Day yelled and grabbed the plate off the floor. He flung it like a Frisbee, and it hit the man in the shoulder. If he'd missed, the plate probably would have broken the balcony door, he threw it so hard. Instead, the intruder screamed as the cabin door banged closed. Knight jumped and tackled the man, pinning him to the floor.

Day breathed deeply as Knight subdued the man. "Grab a washcloth from the bathroom and some towels," Knight said to him before turning to the intruder. "Don't move or make a sound, or I'll snap your neck like a twig." The man stopped moving and went quiet. "You picked the wrong people to mess with, asshole." Knight breathed deeply, and Day turned to get what Knight had asked for. He returned and held the washcloth and towels out for Knight. "Shove the washcloth in his mouth." Day did as Knight asked. Then Knight put the towel over the man's head and shoved his head into the carpet. "What the hell were you thinking?" Knight whispered into the man's ear. "Or let me guess: you weren't."

He got a muffled response.

"You figured that the people who took out whatever pieces of shit you have for friends didn't know how to protect themselves from the likes of you." Knight leaned closer. "You could have left well enough alone, walked away, and melted back into the darkness or slipped back into whatever cesspool you came from. But no, you decided confronting us was your best option. What a fuckbag!" The man started to move, and Knight placed his hands on each side of the intruder's head. "Thirty-eight pounds of pressure." Knight forced the man's head to the side. "That's all it takes for me to snap your neck, and I can do that in my sleep. So if you move again, I'll turn you into shark bait. That's right. I'll snap your fucking neck, wait till it's dark, and dump your body overboard. The family you seem to hold in such high regard will never know what the fuck happened to you. Granted, fish food will at least put you to good use."

Knight's little speech seemed to have the desired effect. The man didn't move, and Day hurried through the room. He gathered the weapon, careful not to touch it with his bare hands, dumped the ammo, and set both aside. "What should I do now?" Day's arm throbbed.

"I hope you didn't reopen those wounds."

He didn't think so. He'd used his good shoulder, and now both of them ached.

"Call Blain, and get him down here. He said to let him know if we needed something official, and we definitely need that, unless you want to dump this useless pile of crap overboard." Knight began to laugh. "Don't want to pollute the sea with our garbage, though."

Day found the card Blain had given them and made the call. "Blain? It's Day, I think we need some assistance from you. Can you come to our cabin?"

"What time is it?"

"Early. Get over here, please." Day hung up and grinned at Knight. "He's on his way."

Knight nodded, and neither of them moved until they heard a knock. Day checked through the peephole and then opened the door for Blain. "I went up on the pool deck for a walk, and when I came back, I saw him sneaking into our room. He appears to be a relative of one of the guys in the shake and bake from a few days ago."

"Shake and bake?" Blain asked.

"Don't like it? How about the guys we Jiffy Popped?" Day felt punchy. "I'll stop now. I think I've had enough for a while." God, he'd definitely had a lot more than he'd expected when he got up this morning.

"Yeah, I think you have," Blain commented and turned back to Knight. "Let me make a call and see if I can't get a few things arranged. Then I'll take custody of him, and we'll get him off the ship and delivered to some friendlies in town. They'll know what to do with him and how to get him to talk. They certainly won't want him in the States. This way they can be a little more forceful, especially if he's a foreign national." Blain was having fun making their guest squirm. Blain stepped away and spoke softly into his phone. He made multiple calls, and a little while later a knock came on the door, and another man, along with a representative from the cruise line, entered the room. Their uninvited guest was handcuffed and bundled away. "I suspect the ship will have questions. Just refer them to me, and we'll take care of everything." Blain paused at the door. "I'll see to it that both of you get a copy of the reports, as well as any information he might give us."

"Thanks," Knight said. "I have a… personal interest in anything he says."

Blain paused. "Okay. Use the card, and call me in a few days. I'll brief you on anything we find." It was obvious to Day that Knight wasn't too happy about being cut out of this, but there wasn't much either of them could do without jeopardizing their cover and as a result encountering a lot of extra scrutiny they didn't need.

"I hope that's the end of all this for a while," Day said once everyone had left.

"That was quick thinking on your part. I hadn't figured you'd ordered room service."

"I was hoping you'd understand. The guy fell for it too." Day sat on the edge of the bed. "There's just one thing that still bothers me." Knight tilted his head quizzically. "How many other people are there who want to kill you? You sure know how to win friends and influence people. I mean, good grief, is there anyone who's met you who hasn't wanted to kill you at one time or another?" Day was exhausted and fell back on the bed, closing his eyes. "Lord knows I've wanted to do that at least once a day."

"Now who's being an ass?"

"That would be you," Day retorted. "You're the king of assholeness, remember? If I could give you a crown I would, but it wouldn't be pleasant." He smiled and kept his eyes closed. The room grew silent. Day kept expecting some retort but heard nothing, not even a footstep. "What are you doing?" Day cracked his eyes open and saw Knight staring at him.

"Thinking."

"About what?"

Knight sighed. "How I betrayed my family."

Day's eyes jerked open, and he sat up straight, wincing when he put too much weight on his shoulder. "How did you do that? You've tried to find out who hurt them for two years. Your life has been on hold. I suppose that's a kind of betrayal, because I doubt either your wife or son would want to see you unhappy." Day was treading on dangerous ground, and he knew it the second Knight's lips tightened, and his gaze hardened to stone.

"You don't understand. You can't ever understand." Knight walked toward the door.

"Stop!" Day said forcefully. "Quit being an asshole. God, you are such a closemouthed SOB. You never talk about anything, and it's like pulling teeth to get anything other than prickliness out of you. There are times, two or three each day, that I want to shoot you. How can I ever understand unless you tell me? I can't read your mind. No one can."

"Cheryl could sometimes," Knight countered.

"Cheryl cared about you the same way you cared about her. I'm sure there were times when you knew what she wanted." The confused look on Knight's face told him all he wanted to know. "I see." As he might have guessed, Cheryl was the nurturer, and she took care of him. "No one can read another person's mind." Day lay back down on the bed. He was tired, and he'd had enough fighting with Knight. It was draining. "Do what you want. I'm going to lie down because saving your ass yet again has worn me out. Both my shoulders hurt now."

Knight humphed and left the room without a word. Day closed his eyes. He should have taken something for the pain, but it really wasn't that bad, and he was getting tired of being drugged out on painkillers. It made it hard for him to think, and Lord knew he needed his wits about him to be around Knight. The man was trying at the best of times. He closed his eyes and wandered his way through the quagmire that was Knight. The man was smart; he could be funny and passionate, caring, and even thoughtful. He'd demonstrated that getting him back to the ship and taking care of him. But the man could also be a monumental horse's rear end. That was for fucking sure. So why was he fascinated by the man? He wished he knew, mostly so he could exorcise him from his thoughts.

After a few minutes, Day's pondering centered on why Knight would think he had betrayed his family. They were gone, and he'd been trying to figure out why they were killed. Maybe it was his failure to do so? Day tried to put himself in Knight's Marine shoes. Duty. Honor. Brotherhood. Knight embodied all those things, without a doubt, and maybe he felt his duty to Cheryl and Zachary hadn't been fulfilled, and worse, wasn't likely to be. Yes, their killer was dead, but the person behind it wasn't. That had to be it.... As soon as he thought he'd come up with the answer, another notion flitted near the edges of his mind but refused to take shape.

When Knight returned, he had two breakfast plates with him. Day got up, and they ate without saying much in the small living room area of their cabin. Mostly, Day continued wondering what was up with

Knight. The gruffness he could take, because Lord knew he could be just as gruff and reticent sometimes. But then Knight would turn around and be nice, bring him food, take care of him. "You know you don't have to do this because you feel…." He wasn't sure what he meant and searched for the words. "You don't have to wait on me out of some sense of gratitude. I was joking earlier. I know if I was in the same position, you'd do the same for me."

"You do? It seems you aren't the one that keeps being put in that position," Knight mumbled and continued shoveling food in his mouth.

"Please. You don't need to go all macho Marine on me. You have my back, and I have yours. That's the way it is."

"Yeah, but…." Knight seemed to want to say more and yet he didn't, confusion clear on his face.

"But you didn't expect that the agent in diapers would be the one having your back. You figured you'd have mine, and that you'd be the one to come to the rescue." Day supplied the answer for him and sat up, put down his fork, and took a drink from his glass of water. "Did it ever occur to you that we worked as a team? I knocked on the door, caught him off guard, and you took him out. I couldn't fight. All I could do was give you the chance to act, and you did. Isn't that what your Marine buddies would do for you?"

"Yeah, but you aren't a Marine."

This was another of those moments where Day wanted to kill him and dump his body overboard. "No, I'm not. But Marines don't have a monopoly on honor, courage, duty, and all those characteristics you hold dear. They also haven't cornered the market on watching someone else's back." Day huffed and then started eating again, figuring if his mouth was full, it would keep him from running on at the lips and pissing Knight off again.

"You're right," Knight said and then smiled after a few seconds. "And you can close your mouth. I don't want to see what you're eating." Day did as Knight suggested and nearly coughed from the whole surprise thing. "I have your back, and you have mine. You did what you were supposed to do, and you did it well."

Day swallowed his retort and continued eating. Once they were done, he sat back on the sofa and closed his eyes. He'd done nothing but sleep for the past couple of days, and it was starting to get to him, even though he was still tired.

"Why don't we put bathing suits on and go up to the pool deck? It's not going to be busy, and you can lie out there and relax. It will give you something to do other than look at these walls."

"I should get some work done."

"I called Dimato while I was out and explained that you were still healing. He said everything would wait until we got back and that he was pleased with the job we did. Well, he put it in Dimato-speak, which means he basically said, 'You screwed the pooch in how you did it, but you got the job done.' Then he said for you to rest, heal, and be ready to work when you came back, and hung up. So let it go and relax. In two days we'll dock at Canaveral and go back to real life."

"Okay." Day was too tired to really argue, so he got up and found a bathing suit. Then he managed to get his pants off and his bathing suit pulled up so it covered his bits and ass. When he turned around, Knight took a look at him and laughed.

"You're a mess." Knight came over and adjusted his suit. "If you're going to wear that thing, then it needs to be straight so you don't flash all the men on deck."

"Thanks. But what if I want to flash everyone?" He might have heard a growl from Knight, but he wasn't sure. "Are you going to change and go up with me or did you want to go into town and have some fun?" It wasn't necessary for Knight to stay on the ship if he didn't want to.

Knight seemed to ignore him. "I'm going to put my suit on, and then we'll go up on deck." He got his suit and changed quickly, giving Day a nice view of his smooth ass. The man was intensely gorgeous—all muscle and power. Day turned away just before Knight turned around because his bathing suit was going to hide nothing.

"I've got a few towels," Day said as he grabbed them from the bathroom, swinging them over his shoulder.

"Good." A bottle rattled, and Knight tapped him on the shoulder. "Take these for the pain before we leave and we can be on our way."

He was sick of pills, but he took them anyway, and then they left the cabin, heading up to the pool area.

DAY SPENT the rest of the day doing very little, and he went right to sleep after dinner. When he woke the next morning, his shoulder felt warm and ached. It didn't get better, so Knight called the doctor, who checked and changed the dressing.

"There doesn't seem to be any infection," the doctor said after he finished. "It's part of the healing process. The best thing you can do is continue to rest, and try not to use your arm too much."

"I know," Day said. "Thank you for your help."

"We were just concerned," Knight commented, and they talked quietly before the doctor left. "I'll order us steaks for dinner and have them delivered."

Knight got on the phone, and from what Day heard, the man had ordered a feast for later that evening. He got comfortable on the bed because he figured Knight would have a fit if he attempted to do anything.

"Do you want to rest?" Knight asked after he hung up.

"I guess so." The inactivity was driving him crazy, but he knew rest and keeping his shoulder immobile were the best things right now. He was looking forward to getting home and having his shoulder looked at by his own doctor, or, more accurately, one of Scorpion's doctors.

"You could go up on deck," Knight suggested.

"It's all right. You go. There's no use you hanging around here while I rest." He was bored to tears, but Knight didn't have to feel the same way. "I'll take some medication, and let it work its magic." The pain had slowly subsided over the past few days. "What I don't understand is why I'm still so tired and weak all the time."

"You lost a lot of blood, and it takes the body time to recover from that. You rest. I'm going up on deck for a while. Dinner is set to arrive at seven, and if you need anything else, call room service." He sounded like a mother hen. Day wasn't sure if he should interpret that as Knight really caring about him or normal partner concern. This whole situation was driving him out of his mind. In some ways Knight had grown more standoffish. He spent more time away than he had before, and while they talked, there were no personal conversations at all. Everything was superficial. At one point he thought they'd been getting close—or at least closer—but now Knight was pulling away. Or maybe the whole thing was just the situation and Day's imagination.

Knight went into the bathroom and came out wearing a pair of board shorts that came down to his knees. It looked like something from the fifties, but Knight filled it out in all the right places. "I'll see you later," Day said as Knight pulled on a T-shirt and then opened the cabin door. "Don't let any of the boys make a move on you."

Knight paused, and their gazes met for a brief second, neither of them breaking the invisible contact until a few seconds later, when Knight turned and left the cabin. Day couldn't help swallowing at the banked heat he'd seen in Knight's deep brown eyes. Day had seen the way Knight looked at him—he wasn't blind—but Knight had done nothing about it. And the few times Day had tried getting close, he'd been ignored. For something to do, he turned on the television but paid little attention to the comedy being shown. He turned down the volume, ignored the picture, and napped.

HE JUMPED awake as the cabin door opened and closed. Day cracked his eyes open as Knight went into the bathroom. A few minutes later he came out, wearing only a towel. "How are you feeling?"

"Better." Day swung his legs over the side of the bed and slowly stood. Knight had pulled open the closet door and stood in the doorway. Day walked up to him and trailed his hand lightly down Knight's muscled back. Knight stiffened but didn't tell him to stop or pull away. "I don't understand what's going on," Day confessed as he continued to run his hands along Knight's smooth skin.

"I don't expect you to understand," Knight whispered huskily. Knight didn't move, and Day closed his eyes and slid his hand around Knight's belly, the bumps of his ripped abs passing beneath his palms. He kept his touch light and gentle, the way people worked with skittish horses in Westerns.

Knight stood still. Day felt each breath he took, quicker and quicker, as he moved his hand downward. He found the fold that held the towel together, tugged at it, and the towel fell away. Day pressed his shorts-clad hips to Knight's backside to show him how he felt at that moment.

Day's heart raced, and he was afraid to say anything. Hell, he was afraid to breathe for fear the sound might break the spell. He had no fucking idea what had been going on in Knight's mind since he'd been hurt, and now wasn't the time to analyze it. He slid his hand lower, sliding his fingers over the nest of curls before closing them around the base of Knight's cock. Knight still hadn't moved, and Day debated whether he should continue. He didn't think his touch was unwelcome, based on the fact that Knight was so hard he could feel Knight's heartbeat through his cock. He was about to let go and step back when Knight slowly began to turn around.

Day let go, trailing his hand along Knight's belly and side as he turned. Then their gazes met, and Knight pulled him into a searing kiss that left Day's knees weak. "Fuck…," he muttered when Knight pushed away.

"My thought exactly," Knight said before crashing his lips to Day's once again. Knight held him firmly and pressed him back and then down onto the bed. Knight broke their kiss long enough to carefully remove the sling, then help get Day's shirt off and pants undone. Something about too many clothes rumbled from the back of Knight's throat, and then Day's shorts were undone and pushed down his legs. "I'm going to fuck you until you can't remember your name." Knight pinched a nipple, and Day groaned and arched his back.

"As long as you remember yours, so I can fuck you into senility in return, old man," Day growled right back. That seemed to inflame Knight. The heat between them intensified, and Day's cock throbbed as Knight pressed to him. This time when Knight's lips touched his, an electric spark jumped between them. What was it about this man's touch that sent his heart racing and his sense flying out the window? Not that it mattered. He used his good hand to explore Knight, sliding down, grabbing a firm asscheek and holding on. Knight might think he could get the better of him, but Day was not going to let that happen.

Knight groaned and climbed off him. Day lay on his back, legs dangling off the edge of the bed, cock throbbing each time his heart pounded. He was so turned on he jumped when Knight stroked up his thighs and mewled from deep in his throat when Knight firmly grasped his cock. "Jesus." Day thrust forward, needing, wanting, but Knight wasn't giving it. At least not at that moment. Instead, he leaned forward and swiped his tongue over the head. Day gasped, doing everything but begging. He was not going to beg for anything from Knight, knowing the stoic man would never beg from him. But he was seconds away from doing just that anyway when Knight sucked him deeper.

"That's it," Knight whispered after backing away. Then he blew on Day's wet skin, sending a zing running through him from head to toe. "Now lift your legs." Day swallowed and did as Knight wanted, resting them on the edge of the mattress. "Good boy."

Day was about to protest, but then Knight sucked him deep, and thinking wasn't possible. The wet heat and pressure threatened to take his breath away. He bucked and ground up against Knight's face, holding his head in a desperate need for more. He got it in a way he wasn't expecting. Knight stroked up his chest, teasing his skin before slipping two fingers in his mouth. Day sucked on them the way Knight sucked him. It was hot as hell, and when Knight pulled them away, he hummed around Day's cock, sending vibrations through him unlike anything Day had ever felt.

He was going out of his mind, but Knight held him still, pressing a finger to his opening and then inside his body. Damn, that felt good, and he clamped down on the finger, thrusting upward into Knight's mouth and then back down. "Fuck…," he droned, unsure which felt better: fucking Knight's mouth or Knight's finger—which quickly became two—fucking him.

"You like that, don't you?" Knight whispered and then sucked him deep and tight, driving his thick fingers into him. Day grabbed for purchase on the edge of the mattress so he could thrust upward, driving his cock into Knight's mouth, and as he pulled back, Knight's fingers filled and stretched him in a delicious way. He didn't know which he liked better, and after a few seconds, he didn't give a damn.

"Fuck me," Day rasped and swallowed hard. "I can still remember my name." He had to issue the challenge. Knight had promised he wouldn't remember who he was, and Day fully intended to make sure he kept that promise.

Knight sucked him harder and twisted his fingers. Day gasped and shook on the bed. He pistoned his hips as fast and hard as he could until Knight stopped him. He pulled his lips away, to Day's consternation, and then the thick fingers withdrew from his body. "I'll take care of you."

Knight stepped back, and Day gaped. Knight was gorgeous, the late-day sun shining through the balcony doors, glistening on Knight's already sweaty skin. Breathtaking was one word that came to mind. Knight rolled on one of the last condoms they had and stepped closer to him. He firmly grabbed Day's legs, holding his ankles, as he slowly entered him. The stretch was amazing, and Day gripped him tight as Knight filled him.

"Dammit," Day hissed. "I won't break."

Knight pressed deeper, his big cock stretching Day and driving him wild. As soon as he felt Knight's hips on his butt, Day sighed and held still, dropping his head back on the mattress.

"For God's sake," Day whispered, and Knight began to move. This was no slow, long, lingering fuck. Knight thrust forward, and Day shook, the driving force reverberating through his entire body. Fuck, it felt amazing, and when Knight changed the angle slightly, he dragged his cock over that spot inside him, and Day saw stars—fucking twinkling stars. "Oh, my God," Day breathed. He had to remember to hold his injured arm to his body because he wanted to reach out with both hands, haul Knight to him, and kiss his breath away. "Don't you dare stop," he growled instead.

"Bossy," Knight countered with a bone-rattling snap of his hips.

"You better fucking believe it. I heard it's called topping from the bottom or something like that."

"I." Knight withdrew and drove into him. "Call it." He did it again. "Being a pain in the ass." Knight picked up speed, driving Day out of his mind. As Knight promised, there were times when he did indeed forget who he was. All he wanted was for the pleasure to go on and on.

Of course it couldn't, and soon Knight's movements became erratic. Sweat poured off him, dark hair plastered to his head, eyes shining as his gaze met Day's and stayed there. Knight's breathing hitched, and Day lay back, giving himself over to the passion Knight provided.

"Jesus!" Knight cried. He thrust quickly and then stilled. He throbbed deep in Day's body, blissful pleasure glowing on his chiseled features as Day tumbled into ecstasy right after. Neither of them moved. Day didn't want to break the magic that linked them. He was beginning to understand how precious the connection between them could be.

Knight withdrew from his body, and Day slowly lowered his legs. He was worn out, and Knight sounded as though he'd run a marathon. He eventually settled on the bed next to Day.

"Damn, you're something else," Knight said. He continued breathing deeply.

Day moved closer, eventually turning over so he could look into Knight's eyes. He didn't know what to say. That was probably as close to an expression of feelings as Knight was going to come. He took Knight's hand and simply held it, closing his eyes.

This had to be the weirdest cruise in history. He and Knight had gotten closer, but Day wasn't sure if it would last. They'd done what they'd come here to do, and now it was time to go back to their real lives. Day wasn't sure he was ready for that, but it hardly mattered. Real life was going to return, and he had no idea what was going to happen when they got home. Over the past week, he'd come a long way in confirming who he was and determining he needed to be true to himself. He'd spent the week surrounded by gay men, which he'd originally thought would be hell, but it had been an eye-opening experience. The closet wasn't going to hold him any longer. "What are we going to do after… this?" Day finally asked. He could get shot and remain clearheaded enough to save Knight, but asking that question had required him to pull together all his courage.

"Well, we need to get our bags packed so they can take them tonight. We have dinner ordered, and tomorrow we get off the ship and go home. We aren't expected to be back in the office until Tuesday, and then after reports and debriefings, we'll go back to our lives." Knight didn't release his hand, but Day heard no mention of the two of them continuing whatever the hell this was in that explanation. Well, at least he had his answer, and now he knew where he stood.

He slowly sat up and then went into the bathroom. He couldn't face Knight right now. The thought of just going home hurt, but fuck if he would let Knight see that. If he was going to hurt, he would do it alone where no one could see him. Day turned on the water and filled the sink. He used a washcloth to clean himself. Showering was problematic with his bandages, so he washed his hair and took a sponge bath. By the time he was done, he felt better. After wrapping a towel around his waist, he vacated the bathroom for Knight to use and began getting dressed.

He found it hard to look at Knight, but he couldn't help it. When Knight disappeared into the bathroom, he carefully got out his bag and began packing his clothes and equipment. It took him a while one-handed, but he was done by the time Knight came out and finished his packing. Knight put their bags in the hall. They still had carry-on luggage, but that was all.

Room service knocked on their door a while later and brought in dinner. Knight signed for it, and they sat and ate in near silence. Knight seemed perfectly at ease. Though Day was inches away from asking the millions of questions on his mind more than once, he stopped himself. He didn't want to appear needy or desperate. If Knight had wanted something to happen after they left the ship, he would have indicated it. So he would go home and return to his own life, maybe a little wiser and slightly more guarded with his heart. He only wished he knew why.

Answers weren't forthcoming from Knight, who was the picture of Marine stoicism. His expression said "don't approach unless you want me to take your head off." When they were done, Day put his dishes on the tray. His shoulder ached from the activity, so he took some pain medication, hoping it would help. Then he pulled open the balcony door and stepped outside. He closed it behind him and settled into one of the lounge chairs watching the stars and listening to the sound of the ship as it cut through the water. "Stop this," he whispered to himself.

"Are you feeling okay?" Knight asked after pushing the door open.

"I'm fine. Just getting some fresh air," he answered

“I’m going to go for a walk,” Knight told him. Day grunted and nodded, turning back to the stars.

“You might as well enjoy the last night,” Day said coldly. He intended to spend as much of it as he could right here. Hell, he wondered if he could spend the night out here. That bed suddenly seemed too damned small and rather cold. He refused to look, but the balcony door didn’t close for quite a while, and then it quietly slid back into place. The lights in the cabin went out, and Day sat in the darkness.

Day smiled. He remembered being about eight, lying out in the backyard. He’d gotten a new sleeping bag for Cub Scouts and he’d begged to sleep in it outside. His mother wouldn’t let him do that alone, so she’d strung a tarp over the clothesline to serve as a tent, and they had sat out looking at the stars. “If you make a wish on the first one you see, it will come true,” she had told him. After his mother got sick, he’d stood outside night after night, wishing on stars—wishes that went unanswered. His smile faded, and he closed his eyes, blocking out the stars and all their unanswered wishes. Eventually the medication kicked in, and he hadn’t even realized he’d dozed off until the lights came on in the cabin. Day got up and pulled open the balcony door, then went inside and closed it behind him.

He had nothing really to say to Knight, so he simply got cleaned up and climbed into bed, then turned away from Knight and closed his eyes. Eventually Knight came to bed as well, but Day showed no reaction at all. At some point during the night, the ship stopped rocking, and he figured they were pulling into port. He shifted to get comfortable, and in a moment of clarity and understanding it hit him: the answer to the question he’d tried to figure out earlier. Knight’s supposed betrayal of his family? It was him. He was the betrayal. Day looked over at where Knight slept. At least he had his reason.

THE AFTERNOON of the following day, after getting off the ship and back to the airport, Day had never been so glad that their covers had been deep enough that their return tickets had been booked even if they hadn’t expected to use them. They’d boarded the plane, and Knight had almost instantly gone to sleep, waking when they landed. After they got their luggage, Day walked over to the parking garage, Knight following behind him. "I'll see you at work on Tuesday." He patted himself on the proverbial back for keeping his voice level and headed to his car. He got his bags in the trunk one-handed and then closed the trunk and drove home. He didn't even look in the rearview mirror.

Day unlocked the door to his place and went inside. It felt good to be home. All that flux about his feelings and crap became much less important. He got his bags inside and unpacked, started laundry, and then debated what to do for dinner. He settled on pizza delivery, and once it arrived, he dropped onto the sofa and ate while watching television. Once he was done, he stretched out on the sofa, television still on, and proceeded to fall asleep.

He never made it to the bed. Day woke hours later to an aching back, the television blaring, and someone pounding on his door. "I'm coming," he called. He turned off the damned idiot box and threw away the rest of the pizza before hurrying to the door. He stifled a yawn before pulling the door open. "What…?" he began when he saw Knight standing outside his door. "Is something wrong?"

Knight looked him over. "Aren't those the same clothes you were wearing yesterday?"

Day looked down. "I guess they are. I fell asleep on the sofa and…." He paused. "Did you come here to harass me about my wardrobe?"

Knight didn't answer and stepped around him, coming inside. "I wanted to make sure you were okay. Will you see a doctor today?"

"Yes," he answered testily. "I'll call when they're in." He stepped over to the sofa and sat down. "Is that all you wanted?" Day motioned toward one of the chairs, and Knight sat as well. Day watched him and waited for an answer. Whatever was going on, Knight would get around to it in his own time and not a minute before.

"No, I…." Knight fidgeted in the chair. "I never know how to say things like this. I can kill a man with my bare hands, and I've done it too, but…." Knight faltered, and Day sat still, wondering what he was getting at. "I've shot men, and so have you. You saved my life, and I never know what to say."

"Knight, you aren't making a lot of sense. Take a deep breath, sort through your thoughts." Under normal circumstances Knight being tongue-tied might have been a good thing, but his nervousness was unsettling. "Just Marine up, and tell me what you came to say."

"I'm not good at putting my feelings into words. See, everything is a mess. I keep thinking I'm betraying Cheryl and Zachary, but I'm not. They're gone, and she would be pissed as hell if she knew I sat home all the time drinking and pining for her. I doubt she'd be happy that the person I like is another guy, but then…."

"So you're saying you like me. That's very nice to know."

"Shit, you're going to really put me through the wringer on this one, aren't you?" Knight stood and walked toward the door. "I'm a Marine—we're men of action, not words. We don't say a whole bunch of flowery shit to impress people. I always figured it was best to be quiet and let my actions speak for themselves. I've never betrayed anyone, and I've never walked away from someone who needed me to have their back. Never!"

Day jumped at the shout. "Okay. I believe you."

"I can take a bullet for someone long before I can tell them that I care for them. Cheryl used to hit me on the back of the head sometimes. That was her way of saying that I was being a total ass and to knock it off."

"Can I hit you like that?" Day asked, and Knight growled like a bear on the hunt. "I'll take that as a no."

"Damn right," Knight said firmly.

"So what are you trying to say? That you care about me?" Day pressed.

"Yeah. All that time we were together on the ship, even the crappy parts, like when you were hurt and I was worried sick—they were good. I liked it. I like being with you." Knight walked back to where Day sat. "I'm not the mushy type. I doubt I ever will be, but you'll never have to worry if I have your back."

"And I'll have yours," Day said. "You can count on that."

Knight nodded. "I still have to find out who…." He swallowed hard. Day knew his wife and son were still a difficult subject for him to speak about.

"I've got your back, remember? We'll figure it out together." Day half expected Knight to protest, and when he didn't, Day figured that was an excellent and telling sign. He stood and then stepped closer. When Knight didn't move, Day pulled him forward, kissing him hard and full on the lips, their tongues dueling for dominance. Neither of them won the duel, but the kiss was most definitely a winner, judging by the way his heart raced and other parts stood at attention. Day pulled back and smiled. "Is that how you really feel?"

"I'm not trying to hide anything," Knight said. "I just never seem to be able to find the words. But I think I have some that will help you understand."

Day raised his eyebrows, wondering what words could be so special.

"My first name is Orville."

Day fully understood the message and implication of that snippet of information, and he pulled Knight into another kiss.

DIRK GREYSON is very much an outside kind of man. He loves travel and seeing new things. Dirk worked in corporate America for way too long and now spends his days writing, gardening, and taking care of the home he shares with his partner of more than two decades. He has a Masters Degree and all the other accessories that go with a corporate job. But he is most proud of the stories he tells and the life he's built. Dirk lives in Pennsylvania in a century-old home and is blessed with an amazing circle of friends.

Facebook: https://www.facebook.com/dirkgreyson

Email: dirkgreyson@comcast.net

http://www.dreamspinnerpress.com

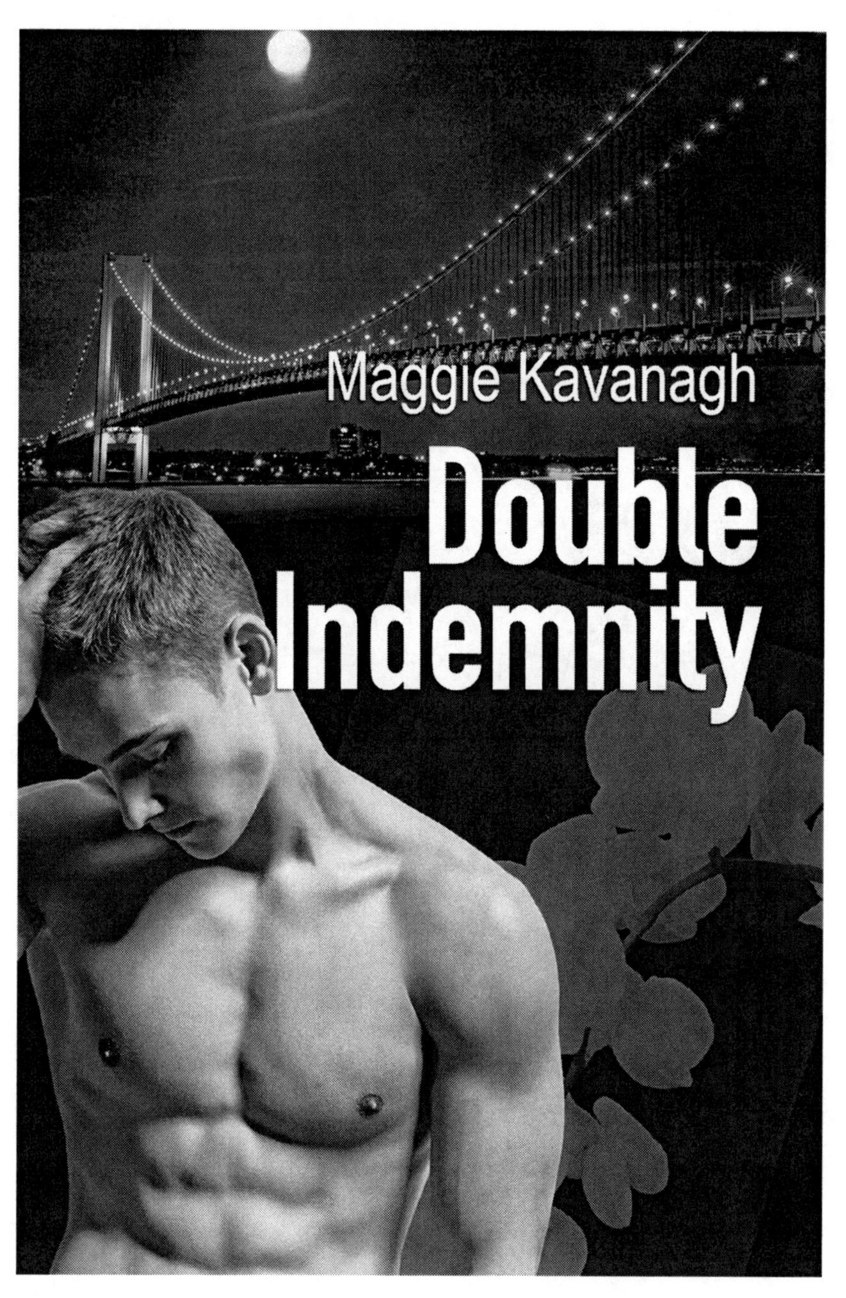
Maggie Kavanagh
Double
Indemnity

He may not be the good guy
he seems to be...
EIVISSA
A.J. LLEWELLYN

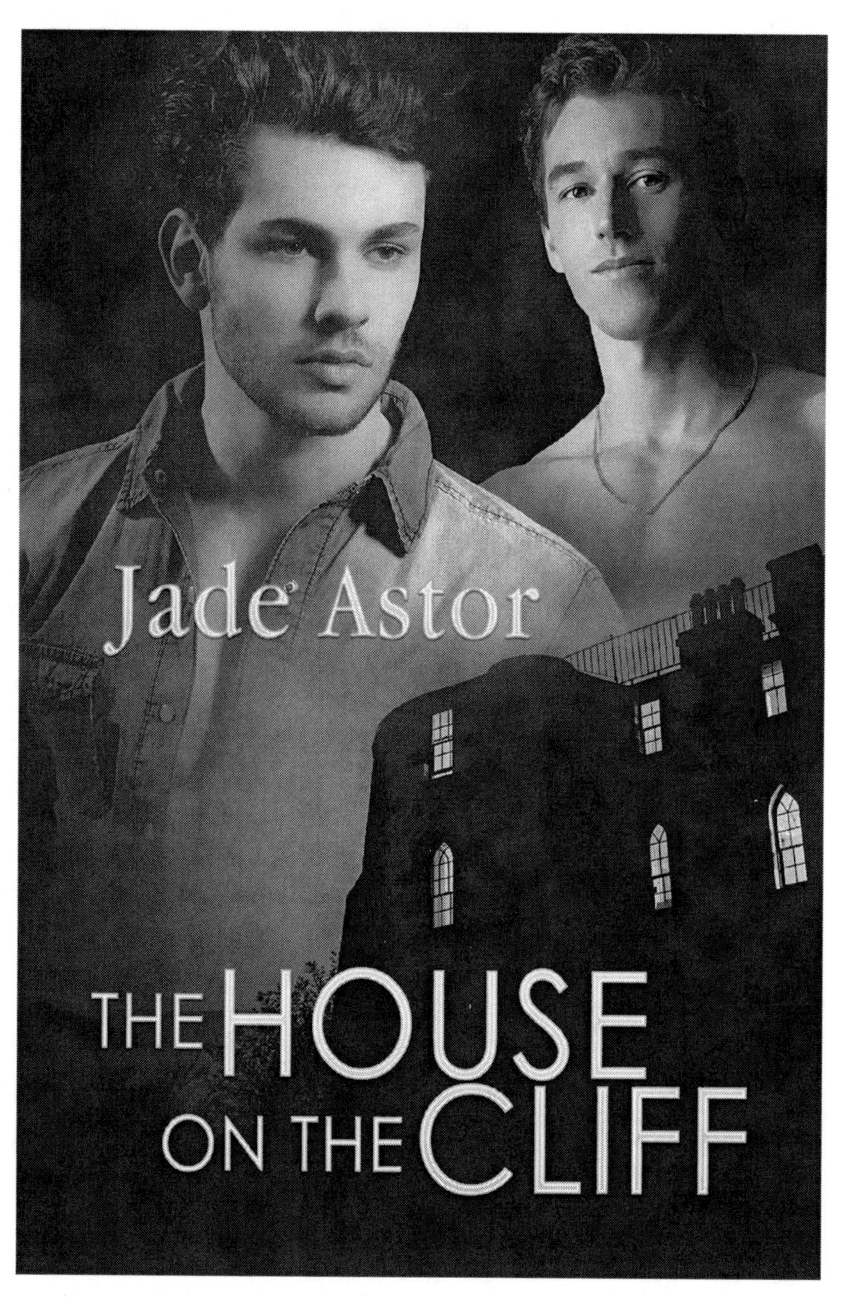
Jade Astor
THE HOUSE
ON THE CLIFF

Miller's
Creek
R.G. GREEN

Steps to Heaven
STAR NOBLE

FOR
MORE
OF THE
BEST
GAY
ROMANCE
DREAMSPINNER
PRESS
dreamspinnerpress.com

CPSIA information can be obtained
at www.ICGtesting.com
Printed in the USA
FSOW02n1837100417
32960FS

9 781632 167064